"A lost sonnet, surely the answer. A sonnet sent by Keats to his brother that hadn't been copied and returned with the others. An unknown sonnet in John Keats's own hand, a discovery far more valuable than any letter or autograph of a known poet.

Suddenly I seemed to have the key to another question that had troubled me earlier: why had Crosley given an emotional reading of someone else's love sonnet? The answer I came up with was a variation of my earlier theory. The recitation had been his cryptic public confession.

★

"Its's a quiet delight to pick up one of Terence Faherty's mysteries."
—*The Indianapolis News*

Terence Faherty

The Lost Keats

W😐RLDWIDE.

.TORONTO • NEW YORK • LONDON
AMSTERDAM • PARIS • SYDNEY • HAMBURG
STOCKHOLM • ATHENS • TOKYO • MILAN
MADRID • WARSAW • BUDAPEST • AUCKLAND

For Tom, Tim, Kathy and Dennis

THE LOST KEATS

A Worldwide Mystery/February 1996

First published by St. Martin's Press, Incorporated.

ISBN 0-373-26192-6

AUTHOR'S NOTE

The characters and events described in this novel are imaginary, but the history is real. The English poet John Keats did have a brother George who emigrated to America. George did settle in Louisville, Kentucky, where he received letters and poems from his poet brother. After tuberculosis had claimed both brothers, George's widow did remarry. Her second husband, John Jeffrey, did send copies of the Keats manuscripts back to England for use by Keats's first biographer. Mr. Jeffrey may or may not have missed one.

A MURDER

THE DARKNESS AROUND ME was hot and fetid and washed with red. My thoughts were as feverish as the night, and I wondered if I might be ill or drunk or dreaming. I was standing in the shadows in the corner of a small room. To my left, tall windows opened onto a balcony and a starless black sky. Through the open windows came a confused murmur of foreign voices from the street below. The voices were overlaid every few seconds by the rumble of distant thunder. These two sounds, the voices and the rumbling darkness, were both background for the room's own sound, the labored breathing of a dying poet.

The man lay sleeping on a couch made up as a bed in the opposite corner of the room from my concealing shadows. The only light in the red darkness came from a candle on a table near the sleeper's head. Around his bed were tall piles of books, standing like silent witnesses. There was a single book facedown on the table, and beside the table a chair. Someone had recently been reading to the sufferer. Perhaps I had been myself. I couldn't quite remember. Something, the closeness of the room or the rising noise of the storm, made it impossible for me to concentrate.

To steady myself, I studied the man on the bed. He was small of stature and wasted, his regular features pale and sharp. The only color in his face was a blue tinge that shaded his lips and eyelids. His skin was dotted with tiny beads of moisture, which reflected and multiplied the candle's flame. These points of light seemed to grow and lose focus, obscuring the sleeper's face like tears in my own eyes, and I wondered if they were a sign of his delirium or a symptom of my own. If it were not for these living beads of light and for his breathing—a gurgling, really—heavy and slow, I would have thought I'd come too late, that the poet was already dead and one with the ageless books.

Outside, the rumbling had slowly grown in strength until it obscured the street voices and challenged the drowned breathing from the bed. The thunder climaxed in a single echoing boom, and then the rain began, steady and hard. The room was lit now by flashes of lightning. For the first time, I could see that it was papered in a choking floral pattern, pale red roses covering the walls and even the ceiling.

One of the lightning flashes cast a shadow over the death scene. I realized then that the books and I were not the only watchers in the room. From off the balcony came a silhouetted figure, a black shadow who moved slowly toward the bed. I waited for the lightning to reveal the newcomer's face, but he was nearly to his goal before it flashed again. The figure bent low over the glistening head and pulled a pillow from beneath it. I recognized the threat in that gentle movement. I cried out, but no one—neither the stranger nor the dying poet—heard me. The shadow, still bent forward in a formal bow, pressed the pillow against the sleeper's face.

In the same instant, the tortured breathing stopped and the candle beside the bed went out. I struggled forward against the moist darkness, fighting to reach the bed, but I was held in place. Then I felt myself falling backward, away from the darkness and toward a hissing, flickering light.

ONE

IT CAN TAKE A LONG TIME to realize that you've made a mistake. And the bigger the mistake, the longer the process can drag on. You might suspect it right away. The little sparks of doubt might flare up first thing every morning or glow on into the night when you're trying to fall asleep. But you recite to yourself the litany of reasons for doing what you did, and it snuffs out the doubt like a magic incantation. The trouble is, the doubt pops into your head by itself and the rationalizing takes effort. More and more effort. It's like fighting a guerrilla army in some jungle you barely know. You win every battle, but the enemy never goes away. In the end, there's no thunder or lightning or trumpet blast. You just raise your head one day and look around and you know in your heart you've screwed up.

It was August 1973. I was enrolled as a seminarian at St. Aelred College and Seminary, a small school tucked away in Huber, one of the southernmost counties of Indiana. It was a part of the world I'd known little about and had never expected to see. But there I was in the graduate school of theology, one year down and three to go. So I knew where I was and where I was going, or at least I should have known. But as those long summer days drifted by I was feeling more and more like a train traveler who had slept through his stop and awakened in a strange land. This traveler's name, incidentally, is Owen Keane.

It was nine o'clock on a Tuesday morning and hot and humid despite the early hour. I was hurrying across the campus for my weekly talk with Father Jerome Loudermilk, a dean of the school of theology and, coincidentally,

my spiritual director. Every seminarian at St. Aelred's had
a spiritual director, a priest with whom he could discuss his
problems and assess his progress. When things were going
well, it was a pleasant enough duty for seminarian and
spiritual director both. When there were problems, it was
a different experience entirely. Lately, my visits to Father
Jerome had reminded me of childhood trips to the dentist.

The results of the self-evaluations and the psychological
testing that were a regular part of life at St. Aelred's were
strictly confidential, and yet my two hundred or so fellow
seminarians had a pretty good idea of who was doing well
or badly. I was an "AR" in the secret vernacular of the
school, an at-risk seminarian, one who was in danger of
leaving or being asked to leave St. Aelred's.

That day, as I jogged across a grassy quad, St. Aelred's
reminded me a little of Boston College, where I'd earned
my undergraduate degree. Both schools had hilltop campuses and ornate Gothic architecture. Both campuses were
old enough, their buildings gray and their trees mature, to
look like they'd been in place forever. The externals of my
two schools were similar, but their atmospheres were totally different. It was more than just the absence of coeds
at St. Aelred's, although that was certainly part of the difference. Boston College had felt new and evolving, hectic,
harried, and growing. St. Aelred's was an older universe
that had expanded to its limits and now had begun to con-
tract.

Father Jerome's office was on the second floor of the
administrative building, St. Bede Hall. I arrived at the office five minutes late, sweating and out of breath from my
run up the stairs. The dean's suite was arranged oddly, with
the secretary hidden away in a cubbyhole off an un-
guarded reception area. Father Jerome's door stood open
on the far wall, but I knocked loudly on the frame of the
hall door just to be safe.

"Come in," Father Jerome called to me. He was seated behind his desk, studying a long white business envelope. He stood as I entered and shook my hand. His thin palm was much drier and cooler than mine, and I noted that he discreetly patted his hand against his pants leg as he came around to my side of the desk. Jerome Loudermilk was a tall, thin man with a long narrow head and a face to go with it. Beneath a fringe of white hair, his brow was lined and concave at the temples. His long, straight nose was squared at the tip and his ears had lobes an inch or more in length that seemed to me to be sagging a little lower each time I saw him.

We sat, as we always did, facing each other in his two visitor chairs. This arrangement was intended to put me at ease, but it always had the opposite effect.

"How is it outside, Owen? Hot as yesterday?"

"Hotter," I said. "And more humid."

"You haven't been here long enough to get used to our Indiana weather. You know what we say about it, don't you? If you don't like our weather, stick around for ten minutes. It will change."

I smiled politely, remembering people in Boston and my hometown of Trenton, New Jersey, who swore by the same tired line.

Father Jerome's next remark wiped the smile off my face. "I was just sitting there thinking about seminarians who drop out," he said offhandedly. "Not a very happy subject for a reverie. Do you know why most seminarians fail, Owen?"

They ask too many questions, I said to myself, thinking of my own problem. Out loud I said, "No, Father."

"They fail because they come to the seminary for the wrong reasons. Some are just taking a flier on the market, as we used to say. They think they might have a vocation, they want to test it, so they try the seminary. Most of them find out soon enough that they were wrong.

"A much bigger group, say seventy percent of the young men who have problems, look to the priesthood as a way of escaping unhappy situations at home. Parents who fight or separate or simply fail to affirm their child's worth. Entering the seminary can be a way of winning a parent's approval, or a way of rising above their disapproval, getting beyond its reach. It's a bad reason, but a common one."

"I get along fine with my parents," I said.

Father Jerome looked shocked at the news. "I wasn't speaking about your situation, Owen," he said quickly. He leaned forward and patted my knee reassuringly. "I've had someone else on my mind. Sorry for rambling, but I need a sounding board now and again as much as you do."

I tried to assume a less rigid position in my chair. "What's the problem?"

Father Jerome raised his narrow shoulders in a shrug that conveyed embarrassment. "It seems that one of our seminarians has taken French leave. One of the boys I was counseling, in fact. I suppose you've heard something of it."

"You mean Michael Crosley," I said.

He smiled sadly. "The campus grapevine is still operating efficiently, I see. Do you know Michael?"

"Not well," I said.

"I'm afraid that would be almost everyone's answer. Not a very open young man. Or a very happy one. That was the point of my observations regarding unhappy family situations. I've been wondering whether Michael might be part of that seventy percent I mentioned earlier."

Father Jerome stretched his long legs out, and I pulled my own back deferentially. "We've had dropouts before, of course," the priest said, "and sudden ones, too, but never one so sudden and so complete as Michael Crosley."

"How do you mean?" I asked.

Father Jerome considered my question for a moment with his long head tilted to his right. His right ear lobe swung down like a plumb bob. I was afraid that he was going to politely change the subject. Instead, he said, "Michael just vanished one night a little over a week ago. It will be two weeks this Friday. Left no note, sent no letter. He packed a small bag, but left most of his belongings. They're still in his room over at the old rectory."

"Have his parents heard from him?"

"Michael's father passed away last spring. His mother lives in Indianapolis, but no, to answer your question, she hasn't heard from him. Mrs. Crosley is surprisingly unconcerned, it seems to me. For the moment, at least. She seems to have been expecting this to happen. I should have been expecting it myself," Father Jerome added.

"Why?"

"First and foremost because I am Michael's spiritual director. I should have recognized the way his thoughts were tending. And there were warning signs I'd heard about that should have alerted me. Michael was missing prayer services and even daily mass. Well, it is the summer session, many graduate students are away on vacations or social missions or they're helping out in their home dioceses. Things are a little slack. Still, I should have spoken to him sooner.

"And there were other, stranger signs. Did you know that Michael had been in a fight recently?"

"No," I said.

Father Jerome looked disappointed, either in me or the local grapevine. "I'm told he appeared around campus with a black eye only days before he disappeared," the priest said. "He refused to explain it. There was one other odd thing. Not a warning really since it didn't happen until the night he left. Michael took away a raincoat that didn't belong to him. It was raining on and off that evening. Still, it was not like him at all."

"Has anyone looked into any of this?" I asked.

"Not very thoroughly. I spoke with a man I know who is with the state police, but there wasn't much he could do. He seemed to think that Michael had taken it into his head to run off to California or New York City, something like that."

Father Jerome smiled and leaned toward me slightly. "I'm afraid that most people see nothing unusual in someone running away from a seminary. The hard thing for them to understand is why someone would come here in the first place."

He settled back with a sigh. "I have just the opposite difficulty, with respect to Michael. I'm not sure I really understand his decision, since he didn't see fit to discuss it with me. That troubles me. It was his choice to make, of course, but I'd like to know why he made it. Was it his family situation, or was there something else? I've tried to make my own inquiries, but I don't really have the time to do a thorough job. Or the talent. I was thinking that you might look into it for me."

"Me?"

"Yes. As an exercise, if you will. Try to figure out what made Michael leave. What made him come here in the first place. Give me something that I can use in my report to the rector. What do you think?"

I thought it was too good to be true. I was wary. "Why me?" I asked.

Father Jerome answered by changing the subject. "I've been in correspondence with Father Barret of Boston College. I'm sure you remember him."

I nodded. Barret was a tall, patrician-looking Jesuit who taught logic. I easily recalled his clipped speaking voice and his apt habit, when he lectured, of addressing a point in the air above his students' heads.

"Father Barret tells me that you were something of an investigator at Boston, that you helped to clear up some unpleasantness at the school."

The reminder of that "unpleasantness" passed through me like a cold wind. "Did he?" I asked.

"Yes." Father Jerome settled back in his chair and addressed the ceiling. "I remember wondering, when you first came to us, how a hot prospect like you had gotten away from the Jesuits." He made the statement wistfully, like a man nostalgic over lost innocence. Then he shook the thought gently from his head. "Are you interested in helping me?"

I was, of course, though I should have known better. I should have given him a polite no, looked blank, denied I'd ever heard of Boston College. But I hesitated. I was suffering through the dog days that summer, both physically and emotionally, and I needed a break. I mistook Michael Crosley's mystery as a possible distraction from my own troubles. Father Jerome's next remark made it clear that he did not.

"I think this could actually help you with some of the hurdles you're facing now," he said.

Hurdles? There was only one left that I could see, and beyond it a long, dark drop. "How, Father?"

"I'd like you to work that out for yourself. Let's call it one part of your investigation."

The old priest's honeyed voice hadn't changed, but I suddenly understood that what he was offering me was not an odd job but a challenge. That changed the proposition entirely. My ego shoved my better judgment aside. "I'll be glad to look into it," I said.

"Good. I can't help you very much, I'm afraid. Michael's self-evaluations and the results of his testing must remain confidential. Other than that proscription, I'll give you a free hand. You've completed your summer classes?"

"Yes."

"Good," he said again. "You have my permission to come and go as you see fit. I'll call over to the old rectory to tell them that it's all right for you to examine Michael's room. And here is something that may help you get started." He produced an index card from the breast pocket of his jacket. "I'd given Michael two service projects this summer as part of his counseling. One was a halfway house for young men recovering from drug-related problems. The other was a nursing home. Here are the names and addresses of those two places."

He handed me the card and then leaned over to his desk to retrieve the white envelope that he'd been examining when I arrived. "And there is one more thing that might prove helpful to you. A favor you could do for me. This is a letter I've written to Beatrice Crosley, Michael's mother. As I told you, she lives in Indianapolis. I don't feel that it's adequate somehow to send this in the mail. Someone from the school should go to see her. I should go myself, but I'm not able to at the moment. Would you mind?"

"Not at all," I said.

"You have clericals, I assume."

"Clericals" were the uniform of the priesthood that St. Aelred's seminarians were permitted to wear only when working off campus.

"Yes, Father, I have them."

"They would be appropriate for your visit to Mrs. Crosley, I think. After that, you can use your own judgment. Incidentally, I asked Michael to wear his normal street clothes when he made his service calls."

The old priest paused for my comment. When I failed to come up with one, he smiled and said, "Good luck, then, Owen. Stop by anytime to bring me up to date."

We shook hands again as I rose to leave. My palm was still moist.

TWO

I HADN'T GOTTEN as far as St. Bede's arched doorway before I was asking myself why I hadn't told Father Jerome all I knew of Michael Crosley. I may not have had all the details of Crosley's sudden departure, but that hadn't stopped me from coming up with my own explanation for it, one that I had been kicking around in my head since I'd heard he'd gone away. The basis of my theory was a clue I'd withheld from the old priest. I'd happened on it, I now calculated, three weeks later, on the very first evening of August.

THAT NIGHT I'd been sitting alone in St. Aelred's campus pub, adding my share to the cloud of cigarette smoke that hung beneath its timber rafters. This overcast seemed far too heavy for the small crowd. Most of the audience huddled close to the brightly lit stage, like campers around a fire. I'd chosen a table farther back, well out of the light. On a better night, the stage would have held a small band or a solo musician, and the room would have been full of music and the steady bass of beery conversation. That night's event was an open-mike poetry reading, and the crowd was quiet and polite and thin.

The pub was called the Unstable. It had originally been called the Stable, a reference to its interior of rough-hewn timbers and reclaimed barn wood. That name can't have lasted more than five minutes before some campus wit came up with the obvious pun, rechristening the place forever. The Unstable was like any other college pub on any campus anywhere, serving beer and wine to students who would otherwise be driving around in search of something worse, except that its customers were almost always male. Lonely, homesick males, to judge from my own experience.

I'd selected my table diplomatically that evening. I was at the Unstable as a favor to a classmate. A favor and a half, I should say, as I disliked poetry readings. I'd elected to sit far from the light in case I was lucky enough to fall asleep, but also as a precaution against involuntary grimacing. I'd grimaced quite a lot already. First through the complete works of an undergraduate who specialized in stories of high school romance told in endless rhyming couplets. Then through some warmed-over Vietnam protests that already sounded dated, only months after the peace agreements had been signed.

When the acquaintance who had invited me finally took the stage, I started grimacing before he'd opened his mouth. He stood before the mike for a long minute with his eyes closed and his fingertips pressed together, composing himself for the ordeal to come like some Olympic high diver. Then he recited a poem that sounded like bad James Joyce played at the wrong speed: words piled on words for their sound alone and references personal and obscure enough to puzzle even the poet's immediate family.

When this torrent finally dribbled out, no one applauded more loudly than I did. The favor was done. I was a free man.

I was lighting a last cigarette and thinking of bed when Michael Crosley stepped up to the microphone. Crosley was tall and stocky with prematurely thinning brown hair and blank blue eyes. His eyes were especially blank now as he stared out into the darkness beyond the stage lights. Even from my distant seat, I could sense the wave of surprise and anticipation that passed over the crowd. If Crosley was known for anything, it was for a piety bordering on caricature. He was certainly not known for reciting poetry in bars.

Crosley hesitated at the microphone as my friend had done, but it wasn't to perform some self-conscious warm-up. He seemed to have genuinely forgotten his purpose. He wore the look of a man recalling something curious and half forgotten. Without losing this strange expression, he began to recite.

> "My soul had been too long at youthful ease;
>   Slow days had come and passed in languid file;
> When I was captured by Eumenides,
>   Thy furies sent to torture and beguile;
> The voice that has become my sacred muse,
>   The orbs that have eclipsed all other light,
> The form of perfect grace that has confused
>   A lifetime's certainty of wrong and right..."

I found that I was leaning across the table, straining to hear Crosley's high, wavering voice. His expression hadn't changed, but I was certain suddenly that he was close to tears.

> "No more will my poor spirit find its rest
>   In faery realms of words and games of love;
> For now, forsaking artifice and jest,
>   Can I but strive to reach the heights above..."

Tears began to roll down Crosley's broad face, and his voice grew husky and strained.

> "While doomed to fall outside that promised land,
> With fingers stretching upward for thy hand."

Crosley stood as still as he had before he'd begun, gazing into the smoky silence and ignoring the audience that began to clap a beat late and then stopped abruptly in expec-

tation of another poem. The polite applause began again as
Crosley turned and walked off the stage.

I continued to watch the bright, empty space where
Crosley had stood. I was trying to fix some piece of the
poem in my memory, but I could only recall clearly the face
of the man who had recited it.

MY FAILURE TO SHARE my clue with Father Jerome might
have stemmed from the peculiar nature of my training as a
detective, which had come largely from paperback mysteries. In those books, the detective always held something
back. Sometimes from his client. Usually from the police.
Always from his spiritual director, if by some strange
chance he had one. A more likely explanation was that I
wanted to impress the old priest, and that meant holding
back the best clue, as some lesser fictional detective did,
until the last chapter of the book.

The emotional recitation of a love poem by a seminarian was certainly the best clue I could think of to the seminarian's sudden disappearance. Crosley had met a girl. In
an agonizing process, which included a public confession
via a poetry reading, he'd chosen his love over his vocation. Good-bye St. Aelred's. Father Barret, my Boston
college logic professor, would have congratulated me.

Or instead, he might have warned me about the danger
of deducing before acquiring all the facts. Any number of
my fictional role models would have seconded the advice.
If I'd been listening.

THREE

THE MAJORITY of the housing on St. Aelred's campus was in dormitories more or less identical to those of the same vintage anywhere, with students sleeping two to a room. There were also smaller residence halls that didn't fit this pattern, reserved for upperclassmen or others who requested private rooms. One of these exceptions was the old rectory, named for its original role as the residence of the rector of the graduate school. The old rectory was a Victorian-looking three-story house, built, like most of the campus buildings, of Indiana limestone. It might have been the formal building material that threw me off. It was hard for me to think of the old house as anyone's home.

I was surprised, then, when the door opened in answer to my ring and I was met by the smell of baking and by Mrs. Wilson, the woman who ran the house. She was an ample lady in a blue cotton dress who wore a flowered kerchief over her gray hair. She greeted me with a smile that faded when I mentioned Michael Crosley.

"Father Jerome just called me," she said, shaking her head. "I told him not to worry himself over that one. No one could have known."

We slowly climbed carpeted stairs to the third floor. Mrs. Wilson's legs were troubling her, I noticed, but her lungs were sound. While we climbed, she gave me the *Reader's Digest* version of her autobiography. "I've been at St. Aelred's for twenty-three years," she said. "My husband Ollie and I came here after he got out of the service. He worked in the dairy, back when it was running, and I cooked and cleaned for the rector—it was Father Ulrick then—in this house. After the dairy shut down, Ollie worked on the grounds crew. He died in sixty-seven. April. Around that time, they changed this place into a residence hall and made me the landlady, so to speak. It's like a pension, except I get to keep busy, which I like. I sometimes think they'll name the place for me when I go. St. Katrinka's Hall." She laughed. "What do you think?"

"That would be nice."

We eventually arrived at the end of a narrow hallway at the very top of the stairs. Mrs. Wilson opened an unlocked panel door marked 3A and stood aside.

The room was small and irregularly shaped and very warm. The ceiling followed the pitch of the roof above it, and I could feel the heat coming down through the white plaster. The morning sun shone through the room's only window, creating a shaft of light in which circulating dust was visible.

Mrs. Wilson made a soft, deprecating sound under her breath and crossed the room to open the window. To do this, she had to lean across a small writing table and chair. The only other pieces of furniture in the room were a bureau and a narrow bed.

One wall of the room was divided into two spaces of unequal size by the rough brick of a chimney. The bed stood on one side of this column. Shelves had been built across the other, smaller nook, and these were crammed full of books. The overflow stood in small piles around the room. The only decoration in the room besides the book piles was an old, dark print of the Sacred Heart of Jesus that hung over the bed.

"Just as Michael left it, dust and all," Mrs. Wilson said. "The garret, he called it."

The hermit's cell would have been more accurate, I thought. "No one saw Michael leave?"

"No," Mrs. Wilson said. "I saw him earlier that evening when he came in soaking wet. Thunderstorms all day that day. Wet footprints and mud all through the house. No one heard him go out. It must have been after ten, because Philip Swickard, the young man whose raincoat Michael took, didn't get in until ten.

"He, Philip I mean, has one of the rooms on the second floor. He got up for the early prayer service the next morning and noticed that his coat was gone. It had been hanging on the hall rack downstairs. Philip was not pleased," Mrs. Wilson said with much emphasis. "Very particular about his things, Philip is. He went all around the house asking the other young gentlemen if they had seen his coat. He found Michael's door open and his room empty.

"I watched for Michael all day, and, when he hadn't returned by the next morning, I called the rector."

"Michael took away some of his own things?" I asked.

"Yes. Not very much. He had a big suitcase and a little one." She opened the narrow door of a closet. "The big one's still here, you see, but the little one's gone."

"You said downstairs that no one could have known about Michael leaving. There wasn't any warning?"

She smiled and pointed to her left eye. "There was the shiner. It made him look like a little boy. He got embarrassed when I asked him about it, so I pretended not to notice."

"Anything else? Anything different in the way he acted?"

Mrs. Wilson considered the bare floorboards seriously for a moment before answering. "There was a change," she finally said. "Up to a month ago, he acted more like a priest than most of the priests I've known. He was too serious, if anything. Too pious. Then overnight he seemed different. Happy sometimes, but mostly down in the dumps. And absentminded, too. Dazed almost. Walking around in a dream."

This was exactly what I'd hoped to hear, as it fit the conclusion I'd already grown fond of, the idea that Crosley had fallen in love. "Maybe that's why he took the wrong coat," I ventured. "Absentmindedness."

Mrs. Wilson smiled broadly. "You've never met Philip Swickard," she said.

"No," I admitted, "but I'd like to talk with him."

The landlady held up a thick forefinger that took a different crooked jog at each knuckle. "That I can arrange. I heard the radio in two-B as we came up. Let me go ask him."

She marched off down the hallway, leaving me alone in the room. I used the waiting time to look around more carefully. There was nothing hidden in the large suitcase or in the closet itself. I went through the pockets of the few items of clothing hanging there, finding only crumpled tissues and empty candy wrappers. I noted that Crosley's clericals still hung there, looking sad and ordinary. I then turned my attention to the bed, finding nothing beneath the pillow or the mattress, and only a pair of black oxfords under the bed itself. The three drawers of the little bureau held underwear, socks, and shirts. Each drawer was half empty, which was consistent with the idea that Crosley had packed a small bag.

I examined the crammed bookshelves briefly, recognizing a few of the titles from classes I'd already taken. Then I noticed a single volume that stood out from the crowd. It sat alone, as though in a place of honor, on the top of Crosley's writing desk. I pulled out the unpadded wooden desk chair and sat down to examine the book. It was *John Keats* by Walter Jackson Bate. The book's cloth cover was protected by a plastic jacket, and there was a Dewey decimal number on the spine. I opened the back cover and confirmed that the book had been borrowed from St. Aelred's library. It was a week overdue. I flipped through the book from the back to the front, stopping when I came to a page marked with a piece of paper. The bookmark interested me more than the place it kept. It was a slip of plain pink notepaper. On it was written a phone number and a name—*Melissa Donahue*.

"Bingo," I said aloud.

I opened the desk's single drawer, looking for a pink notepad. Instead I found a large spiral notebook with Crosley's name on the cover. Its three sections held class notes for three different courses Crosley had taken. The notes were kept in a neat, characterless hand that was entirely different from the careless, flowing style of the writing on the pink paper. I flipped through the notebook, looking for a doodle or a marginal question or some personal touch left by the man who had taken the notes. There was nothing like that. I had just replaced the notebook in the drawer when a discreet knock came from the open door behind me.

Mrs. Wilson was filling the doorway. "I have Philip here," she said, indicating the hallway behind her with a movement of her kerchiefed head. "Do you need me for anything else?"

"Is there a phone book I can borrow for a moment?" I asked.

"In the front hall downstairs," Mrs. Wilson said. "Under the phone." She sounded slightly mystified, which I found gratifying.

"Thanks for your help," I said. "I'll be down to look at it in a minute."

She nodded and backed out of sight. Her place in the doorway was taken by a young man dressed formally in a white shirt and dark blue trousers. I saw immediately why Mrs. Wilson had found the idea that Crosley had taken Philip Swickard's coat by accident so amusing. Swickard was no taller than five foot two, a foot shorter than Crosley, and he might have weighed a full hundred pounds less. "I'm Philip Swickard," the young man said, making it sound like a proclamation. "And you are?"

"Owen Keane. I'm looking into Michael Crosley's absence for Father Loudermilk."

Swickard's expression suggested that I'd have to be getting my orders directly from Pope Paul before he'd be impressed. He remained in the doorway with his arms crossed before him. I tilted my chair back on two legs and crossed my arms in imitation. "I understand that Crosley took your coat when he left," I said.

"Yes," Swickard said. "It was a London Fog. Black. Brand new." I thought he might quote me the retail price. Instead he added, "I guess I'm lucky he left my car."

"Your car?" I prompted.

"My Chevy Nova. Blue. Seventy-one. Crosley was always borrowing it for the service work he was doing. And once to run down to Evansville. He'd fill the tank up, but he'd never clean the windshield off. Dust and smashed bugs so thick you couldn't see to drive.

"My keys were in the pocket of the raincoat. I leave them there a lot. I really panicked when I couldn't find the coat. I mean, the car was right where I'd left it—I checked that right away—but I only have the one set of keys. Then Bill Feltig from two-A came in swinging the keys on his finger. He said he'd found them out in front of the house, lying in the gutter."

None of that made much sense to me, so I backed us up to the last important thing Swickard had said. "Why did Crosley go to Evansville?"

"He had to visit someone. Didn't say who. Told me it was real important and that he'd clean the car up when he was done, which he didn't."

"When was this?"

"A couple, three weeks ago."

I now knew the girl's name, her phone number, and the town where she lived. I decided to bounce my theory off Swickard, as much to impress him as to satisfy myself.

"Did Crosley ever mention a special friend?" I asked. "A girl maybe?"

Swickard answered with a loud, mirthless laugh. "Michael Crosley? You've got to be kidding. That guy wouldn't bend over to pet a puppy. He didn't have any friends, never mind special friends. Saying hello was a major social interaction for him. He was above that kind of stuff. And a girl!" Swickard treated me to another harsh laugh. "He'd have a hard time identifying one. You're way off base, fella. Way, way off."

I found that I'd let my chair down on all four legs sometime during Swickard's speech. I stood up now so I could end our interview looking down at him. "Thanks for your help," I said.

My confidence had almost bounced back from Swickard's laughter by the time I reached the first floor. I found the phone book under a black desk phone on a small combination chair and table. I noted the number on the phone dial for future reference. Then I sat down and opened the phone book on my knees. In the front of the book was a listing of all the exchanges in Indiana. I found the Evansville heading and then looked below it for 842, the first three digits of the phone number I'd found upstairs. It wasn't there. I scanned the entire page, finally finding 842 buried in the large group of Indianapolis prefixes. So Evansville had nothing to do with Melissa Donahue. Why then had Crosley gone there?

I found that I was staring at a row of narrow metal mailboxes that were set in the opposite wall. MICHAEL CROSLEY, 3A was printed on the last box in the row.

"Need anything else?" Mrs. Wilson had padded up beside me on the thick carpet while I pondered.

I tried to look less confused than I was suddenly feeling. For something to say, I asked, "Has any mail come for Michael?"

"No," Mrs. Wilson said. "I checked yesterday when the mailman was here. There was nothing."

That fit at least. If Crosley had run off to be with his girlfriend, there would be no letters from her piling up. My ego began to reassert itself. "Don't worry, Mrs. Wilson," I said as I rose to leave. "I think we'll have this straightened out in no time."

FOUR

AFTER GIVING MY EMPTY assurances to Mrs. Wilson, I returned to my dormitory, St. Meinrad Hall. Because it was August, the dorm was almost empty. My own roommate had returned to beautiful Pittsburgh for the month, and I was enjoying the privacy. On my walk, I toyed with the idea of applying for Michael Crosley's vacated garret, but I knew I wouldn't do it. I already felt too alone at St. Aelred's, too cut off from my fellow seminarians. It wouldn't be a good idea, I decided, to add physical separation to spiritual isolation. That might have been the trap that Crosley had fallen into.

Besides which, leaving St. Meinrad would have meant giving up Brother Dennis. At Boston College, he would have been called the resident assistant of the dorm. At St. Aelred's he had an archaic and vaguely English-sounding title: housemaster. Brother Dennis was a member of St. Aelred's small but vital monastic community. Unlike the undergraduates and seminarians, who dressed and often acted like college students anywhere, the monks really seemed to belong in St. Aelred's Gothic world. Except when working outside in summer, they wore black hooded robes and maintained daily ritual observances—matins, noonday prayers, and vespers—that were echoes of past centuries. St. Aelred's modest standing as a tourist attraction was entirely due to the monks. The chanted services were attended by day trippers from as far away as Indianapolis and Cincinnati.

The monks also maintained a gift shop through which their own crafts were sold. This shop was almost the last vestige of an old tradition of self-sufficiency at St. Aelred's. In the past, the college had had its own sawmill, hospital, power plant, and printing press, as well as the dairy at which Mrs. Wilson's Ollie had once worked. The monks still maintained a press and a small hotel for visitors, but, to a large extent, the practical pursuits had given way to more artistic endeavors: painting, musical composition, weaving, pottery making. These produced an income for the monks and seemed—to me at least—more in keeping with the spiritual life.

Brother Dennis would have objected strongly to being called an artist. In addition to being a housemaster, he was a potter. He turned out practical, unadorned clay pots and jars whose only claim to originality came from their never being quite right. Never exactly round or perfectly flat on the bottom, the jar tops too big or too small or pinched slightly so they wouldn't sit flush.

These irregularities seemed to me to be the perfect signature for their creator. Brother Dennis was himself unadorned, practical-looking, and utilitarian. He was of medium height and rather narrow in the shoulders and chest but very muscular with large forearms and hands. Like his wares, he was imperfect, too handled by life before he'd been set in the kiln. His nose had been broken more than once, and now sat at an angle that suggested his face was about to enter a left turn. His brows were thick and scarred and his left eyelid drooped. The knuckles on his hands were also scarred and they were bulbous.

Brother Dennis had a personality to match his face, open and friendly, but battered somehow and rough-edged. No one seemed to know his full history. I sometimes wondered if he still knew it himself. At one time, I'd fancied him an ex-prizefighter who had accidentally killed a man in the ring, but that explanation alternately sounded too romantic and too prosaic. He was more like the survivor of some great catastrophe who had been patched together afterward but was ever incomplete. He was infinitely curious about his seminarian charges and protective of us. He gave us all nicknames. My own started life as my initials and eventually evolved into "Okie," making me sound like a displaced farmer from the thirties.

Brother Dennis met me now on my return to the dorm. He set the trash can he was carrying down on the top step of the entryway as I approached.

"Okie," he said. "You've just missed an important phone call. You're to call right back. Go in and do it now."

I was smiling as I often did at the communications challenge Brother Dennis posed. "Who am I supposed to call?"

Brother Dennis tapped his forehead with the palm of his hand. "That would help, wouldn't it? It was a young lady calling long distance from New York City. I wrote it all down for you. Her name is Mary Fitzgerald."

"Mary?"

"Aha. I thought so. What was she, now? Your old sweetheart, I bet."

"Yes," I said. "She was."

Brother Dennis's battered face fell in pieces. "Oh. I'm sorry, Okie. I was only kidding with you. I didn't know. Honest."

"It's all right," I said. "No problem. Mary and I are still friends." That didn't seem adequate somehow, so I added, "Good friends."

"Tell me about her." It was the kind of personal inquiry that any conversation with Brother Dennis was likely to contain.

"She's a sweet person. Positive, outgoing. We were English majors together at Boston College. Neither of us put it to very good use. She's taken a job with a big company."

"So have you, Okie. The biggest."

"Right. Mary's with IBM."

"Ah yes. Computers. She's smart then, and analytical."

Actually, Mary sold typewriters, but the conclusions the monk had drawn were accurate. In any case, he had already moved on to the next category.

"What are her hobbies?"

"She plays the flute. And she likes to skate."

"Ice?"

"Roller."

"Is that right?"

"And she does a lot of charity stuff. She's always volunteering for something."

Brother Dennis nodded approvingly. "Big-hearted. I knew it. What does she look like? Paint a picture for me. From her voice on the phone, I thought she had dark hair. Almost black. And big dark eyes."

I smiled again. "You must have had a bad connection. Her hair is light brown, with golden highlights in the summertime. She'll have those now, if she hasn't been spending too much time in an office. She wears it straight, almost shoulder length."

"Color of eyes?"

"Blue."

"What does that tell me? What color blue?"

"Like the sky in April."

"Ah. That's better. You're warming to your subject. What else?"

"She has strong cheekbones and a small mouth."

"But well shaped, I'll bet," Brother Dennis interjected.

"Yes, a small, well-shaped mouth."

"What's her figure like?"

I was now seriously regretting that I'd gone along with this interrogation. "It's nice. She's tall and thin."

"Don't say 'thin,' Okie. Say 'lithe.' She's not flat-chested, is she?"

"No," I said, irritated by both the question and the suggestion.

"Good. How about legs?"

"Two. Roughly the same length."

Brother Dennis processed the information I'd given him and shook his head. "Doesn't sound like the girl I talked to. Have you got a picture?"

I would have said no, but Brother Dennis's simple directness was irresistible. I pulled out my wallet and made a show of searching for Mary's picture. Then I pulled it from the compartment where I always kept it.

The photo looked like a postage stamp in the monk's hand. "You forgot the mole on her cheek."

And the one on the small of her back, I thought. Aloud I said, "Sorry. I must have been idealizing."

He handed the picture back. "Still can't believe that was the girl on the phone," he said. "This girl sounded much darker. Maybe I'm confused. Maybe I was hearing the way she was feeling. Did you two have a fight?"

"No."

"How did you break up?"

Badly, I thought. We'd stopped talking out our plans together. I'd worked out my own in secret and sprung them on her without warning. I searched for some cliché to express all that. "We drifted apart," I said.

Brother Dennis shook his head. "Something's not right. Better call her first thing."

"Thanks for the message."

I left him and went inside to my room. There I was confronted by Mary's ghost again. Her name and number were taped to my door, courtesy of Brother Dennis. As was his custom, he'd added to the note a line from Scripture, carefully identified as being from the book of Proverbs: "A word spoken in good season, how good it is!"

"That season's long past," I said as I took the note down.

FIVE

SHORTLY AFTER LUNCH the next day, I changed into the summer version of my clericals: a short-sleeved black shirt with a white plastic tab inserted in the collar, black dress pants, and black shoes that needed polish. Then I pocketed Father Jerome's letter to Mrs. Crosley and walked down the hill to the parking lot behind the old dairy, where I kept my car. Many St. Aelred's students stored their cars in the big gravel lot, but mine was easy to spot. It was the only red '65 Karmann-Ghia with New Jersey plates on campus. Red and gray, I should say. I'd been filling in some holes in the rocker panels and around the headlights with fiberglass filler in my spare time. I'd gotten as far in the process as sanding down the patches and painting them with gray primer. The resulting mottled look pleased my eye, giving the Volkswagen a rugged air that made it seem more like the sports car it pretended to be.

The inside of the little car was as hot as Brother Dennis's kiln. I rolled the windows down, using the sole surviving window crank, an heirloom I stowed in the glove compartment for safekeeping. I'd customized the car's interior with a fat walnut gear shifter, matching radio knobs, and a black imitation leather steering wheel cover held in place with flat plastic lacing. The driver's seat was split at the seams and repaired with electrical tape, and just settling into it again felt like a visit home. I rattled the gear shift lever to confirm that the car was in neutral, and fired up the engine.

I had a full four hours to make my appointment with Beatrice Crosley in Indianapolis. After my exchange with

Brother Dennis the day before, I'd called Information and gotten Mrs. Crosley's number. Then I'd spent the afternoon dialing and waiting and wondering whether I should be calling at all. There was always the chance that Michael's mother would refuse to see me, but I didn't want to turn up on her doorstep unannounced. Finally, around five o'clock, Mrs. Crosley had answered. Over the phone, she had sounded as unconcerned as she had to Father Jerome. She had agreed to see me at five o'clock the following evening when she got home from the bank where she worked.

Navigating with the same road map I'd bought at the state line on my arrival in Indiana, I drove east for ten winding miles on State Road 62. Then I turned north on Highway 37 and settled back to enjoy the passing show. Many people will tell you that Indiana is flat, and much of it may be, but the southern third is hilly and green. The scenery I drove past for the first hour reminded me of eastern Pennsylvania, except that the farms were fewer and not so well cared for.

Following 37 northward was like tracing a river from its source to its mouth. The road was a modest two-lane until Paoli, where it grew wide shoulders and acquired smoother asphalt. Just south of Bedford, the road grew again, to four lanes of concrete with a steel guardrail down the middle. There were frequent signs for quarries and stone companies now. Where the road cut through small hills, the sides of the cut were crumbling facings of exposed limestone and the edges of the road were littered with fallen debris.

The highway bent well around Bloomington, and I saw nothing of the state university I knew was hiding there. North of Martinsville, the hills began to diminish and the horizon slowly retreated. By the time I finally neared Indianapolis, the road was flat and straight enough to give me the same view for miles. The smokestack of a power plant first appeared in the hazy distance as a striped pole with a plume of white attached. When I reached the city's out-

skirts, the stack had grown into a giant, and I felt insignif-
icant and a little lost in the late afternoon traffic.

Mrs. Crosley's directions kept me on the south side of the
city but took me to its eastern corner, a section called Beech
Grove. It was a residential area of modest homes bordered
on one side by a huge train yard. I was a good hour early
for my appointment. I found a Dairy Queen restaurant that
advertised a "brazier" on its sign and stopped for an early
dinner.

There was a phone booth outside the restaurant. After
eating, I carried the last of my milk shake outside and
paged through the booth's phone book. There was less than
a full column of Donahues listed. It was no job at all to find
Melissa's number, although her name didn't actually ap-
pear. Instead, the listing was for an Earl H. Donahue, 7241
Kingsway Drive.

BEATRICE CROSLEY'S HOME was on Fourth Street. The
house was a small ranch with brown shingle siding and a
tiny, slightly less brown front yard. It was only a quarter to
five, but I tried the bell anyway. Mrs. Crosley must have
been running ahead of schedule, too. The windowless front
door opened almost immediately.

She was a short woman, about five five, with an extra six
inches of brown hair coiled on top of her head for good
measure. Her eyes were a darker blue than her son's and
each was surrounded by a puffy redness. Her thin lips drew
themselves out in an even thinner line as I introduced myself.

I had intended to withhold Father Jerome's letter until I
was sure that I'd be invited into the house, but now I
handed it to her impulsively. She held it in front of her
without looking at it.

"I've just now gotten home from work," she said, "and
the house is still stuffy from being closed up all day. Why
don't we go out on the patio."

We began the trip to the patio through a small, neatly furnished living room, where I spotted a framed portrait of Michael Crosley. I decided that it was his high school graduation picture, based on his hairline, which was more or less intact. There was something else unusual about the photograph. After we'd entered the adjoining dining room I realized what it was: the photographer had somehow gotten Crosley to smile.

We exited the house through sliding glass doors set in the dining room's back wall. The "patio" was a ten-by-ten concrete slab that listed a little to port on the shaggy lawn. Two webbed folding chairs and a circular aluminum table stood in the center of the slab.

"Please sit down," Mrs. Crosley said. "Can I get you anything? Iced tea?"

I said yes to that, and she disappeared back into the house. I looked around while I waited. The backyard was only slightly larger than the front. It was bordered on three sides by unmatched fences belonging to the neighbors: chain link to my right, split rail to my left, and stockade in front of me. The neighbor's dog, a yellow Lab that stood on three legs, eyed me warily through the chain link. Mrs. Crosley's long grass was uniformly dry, except for a healthy green fringe around her garden, a large plot in the center of her lawn, where several rows of tomato plants were held upright by stakes, their branches sagging under their load. I recognized peppers and squash among the other plantings.

I stood up to help Mrs. Crosley negotiate the sliding door. She was balancing two glasses and a pitcher containing a week's supply of iced tea. To break the silence after we had seated ourselves, I said, "You have a nice garden."

"Thank you," she said. "I really don't know why I even planted one. It's so much work, and I end up giving everything away. It was really my husband's hobby. I guess I couldn't stand not having one this summer."

"Mr. Crosley passed away last spring?"

"Yes. Quite suddenly. Heart attack. I never thought that would happen to him. He was always so quiet. Never one to show his feelings usually. Not angry or excitable ever, hardly."

She looked from the garden to me. "You said on the phone that you're a friend of Michael's."

I had said that, but I didn't want to be held to it now. "An acquaintance, really," I replied. "We share the same spiritual director, Father Loudermilk."

Mrs. Crosley nodded. "A nice man. I've spoken with him on the phone."

"I last saw Michael about three weeks ago at the campus pub. I was surprised to hear a little later that he'd left St. Aelred's."

"I wasn't," Mrs. Crosley said. She looked back out toward the garden. "Michael was very affected by his father's death. More than he let on. More than he even knew, maybe." That last observation confused us both. Mrs. Crosley stared into the distance while she tried to work it out. "Mikey and his father didn't get along very well. They were too different for that. Mikey was always studious and sensitive. Bookish. Martin, my husband, was not. I don't imagine he read a book a year. Martin worked up at the RCA plant on Sherman Avenue. He operated a presser, a machine that makes record albums. In twenty years there, he barely missed a day.

"Martin always belittled the things Michael thought important, his books, his academic successes. He wanted Michael in sports, you know, football and wrestling. Michael tried. He was big enough for it, but he didn't have the instinct."

Mrs. Crosley paused to refill my glass. She set the glass pitcher down and studied it for a moment, wiping idly at the condensation that had formed on its fat sides. Then, still staring at the pitcher, she said, "I'm sure you've no-

ticed that sons often take after their fathers. Get their
identities from imitating their fathers, I mean. You've seen
a little boy, I know, toddling along after his dad, wearing
the same kind of ball cap or maybe cowboy boots like his
dad's. But the opposite happens, too. Boys define themselves by consciously not being what their fathers are.''

She looked at me and almost smiled. ''That was the way
it was with Mikey. Mikey was one pole of the compass, and
his father was the other. When Martin died, Mikey lost that
point of reference for his identity. And he lost his best reason for being at St. Aelred's.''

I must have looked confused again, because her dry voice
picked up speed as she tried to explain.

''When Michael first told us about the priesthood, I
knew he was just feeling us out, you know, saying the thing
aloud to hear how it sounded. But then his father laughed,
as though Mikey had said he was going to be a lion tamer
or an astronaut, and I could see Mikey's eyes harden. I said
to myself, 'He'll be a priest now if it kills him.' ''

Mrs. Crosley's gaze returned to the garden. ''You understand now why I say that Michael lost his vocation when
his father died. His goal was never to be a priest, really. It
was to be the total opposite of his father, the mirror image
of Martin Crosley. He's lost without that goal, I'm afraid.''

I thought for a moment of Father Jerome's observation
that a vocation was often an answer to a bad family situation. ''Where do you think Michael's gone?'' I asked.

Mrs. Crosley considered the question seriously. ''He's
gone looking for himself,'' she finally said.

She turned to me, smiling definitely now, but with a dark
look in her eyes that negated the smile. ''He's searching for
Michael Crosley,'' she said, ''and when he finds him, he'll
come back. To me at least,'' she added. ''I wouldn't want
to create any false hopes for Father Loudermilk. I don't see
Michael ever going back to St. Aelred's.''

Without thinking, I turned down her gestured offer of more iced tea, and Mrs. Crosley began to push her chair back from the table as though I'd announced my departure. I tried to think of the other questions I wanted to ask.

The first one that came to mind was the question that had so delighted Philip Swickard. "Has Michael mentioned meeting anyone recently? A special friend?"

Mrs. Crosley checked herself in the motion of rising. "A girl, you mean?" she asked.

I nodded, and she slowly settled back into her chair. I was grateful that she hadn't burst into laughter at the idea, but when she spoke, she came down solidly in the Swickard camp.

"Michael's never been the kind that made friends easily. To tell you the truth, he's never seemed to want them. He never really had special friends while he was growing up. Certainly not girlfriends. I often hoped that Michael would meet someone. Prayed that he would. Why do you ask? Did Michael mention someone to you?"

"No," I said quickly. Like Mrs. Crosley, I was concerned about creating false hopes. Michael Crosley could tell his mother about Melissa Donahue when he was ready. "It was just an idea I had," I added.

Mrs. Crosley waited expectantly, her hands on the arms of her chair. "Was there anything else?"

"Evansville," I said. "Michael mentioned the place once. Can you think of any reason why he might have gone there?"

Mrs. Crosley frowned. "Evansville was my husband's hometown. His brother, John, still lives there."

"Could Michael have gone to stay with his uncle?"

"No," she said emphatically. "I called John right after I heard from Father Loudermilk. He told me that he hadn't seen Michael since Martin's funeral. John promised to call me right away if he heard anything."

She stood up completely now, and I acknowledged receipt of her message by saying, "I'd better be getting back."

Mrs. Crosley was smiling her phony smile again by the time we reached her front door. "Tell Father Loudermilk that I'll call him as soon as I hear from Mikey," she said. "I expect to hear from him shortly."

I was thinking of Melissa Donahue when I answered. "I'm sure you will."

SIX

AFTER LEAVING MRS. CROSLEY, I stopped at a filling station to top off the Ghia. The young man working behind the counter wore a blue uniform shirt with JIM embroidered on an oval-shaped patch over the pocket. I asked Jim about the Kingsway address. He produced a greasy map of the city from under the counter and studied it for a minute, holding it an inch or so away from his nose and repeating "Kingsway" over and over again as though he were calling a dog.

I finally circled around behind the counter so I could read the map's index over Jim's shoulder. "Look under C-two," I said.

Jim laid the map out flat on the counter and traced the coordinates with his index fingers. They came together in the upper right-hand corner of the map.

"Castleton," Jim said. "That's a ritzy area up by Castleton Mall. That's the new shopping center, all enclosed, so you can walk around from store to store and never go outside."

"No kidding," I said.

"No kidding."

Jim rattled off some directions that I hurriedly copied on the Dairy Queen napkin I'd used to note the Donahues' address.

"Don't be a stranger now, Father," Jim said as I left.

My hand went up involuntarily to the collar I wore. "Thanks," I said.

I drove out onto I-465, the loop of highway that circled Indianapolis like the wall around a medieval city. I followed the highway east briefly and then north for twenty minutes. The road ran past some light industry, small offices, fields of corn and soybeans, and scattered subdivisions. I kept an eye out for the Indianapolis skyline, but I never saw it. They might have already taken it in for the night.

Halfway to Castleton, I passed the exit for I-70, the interstate that had carried me in from the East when I'd first come to Indiana and St. Aelred's. I felt a momentary impulse to get back on 70 and head home, to do what Michael Crosley had done, to go off and find myself. The feeling passed quickly. For one thing, I had no idea where I'd go to find Owen Keane. And I was intimidated by the thought of setting out alone. The moment left me marveling anew at Crosley's decision. What had happened, I wondered, to make him take so awesome a step?

I left I-465 at the Shadeland Avenue exit and drove north until I spotted 75th Street. I made a right onto 75th and then the next right, which was Kingsway. Almost immediately, I felt an irrational regret that I hadn't gotten around to painting over the Ghia's gray primer spots. The Donahues' neighborhood was very quiet and very nice. Large brick colonials sat well back on green, shady lots. There were no cars parked on the wide streets, but the ones I could see in the driveways I passed were large domestic sedans with a smattering of smaller, racier imports.

Here and there, kids were shooting basketballs at driveway hoops. I wasn't surprised to see that activity. In my year in Indiana, I'd learned that basketball was the unofficial religion of the state. Three worshipers were playing in the Donahue driveway, all boys around ten years old. One of them, a blond kid with bony knees and huge feet, dribbled a basketball around expertly while two slower, taller friends tried to guard him.

The kid with the ball stopped in his tracks when I pulled up at the curb. He held the ball on one skinny hip and watched as I climbed out of the VW. His two opponents took up positions behind him.

"Nice car," the blond called out with enough sarcasm to flatten one of my tires.

"A gift from Elvis," I replied as I ascended the walk.

I was ringing the bell before the kid selected his retort. "I'll bet," he said.

The front door was opened by Earl H. Donahue himself, or so I deduced. The man was middle-aged and still dressed for work, in light blue suit pants, a lighter blue shirt, and a wide blue and pink striped tie. This natty collection was all but undone by his shoes, huge black wing tips with thick soles. Mr. Donahue's hair also contained internal contradictions. It was brown and he wore it fashionably long over his ears, but combed straight back off his forehead in keeping with some earlier style. The face beneath the contradictory hair was fleshy and unlined and unsmiling.

I noted that he carried an open newspaper and jumped immediately to another deduction. "Sorry to interrupt your reading."

Donahue cut me off. "Look, Father, we're Presbyterians. So if you'll excuse me . . ."

"I'm not a priest," I said. "I'm a seminarian. My name is Owen Keane. I believe Melissa and I have a mutual friend." That didn't budge Donahue, so I added, "Michael Crosley."

Donahue smiled even less. I don't know what I'd been expecting when I'd approached the Donahues. Perhaps that Michael Crosley would answer the door himself. It should have occurred to me, I suddenly realized, that Michael might not be the only runaway. Perhaps Melissa had gone off to California with him.

I'd no sooner had this second thought than Donahue invalidated it. Without taking his small, suspicious eyes from me, he turned his head slightly and called "Melissa" over his shoulder.

I noted a movement in the yard and turned to find that the basketball trio had come around behind me to watch the fun. When I turned back to Donahue, he'd been joined by a young blond girl. My artistic roommate from Boston College, Harry, would have described her as statuesque, and he would have been right. She wore an extremely short plaid dress and was shoeless, but she equaled her father's five foot ten. I judged her age to be sixteen or seventeen. Going on twenty-nine.

"Here's another surprise for your mother and me," Donahue said, indicating me with a nod of his head.

"Daddy," Melissa said, sounding as embarrassed as I suddenly felt. "I've never even seen him before."

"That's right," I tried to say.

Donahue wasn't finished. "I didn't say you knew him. But he tells me you may have a mutual friend, a Michael somebody. What was it again?"

His question gave me the floor, and I paused for a second to enjoy it. "Crosley," I finally said. "Michael Crosley."

Donahue turned back to his daughter. "I thought we'd grounded you," he said. "I thought that meant no more new boyfriends."

"I don't know any Michael Crosley," Melissa said.

"So what's this Crosley guy? A hippie? A biker?" When she didn't answer, he turned to me. "Well?"

"Michael's a student at my college, St. Aelred's. Was a student, anyway," I added. "He may have dropped out."

"A student?" Donahue repeated, his square face reddening. "You mean he's a seminarian?" Without waiting for an answer, he turned again on his daughter. "A seminarian, for God's sake. Who's it going to be next, Billy Graham?"

"I don't know any Michael Crosley," Melissa said again. She was standing toe-to-toe with her father, her light voice firm. "I've never even heard of him."

Donahue wasn't buying. "That's not his story. How about it?" he fired at me.

I felt bad about the hole I was digging for the girl, but I had to know the answer. "I'm trying to trace Michael Crosley," I said, addressing Melissa. "He disappeared about two weeks ago. I found your name and phone number in his room." I watched her carefully for some sign that she was faking her ignorance or for a secret signal that she couldn't speak plainly in front of her father. All I saw in her blue eyes was sincere confusion.

"Your phone number," Donahue repeated in amazement. "What are you doing, running ads now?"

That cut it for me. I drew myself up and waded in to Melissa's defense. Sir Owen, the Unreflecting. "Mr. Donahue, I think you're being unfair to your daughter."

Donahue's "Who asked you?" was no more than I expected, but it was overlaid by Melissa's "Mind your own business!" which took me by surprise.

"You heard my daughter," Donahue said. "She doesn't know you or your friend and she doesn't want to know you. Take your story and go back where you came from."

They were standing shoulder to shoulder now against the common enemy, Melissa's unfriendly glare only a more attractive version of her father's.

"Sorry I bothered you," I said.

The door slammed shut before I'd gotten off the porch. Through it, I could hear round two of the Donahue title bout starting up. I didn't feel quite as guilty about it now.

The towheaded kid was waiting alone down by my car. I could hear his two friends dribbling and shooting over in the driveway.

"Not staying for dinner?" the kid asked.

I was about to tell him to go dunk himself when I had a more constructive thought. I took out my all-purpose Dairy Queen napkin and tore off a corner. On it, I wrote my name and the number of the phone in St. Meinrad Hall. I handed it to the kid.

"Do me a favor," I said. "Give this to Melissa."

"What's in it for me?" the kid asked.

I was settling in behind the wheel by then. "I'll leave you the Ghia in my will." He smiled at that. The engine fired on the first try, and I sped off.

I was tired, and the Ghia's headlights had yellowed with age, so I decided that it would be safer to take the interstate back to St. Aelred's. I left Indy on I-65, following the signs for Louisville. Dusk lasts forever in Indiana in the summertime. I drove south in the soft, darkening blue, dodging semis, and killing a good-sized bug with my windshield every mile or so. Philip Swickard would have loved it.

I didn't want to think about Melissa Donahue or Michael Crosley or even Owen Keane. I switched on my AM radio and tried to find an East Coast station. Sometimes, late at night, I picked up WABC from New York City, and it was like a letter from home. It was too early now, though, for that trick to work. Instead, I lucked on to a station that was broadcasting a night game between the Detroit Tigers and the Chicago White Sox. The happy play-by-play stayed with me all the way back.

SEVEN

I AWOKE THE NEXT MORNING with something resembling a hangover, which was strange as I hadn't had so much as a beer the day before. I finally decided that one bad deduction too many had given me the headache. I'd driven up to Indianapolis with the case already solved and Father Jerome's praises sounding faintly in the back of my head. Now my head hurt, front and back, and I found myself on square one again.

I felt better after the seminarians' morning prayer service. It was sparsely attended owing to the summer break, but that was fine by me. I usually found St. Aelred's namesake church too ornate by half. That morning, the rows and rows of empty seats counteracted some of the clutter, and the place seemed airy and fresh. A line from the Psalm reading, "Thou renderest to every man according to his work," encouraged a renewed effort. I decided to give Crosley's mystery another try, starting from scratch if I had to.

Playing detective in my clericals hadn't been a big success, so I left them in my closet, sticking instead with the outfit I'd worn to the service: jeans and a faded green T-shirt. Father Jerome had given me permission for the switch when he'd told me to use my own judgment concerning my attire. He hadn't been as free with Crosley, evidently, having asked him not to wear his clericals. It finally occurred to me to wonder why. The priest had mentioned that detail as though he were offering me a clue. So far, it was a clue I didn't understand.

Father Jerome had also given me two leads that I had yet to follow up: Crosley's two service projects. I decided to tackle them in the order in which the old priest had listed them on the index card he'd given me. That made the first stop Green Streets, the halfway house in New Albany.

A lot of towns in Indiana were named for other places. Hoosiers have their own Brooklyn, Richmond, Atlanta, Princeton, Hamburg, Liverpool, and Milan. Once, during an idle evening, I'd even located a tiny village called Trenton on my map. My homesickness for the original Trenton explained the phenomenon for me. It was easy to imagine settlers trying to recapture some sense of home through the use of a borrowed name. Indiana's many "New" towns conveyed this feeling strongly: New Lisbon, New Chicago, New Salem, New Paris.

New Albany, Indiana, was on the Ohio River, across from the edge of Louisville's suburban sprawl. It must have been quite a little town in its day, that day being way back when rivers were the only interstates. Now New Albany was a shady, sleepy place, with a few crumbling mansions like grounded riverboats to remind it of its glory days.

The Green Streets house was not a mansion, but it was close. I pulled up in front of the big white house after an hour of driving and four stops for directions. The front yard rose steeply from the street. I climbed a short flight of flagstone steps to the front walk. This ran straight to more steps, wooden ones this time that led to a deep front porch. On the porch, a man of about thirty was watering geraniums that grew in a long wooden box. The box was white and, like the house, it looked as though it had been repainted especially for my visit.

The man with the watering can looked up as I reached the porch steps. He was short but built like an ex-football player, an impression somewhat contradicted by his round wire-rimmed glasses and fragile hairline. He wore paint-splattered jeans and a blue work shirt whose long sleeves were rolled up above his elbows. "Help you?" he asked.

I told him my name and that I'd come from St. Aelred's.

He pointed at me with the long spout of his watering can. "You're here about Michael Crosley, then," he said. "We missed him last week. Are you his replacement?"

"Not exactly," I said. "Michael left St. Aelred's on short notice. No notice, in fact. I'm looking into it for the school."

I must have been trying to sound important with that last disclosure, because the man smiled. "What are you?" he asked, "the sergeant-at-arms?"

"Just another seminarian," I said, "but I moonlight as hall monitor. Is anybody in charge around here?"

The man's smile broadened. "That would be me, I guess. I'm codirector. Bill Koffman." He switched the watering can to his left hand and extended his right. "Come on up and have a seat."

He led me to a pair of armless wooden lounge chairs whose paint was so fresh it still looked wet. "Neat ship you run here," I said.

"Thanks." Koffman bobbed his head up and down in agreement as he spoke. "The neighbors aren't too fond of us—group homes have a bad rep in general—but they can't accuse us of letting the place run down. About all there is for the guys to do is paint and cut the grass, so we really keep up on it. We're supposed to have some occupational training stuff someday soon." He shrugged. "When there's money. Things are pretty tight now."

"Who pays the bills?"

"The state mostly. We also get some charity money, United Way, the Archdiocese of Indianapolis, that sort of stuff."

"You're a halfway house for kids with drug problems?"

Koffman bobbed his head again. "And law problems. Teenagers who are transitioning from some correctional facility. Generally kids who were stealing to support a habit. No dealers. No real hard cases, in fact. Just a few who think they are."

Koffman settled back, his legs stretched out at forty-five-degree angles on either side of his chair. "I don't really like to call this a halfway house. The name's all wrong for us. Halfway houses are supposed to be a half step between prison and the real world, someplace where convicts can get used to a little freedom before they're dumped on the street. I think of Green Streets as an 'alternative house.' Most of our kids come from cities, Indianapolis mostly, Terre Haute, Evansville, places like that. They're on their way back to some real bad scenes. It's all they know, mean streets and jail. Green Streets is supposed to give them a glimpse of other ways to live. Give them the idea that there's something worth climbing out for."

"It sounds like a good idea," I said.

"Looks good on a grant application anyway. In practice, the place bores the kids stiff." He had folded his hands on top of his stomach, and now he actually began twiddling his thumbs. "I may not have the smarts for the job."

"What's your background?"

"Behavioral psychology. What's yours?"

Koffman's interest took me by surprise. "English, once," I said. "Theology now."

"Now and forever, right?" Koffman asked, grinning.

"Michael Crosley doesn't seem to think so."

Koffman shook his head. "Took me in, that's for sure. I expected him to be canonized any day. Unworldly kind of guy. I can never imagine him naked. Can you?"

"Not offhand."

"Karen, my wife, got Crosley's number the first time she met him. 'One seriously confused character,' she called him."

"Your wife lives here, too?"

"Yep. She's the other codirector. Koffman and Koffman they call us in the trade. I don't know who gets top billing."

I heard the screen door behind me open. "Somebody talking about me?"

I turned and saw a woman with long, straight brown hair highlighted by a premature streak of gray and a broad face that was heavily freckled. She wore a shapeless denim dress and sandals. I wondered as I shook her hand whether she had just come to the door or had been quietly listening for a time.

She solved this mystery herself when she spoke again. "So Bishop Crosley has escaped," she said. "I can't say I'm surprised. That kid's a textbook case of identity confusion."

"Meaning what?" I asked.

Karen's small, freckled nose wrinkled as she searched for layman's terms. "He wasn't who he thought he was," she said. "And the real Michael Crosley was somebody he wouldn't have associated with. Somebody he would have looked down on."

"What makes you say that?" I asked.

"Woman's intuition," her husband said, leaning forward in his chair to take her hand.

Karen slapped his hand lightly. "I spoke with him," she said. "He was supposed to be here counseling our Catholic kids, one of the strings attached to the money we get from the archdiocese. Michael was pretty useless at it, really out of his depth. So he mostly spent his time talking to me. I never met a square peg trying harder to jam himself into a round hole."

She examined me critically for a second. I thought she was assessing my relative squareness until she spoke again. "So what are you trying to do? Drag him back inside the electric fence?"

That idea rankled, as it seemed intended to do. I studied the tiny beads of sweat on her upper lip before answering. "Nobody wants to drag him back. We'd just like to understand what's happened."

"Good luck," Karen said. "Michael probably doesn't understand it himself."

She looked like she might be through pronouncing on Crosley, so I fed her another straight line. "You say Michael isn't much good at counseling."

"No good at all, actually," she said. "He's had some basic psych courses, and he can parrot it back decently, but our kids know they're dealing with a lightweight. It's a shame, you know. In some ways, Michael is perfect for this job. The biggest problem for our average kid is low self-esteem. That's also one of Michael's problems."

"Is that why he's such a loner?" I asked.

"In part. That has more to do with his parents. Michael saw their marriage as an impersonal, loveless thing. Especially from his father's point of view. Observing that marriage is how Michael acquired his theory of human relationships. And his miserable sense of self-worth."

Karen reached out as she spoke and put her hand on Koffman's shoulder. "The self-esteem problem should help him to identify with our kids, but, as I said, Michael doesn't know himself that well. He can't relate to the residents here, and they know it."

"They've been pretty rough on him, I'm afraid," Koffman said.

"Physically rough?"

"No," Koffman said quickly. "Nothing like that."

"Crosley was in a fight just before he took off." I said it to see the Koffmans' reaction. Their exaggerated incredulity reminded me of Philip Swickard's response to my suggestion that Crosley had fallen in love.

"Michael Crosley?" Koffman asked. "I can't imagine that." He sat trying for a moment, his eyes focusing on the thin air between us.

"It didn't happen here," his wife added. "We would have heard about it. Now that you mention it, one of his eyes did look a little dark last time he was here. I asked him about it, but he didn't want to discuss it."

"When was that?" I asked.

"Two weeks ago today," Karen said. "A Thursday. He always came on a Thursday. I remember thinking this morning that he might be back today."

"He was here the day before he left St. Aelred's, then."

"Huh," Koffman said.

"Did he speak with any of your kids that day? Somebody I could talk with now?"

The two directors held a short conference via mental telepathy. Then Karen said, "Ronnie's around, I think. He had as much to do with Michael as any of the boys. I'll get him."

After she'd gone back inside, Koffman motioned me closer and said, "Don't let any of Karen's little jabs get you down. She doesn't have much time for religion. Any religion." His intonation added an additional message that undercut his apology, something like: "And who can blame her?"

We waited in silence until the screen door opened again. The Koffmans and I had spoken loosely, calling the residents of Green Streets "boys" and "kids." The young man who came out through the screen door was no kid and hadn't been one for some time. He was of medium height, well tanned and thin. His dark, curly hair was unfashionably short, and I wondered if it was struggling back from some reform school haircut. He needed only a golden earring and a bandanna to look like Hollywood's idea of a gypsy. His face was almost unnaturally flat. The only suggestion of depth came from his dark—almost black—eyes.

Those deep eyes stayed on me while Koffman rose and introduced us. Then Koffman said, "Nice meeting you, Owen. Ronnie, I'll see you later. I think I'm on lunch detail today."

Ronnie continued to evaluate me silently after Koffman left us. I decided to help him sum up. "I'm another one of those holy jerks from St. Aelred's," I said. "I don't know much about the real world, and I wouldn't last for two minutes in your old neighborhood."

Ronnie smiled briefly, showing small, very white teeth. "What do you want, Padre?" he asked.

"For starters, I'd like to know what you think of Michael Crosley."

"Seems like you already know that. Where's he been, anyway? Did he give up on us?"

"He may have given up on everything. He left St. Aelred's rather suddenly almost two weeks ago. He hasn't been back."

I could have accepted without comment a variety of reactions from Ronnie, ranging from studied indifference to satisfaction that Crosley had turned out to be a pious fraud. What I actually got—sudden anger—surprised me.

"That creep," Ronnie said. He folded his arms across his narrow chest and stared through me out into the yard.

"What's it to you?" I asked.

"Not a damn thing, Padre." Ronnie's placid exterior fell back into place and he looked at me again, indifferently.

"Did Crosley ever mention any plans to you? About any place he might have been thinking of going?"

"He only talked about going to heaven," Ronnie said. "He could make it sound like a real bad idea. He was a real baby, that one. A kid. He asked me questions about doing drugs that any fifth grader from my old street could have answered. I felt sorry for him, I really did. I tried to be nice to him when the other guys ranked on him. I thought he was okay underneath." He shook his head in amazement at his misjudgment.

I stood marveling for a moment at Ronnie's reaction. He seemed genuinely let down by Crosley's departure, much more than Beatrice Crosley had been. More than Father Jerome. More than I was myself, I realized with a small shock.

While I was busy musing, Ronnie was getting tired of my company. "To hell with Crosley," he said as he turned away. "To hell with the whole lot of you."

EIGHT

I HAD AN EARLY LUNCH in a New Albany pizzeria called the Pizza Prince. The place ground up its pepperoni and sliced its pies into two-inch squares like greasy canapes, making me feel once again like a stranger in a strange land. After lunch, I drove northwest on State Road 64, back to Huber County. Just across the county line, I turned south on 66 to a little dot on the map called Evay. It was the site of Michael Crosley's second service project, the Good Fellows Retirement Home.

The dot on my map turned out to be a fairly accurate representation of Evay, which wasn't much more than a crossroads with a few old houses and a white-tiled filling station where some rusty domestic monsters had dragged themselves to die. It was no job at all to find the retirement home. I spotted the wide one-story building on a slight rise just outside of town. I parked the Ghia in a gravel lot that fronted the building. The stone looked like it had just been put down, and it was bright enough in the midday sun to hurt my eyes.

The Good Fellows Home was newer than I'd expected it to be. The brick building's architecture was American Colonial. A copper-topped cupola rose from the center of its roof, and its large, regularly spaced windows were flanked by white shutters. The double doors opened onto a reception area whose worn carpet belied the building's fresh exterior. The reception desk was staffed by a young woman in a green print dress who was speaking on the phone.

While I waited for the call to end, I examined a faded diagram of the building that hung on the bright, geometric wallpaper. The diagram showed a large square surrounding a courtyard. Each side of the square was called a wing on the diagram and identified by a point of the compass. The east and west wings each had many small rooms arranged along a central corridor. The rear of the building, the north wing, had a laundry, an infirmary, a kitchen, and a dining room. I was standing in the south side of the square, which contained offices and activity rooms.

The receptionist hung up her phone. She had a nice tan and straight, light brown hair that disappeared behind her shoulders. She wore a plastic name tag that identified her simply as "Ann." Her "May I help you?" made me suspect that she had emigrated north from nearby Kentucky.

I wasn't as honest now as I had been at the Green Streets house. Karen Koffman's suggestion that I was a prison guard on the trail of an escapee still bothered me. "I'm from St. Aelred's," I began. "One of our students was visiting residents here at the home. I'm filling in for him today. He's away." Perhaps on the moon, I added to myself.

"Which of the residents has he been visiting?" Ann asked.

I had to admit that I had no idea.

Ann wasn't daunted by the news. She pushed her chair back from the desk. "Mrs. Wasson will know. She knows everything. I'll just be a minute." When she turned her back to leave me, I noted that her hair fanned out like a cape and stretched all the way down to the small of her back.

I was still thinking of Ann's hair when she returned, accompanied by a stout black woman in a nurse's uniform. Salt and pepper curls escaped without design from beneath her cap, and her merry eyes examined me over the half-moons of her reading glasses. She walked in a rapid, businesslike pace in her flat, white shoes, extending her hand to shake mine when she was still five steps away.

"Standing in for Mr. Crosby, are we?" she asked, seriously undermining her reputation for omniscience.

"Crosley," I said. "Michael Crosley."

"Right." She smiled as though I had given a password correctly. "He called on our Catholics, isn't that right? Let me see. Off the top of my head, I know there's Mr. O'Connor in the west wing and Mrs. Steiner in the east wing. I can look the room numbers up if you like, but we have the residents' names printed on their doors."

"I'm sure I'll find them."

"Let me show you the way." She held the inner door to the reception area open for me and escorted me down a quiet corridor. As we walked, I began to hear voices, some talking, some moaning, some calling out.

"This is a big place for such a small town," I said.

"Yes," Mrs. Wasson said, "but of course, we just happen to be located here. We serve the whole southern part of Indiana and a small section of Kentucky. The Good Fellows were a major force in this part of the country once upon a time."

"The Good Fellows?"

"A fraternal organization. Started by veterans of the Civil War. There were lodges in most decent-sized towns in Indiana around the turn of the century. The membership peaked after the First World War and then started to fall off. Now about all that's left are the nursing homes scattered here and there around the Midwest."

"Your residents are all lodge members?"

"No. We also serve the spouses of members. And we have some fee residents, too. We have to. Have to pay the light bills, you know."

I was tempted to ask the happy nurse what would happen to the place when the last Good Fellow died, but I didn't get the chance. We turned the corner into the west wing, almost running into an old man in pajamas and an open robe shuffling forward with the aid of a walker. Be-

yond him was a long hallway containing several other am-
bulatory residents and others in wheelchairs. Some of the
open doorways we passed held people content to sit on their
"front porches" and watch the traffic pass by. Almost
everyone we saw called out a greeting or a request to Mrs.
Wasson, the requests often vague and unanswerable. She
smiled and nodded and more or less ignored everyone.

"Here's Mr. O'Connor's room." She looked inside
briefly. "His roommate is gone for the moment. I'll leave
you here. Perhaps we'll talk again before you go."

Despite the heat of the day, the windows were closed in
Mr. O'Connor's room and the blinds were drawn. The man
himself was asleep in his bed, a sheet pulled up to his chest.
His mouth was open, and he breathed through it, making
a soft noise like the sound of the ocean in a seashell. The
skin of his face was pale and tight, its only spot of color a
red blush at the tip of his sharp nose. His muscular arms lay
outside the sheet, and one was badly bruised. From an in-
travenous, I decided. There was an acrid smell of urine in
the room. A plastic hose emerged from beneath the sheet
and ran to a plastic bag hanging at the foot of the bed.

"Mr. O'Connor," I said softly.

I was relieved when he didn't wake. I did what I was sure
Michael Crosley had done when he visited Mr. O'Connor.
I said a prayer and slipped out quietly.

I continued my circumnavigation of the building, walking to the end of the west corridor and turning right into the
north wing. I noted as I passed the corner that the fire
doors at the end of the corridor were propped open to catch
the breeze. As I wandered, I thought of my own grandfa-
ther, who had passed his last years in a nursing home with
few visits from me. The memory made me sadly sentimen-
tal and set me up nicely for what happened next.

When I reached the east wing I slowed my pace, scanning the doors I passed for Mrs. Steiner's name. Most of

the doors had two names, written in marker on construction paper circles.

I hadn't gotten very far when someone called out to me. "Hey! Help me. I'm in here, boy. Help me."

I backtracked to an open door on the courtyard side of the hallway. In a wheelchair by the windows sat a fragile-looking woman with short white hair and a face that was wrinkled elaborately. Her skin was also weathered in color, to a dull red. She wore thick horn-rimmed glasses that made her eyes huge and indistinct.

"Would you like me to find you a nurse?" I asked.

"Can't you write?"

"Pardon me?"

She shook her head impatiently. "Write. I need someone to write for me. I don't need a nurse."

"Maybe one of the aides . . ."

"One word, that's all I need. I'm not writing home for money. I'm not writing my congressman. One word. Are you too busy for that?"

"No," I said.

"Good. Find yourself a pen and come back here. Sooner you start the sooner you're finished."

"I have a pen," I said, pulling one from the pocket of my shirt.

"Good," the old woman said. "There next to your long nose. Somebody put a name on my door and it isn't mine." I turned to examine the red circle taped to her door. It read "Sarah Morell."

"What is your name?" I asked.

"Olivia."

"And your last name?"

"Morell. Can't you read? Cross out Sarah and write Olivia. Print it, I mean. Big letters."

"It's done."

"How'd you spell it? No offense, Bill, but the public schools aren't what they used to be."

"O-l-i-v-i-a. And my name is Owen."

"Thanks. You can go now, Billy. I'll call you when I need you."

I conceded the small point of my name in my hurry to leave. I'd only gotten a few steps away before she needed me again.

"Billy," she called. "Billy come quick. Help me. Quick."

I poked my head back through the doorway. "Yes?"

"I need some water real bad. My jug is empty. Get me some water, Billy."

"I'll call an aide," I said.

"I don't want to go to the bathroom, for God's sake. Water, Billy, water. Is that too much to ask?"

Of course it wasn't. I entered her room and took a blue plastic jug, from the bureau. The jug was sticky to the touch. There was a brush and comb on the bureau. The nightstand next to the high bed held a small radio. Nothing else softened the room, which was half hospital, half cheap motel.

"You have a nice room," I said.

"Sooner you're gone the sooner you're back. Don't lose your way," she called after me.

I wandered back into the north wing. There I found a nurse's aide who seemed to be late for an important appointment. I told her that someone had gotten Olivia's name wrong. She game me a fresh pitcher of water and a small carton of ice cream, a compensation to Olivia for the mistake.

I heard the old woman calling for me when I was several doors away. "Billy! Billy! Where are you, boy? Save me. You're the only one who can save me, Billy."

I stopped two steps into the room. Her wispy white hair was gone, replaced by a curly blond wig. "Here's your water," I managed to say.

"Water? Pour it down the john, Billy, and get out after him. Don't root in your shoes, boy. He's getting away!"

"Who?"

"I didn't ask his name. I didn't open the window to shake his hand. He frightened me, Billy. Look at my hands quiver!" She raised one hand from the arm of her chair and waved it at me.

"Who scared you?" I asked slowly.

"A man out there in the courtyard. He was peering in the window. Peering, Billy. Use your imagination." She helped me by leaning forward in her chair and widening her hazy eyes unnaturally.

"Well, he's gone now," I said, walking to the window.

"Gone? I'm the one with the cataracts, boy. Who do you think that is, over there in the corner?"

She pointed to a man who was sitting on a bench between small evergreens. He was a fat man in a gray robe and yellow trousers with an unlikely straw hat on his head. His hands rested on a cane, his gaze on a spot of brown grass a few feet before him.

"He was probably just looking around the courtyard," I said. "He probably didn't mean to stare."

"Stare? I said he was peering, Billy! Think back, you'll remember. Peering, with his nose an inch from this window. He only ran away when I started to yell for you."

"He doesn't look like he's run in years."

"A minute ago you couldn't even see him. Now you're telling me his joints are bad. Stop guessing and do something!"

"Do you want me to talk with him?"

"Yes. If that doesn't work, you'll have to knock him down."

"I'll try to find a nurse," I said.

"Wait a minute, Billy. What have you got there?"

"Ice cream. An aide sent it for you."

"Were you saving it for my birthday? Never mind. I don't think I can eat anything. I'm too upset. Leave it here on my tray."

"I'll find a nurse."

Mrs. Wasson found me as I left the room. Her eyes were positively twinkling. "Mr. Kane. Are you the one who wanted Mrs. Morell's name card changed?"

"Keane," I said, feeling like the butt of an elaborate practical joke. "There's no rush about the name change. I've already fixed it. You might want to check on that man sitting out in the courtyard, though. Mrs. Morell caught him staring in her window."

"Peering!" the old woman called out from behind me.

"What a day," the nurse said. "Excuse me, please." She stepped past me into the room, pulling the name card from the door in a quick motion that left a little curl of tape behind. "Sarah, what have you been up to?" she asked.

The old woman was scraping the bottom of the ice cream carton with a plastic spoon. "Mrs. Morell to you," she said.

"I've asked you not to bother people with your stories, Mrs. Morell. You know your name is Sarah, and you know that Mr. Cranny can hardly get up from that bench."

"I don't believe we've been introduced," the old woman said.

Mrs. Wasson sighed for the balcony and turned to leave. "I'll be back with your pills before dinner," she said over her shoulder. "Annie will make a new name card for your door." This last comment was directed to me as well. She took my arm and led me away from the room.

"Thank you for wanting to help," she said. "It's a shame you didn't pick a resident who could appreciate the effort. I'm afraid Sarah is in her own world these days. She manages to latch on to everyone who visits us."

"Including Michael Crosley?" I asked.

"Yes. He was always in there listening to her stories." She escorted me to the end of the hallway. "I've just learned that Mrs. Steiner is away today visiting family. Maybe you can come back some other time to see her. It was nice meeting you." Her smile widened momentarily as she released my arm.

I stood at the corner of the hallway for a moment, studying a cheap print of a primitive farm scene done entirely in shades of blue. Then I walked quietly toward Sarah's room, stopping short of her door to listen.

"Help, Bill. Help." Her voice had lost its force. I might not have heard it at all if I hadn't been expecting it. "Where are you, Billy? Where are you? Alone. Alone with these awful men. Save me, Billy. Save me, anybody. They'll rob me. They'll take everything. Get them out of here. Help. They'll take my glasses. They'll hide my glasses and laugh at me. They'll take my money. Help me, Billy!"

I stepped back into her open doorway. "Try to settle down," I said. "You'll have Mrs. Wasson back in here."

She didn't seem surprised or happy to have me back. "Shush," she said. "Control your voice. They'll hear you."

I tried to look stern. "I'm not asking 'who' anymore."

"Burglars. Downstairs. I told you that kitchen door was no good. Buy a decent lock, I said. Buy a dog. Now what are you going to do? Have you got a flashlight?"

"No."

"Buy a flashlight, I said. Never mind. Go downstairs and chase them out, Billy. Bark like a dog. That'll scare them. Save the silver, Billy. You're the only one who can do it."

"I'm not Billy, Mrs. Morell. There are no burglars downstairs. There's no downstairs."

"That's yellow talk, Billy. Don't run on with that story. Don't hide your head in your drawers. It's not going to make your troubles go away. Bark like a dog. A big one."

"I'm here asking about a friend of mine. I think you know him. Michael Crosley." When she didn't answer me, I started to leave the room.

She stopped me easily. "I know Michael, Owen," she said.

My own name sounded unfamiliar coming from her. She spoke it softly and blinked at me repeatedly from behind her glasses. Her Marilyn Monroe wig had slipped to one side of her head.

"You called me Owen," I said.

"That's your name, isn't it?"

"Yes," I said. "What's your name?"

"Mrs. Morell."

"Olivia?"

"Sarah."

There was still the chance that this Sarah was just another change of costume. I let her quiet voice convince me otherwise. "This is a lonesome place, isn't it, Sarah?"

"Yes."

"You don't like it here."

"No," she said. "It scares me."

"Tell me about Michael Crosley."

"Big guy. Blue eyes like saucers. Carries a Bible."

"Has he been here recently?"

"Not for weeks. I told him something, and he went away. He promised he'd be back, but he's never been back."

I stepped up to her wheelchair, feeling a hot wind through the open window. "What did you tell him?"

"It's a secret," Sarah said. "If I tell you, you'll go away, too."

"I'll come back to see you," I said.

Sarah looked me over carefully. At close range her blue eyes were distinct and shrewd. "Come back tomorrow, then," she said. "And maybe we'll talk."

NINE

WHEN I GOT BACK to my room that evening, I found a note taped to my door. It read: "Okie, Mary Fitzgerald called again. Call her back pronto." Instead of a signature, Brother Dennis followed Mary's phone number with another quote from Proverbs. "Hope deferred maketh the heart sick."

The bit of paper on my door was like some hex sign that prevented me from crossing the threshold. I thought of going over to the church for the monks' vespers service, but I decided that their re-creation of the past would only lead me into my own memories and thoughts of Mary. I wandered instead to the Unstable, in search of a quiet beer. Then too, there was always the chance that Michael Crosley would pop in to recite another poem, or perhaps to read a few chapters of his autobiography.

My investigation needed some improbable break like that. Father Jerome had challenged me to find out why Crosley had left and why he had come to St. Aelred's in the first place. I'd made a little progress on the latter question. I was inclined to accept Beatrice Crosley's assessment that her son had chosen the priesthood as an act of rebellion against his father. It fit in nicely with Father Jerome's remark that seminarians often sought their parents' approval or some immunity against their disapproval. But on the question of why Crosley had left, my mental jury remained stubbornly out.

The Unstable was still suffering through its late-summer-term slump in business. Only a few of the tables were in use, and those were mainly near the small stage where Crosley had held forth. Tonight the stage was occupied by a local musician—I knew him only as Albert—who sometimes stopped by to play his guitar. It was a twelve-string acoustical one, and he was playing some complicated, Spanish-sounding piece that required him to slap the side of the instrument from time to time. I bought a mug of beer, selected a lonely table, and sat down.

I lit a cigarette and picked at an imaginary bit of tobacco on my lower lip. The gesture was a conscious imitation of Humphrey Bogart that was all the more absurd as I only smoked filtered cigarettes. As I sipped my beer, I slipped from thinking of Crosley's vocation to wondering about my own. Why had I come to St. Aelred's? Was I in the other group Father Jerome had mentioned, the ones who came on speculation, on the chance they had a calling? I liked to think I was. I had questions I wanted answered. I wanted to know what there was to know. What better place for a questioner like me than a school that held the secrets?

Why then St. Aelred's? When I'd first approached the priesthood, it hadn't been through the Jesuits at Boston College. They knew me too well. I'd gone instead to a priest in my old home parish, a gentle monsignor whom I'd always liked. He'd passed me on to the local archdiocese, and I'd moved upward through interviews and testing and been found worthy. In the end, they'd given me a list of seminaries with which the archdiocese did business. One was a major university in Washington, D.C. Another was a school I knew in nearby Philadelphia. The third had been my choice, sleepy St. Aelred's in Nowhere, Indiana. Founded before the Civil War and one of the largest seminaries in the country, it was now a quiet backwater. Why had I chosen it? From what, from whom was I hiding?

The answer, if there was one, didn't come. I ground out my cigarette and returned to the subject of Michael Crosley. Although I was willing to accept his mother's insight on his reason for pursuing the priesthood, I was distrustful of her ideas on why he'd quit, if in fact he had quit. He'd lost his reason for being a priest, she'd told me, when his anti-role model, his father, had died. I wasn't buying that. For one thing, I don't believe that a father had to be alive to be an influence. If Crosley had unresolved business with his father, it was likely to continue eating away at him now that Martin Crosley was dead. And there was another reason for my distrust. Mrs. Crosley's thinking had been colored by the rosy hope that Michael was coming back to her. That hadn't happened, and I didn't see it happening.

It was just another of my hunches, unsupported by hard evidence. I'd found very little evidence in my three days of playing detective. There was the testimony of just about everyone that Crosley was the original cold fish. There was Mrs. Wilson's story that Crosley had been acting strangely before he'd taken off. There was the slip of pink paper containing the name and phone number of a girl who violently denied knowing Crosley. There was the Koffmans' opinion that Crosley had been a mixed-up kid who didn't know himself. That judgment didn't carry much weight with me. As I finished the last of my beer, I wondered who really did know himself.

There was also the reaction of Ronnie, the Green Streets resident, to the news that Crosley had left St. Aelred's. He'd been angry. Why? He surely hadn't been looking up to Crosley as some kind of example. He'd called him naive, a baby.

Finally, there was my latest hot lead, a lonely old woman in a nursing home who heard imaginary burglars in an imaginary basement. She claimed to have told Crosley something that had made him go away. In reality, she had probably told him a dozen crazy stories and had finally worn him out. I could picture Sarah now, sitting alone in her room, weaving some tall tale for my return visit. I decided that I probably deserved it.

I was trying to decide between a second beer and bed when the beer appeared magically before me. Actually, it was placed there unmagically by Jim Carroll. Carroll was an employee of the college. Part of the time he worked in one of the college kitchens and part of the time he was the manager/bartender of the Unstable.

"On the house," Carroll said. "Business stinks tonight. I've been hoping some customer would ask me to join him."

I noted that Carroll carried a second mug of beer. "Please join me," I said.

Carroll sat down, his back to the stage lights. "No poetry tonight," he said mysteriously.

"No," I said.

"Last time I saw you in here was for the open-mike poetry session. Big pain in the butt, those things. We only sell five beers and every ashtray in the place gets filled up." The complaint reminded Carroll of something. "Got a cigarette?"

I shook one out of my pack for him, took one myself, and lit them both with my steel Zippo.

Carroll was as close to a shady character as St. Aelred's had. A sixties burnout with a ponytail and an unkempt beard, he always looked to me like a man who needed a good night's sleep and was making do instead on coffee and cigarettes. Other people's cigarettes.

"You remember that night?" Carroll asked. "The poetry reading night, I mean."

"Yes."

"It was the night young what's-his-face read the sonnet. Crosley, the kid who skipped."

"It was a sonnet?"

"Of course," Carroll replied impatiently, making me feel undereducated. "Fourteen lines ending with a rhyming couplet. Got to be a sonnet."

"Next time I'll count."

"It was a real break from the crap the kiddies normally read. 'Elevator poetry,' I call that stuff."

Carroll leaned forward slightly. "I hear you're looking for Crosley."

I wasted a second or two wondering how the campus grapevine could run so well with so many students away. Then it occurred to me that Carroll the bartender would know the secrets if anyone did. Perhaps even Michael Crosley's secrets. I answered him with my cigarette hanging from one side of my mouth, detective style. "Could be I am."

"Look for the woman," Carroll said. "Stands to reason, right? You saw how broken up Michael got reading that love sonnet. 'While doomed to fall outside that promised land,'" Carroll recited, his eyes closed, "'With fingers stretching upward for thy hand.'"

"You know the poem?" I'd taken it for granted that Crosley had written it.

"No," Carroll said. "Only heard it that one time. That last couplet really stuck in my mind. 'Stretching upward for thy hand,'" he repeated, holding his free hand aloft. "Look for the hand."

He winked and stood up. "Catch you later," he said.

Albert was now playing a slow, romantic song, background music for the love scene in a western. The music and Carroll's hot tip brought me back to Melissa Donahue. I'd hoped that she might call me for the conversation she'd been afraid to have in front of her father, but so far she hadn't. Maybe I should have been calling her now instead of rinsing my brain in beer. Maybe I should have been waiting in her ritzy neighborhood to tail her when she left the house.

"Maybe I should forget the whole thing," I said to the empty chair across from me. It was the best piece of advice I'd had that day. I finished my free beer and called it a night.

TEN

AT TEN THE NEXT MORNING, I entered the double doors of the Good Fellows Retirement Home to grasp at the straw held out by Sarah Morell. Ann, the receptionist with the amazing hair, gave me an encouraging smile. I was tempted to ask her what she did with all that hair when she slept. I had visions of it draped across the headboard of her bed like a satin sheet. Not the kind of vision a seminarian ought to be having, so instead of asking, I returned her smile and handed her another phony story.

"I missed Mrs. Steiner yesterday," I said. "She was away. I've come back to visit her, if that's all right."

"Have fun," Ann said.

I made my way into the east wing of the home, keeping watch for Nurse Wasson as I went. Because of my nervous scanning, I accidentally spotted Mrs. Steiner's room. The room was empty, and I moved on feeling both guilty and relieved.

Sarah Morell's room was occupied. She was again in her wheelchair next to her window, but the chair was turned in the opposite direction now. To face the morning light, I decided. Sarah wore a faded pink housedress and slippers. I noted that her curly blond wig was gone.

The wig may have been in her thoughts, too. When she noticed me in the doorway, her hand went up to her short white hair and patted it softly.

"I'm early," I said. "Sorry."

"I didn't think you were coming at all," Sarah said.

"We have to have our talk about Michael Crosley."

Sarah turned her head to look out the window. "I didn't expect it was to visit me. Nobody visits me."

I was embarrassed, but I didn't let her self-pity deflect me. "Crosley visited you," I said. "He listened to a lot of your stories."

"He said he wanted to help with my troubles," Sarah countered, making it sound like a cruelty. "Then he went away and left me."

"What troubles?"

The old woman raised her large hands and then let them fall into her lap. "Money troubles. Costs money to stay here and there's never enough coming in. That's what Frank always says."

I had been standing just inside the doorway. Now I came into the room and sat on the edge of Sarah's bed. "Who's Frank?"

"My nephew. He runs my farm for me. Frank and his family. It's been Morell land since the homesteading days. I guess farming doesn't pay anymore."

She turned her gaze from the window and noticed me on the bed. "Make yourself at home."

"Thanks." I was a little disconcerted by the change in Sarah. Yesterday she'd been way ahead of me, inventing new hoops faster than I could jump through them. I missed Olivia, her character from yesterday, enough to ask after another of her creations. "Who is Billy, by the way?"

"What?"

"You called me Billy yesterday. Who is he?"

"Nobody." She seemed tired and sad and uninterested. Was it because I had exploded her fantasy world, I wondered, or because Michael Crosley had really hurt her somehow?

"Do you feel like getting out of your room for a little while? We could go out into the courtyard."

Sarah scanned the courtyard, perhaps on the lookout for Mr. Cranny, the octogenarian Peeping Tom. "All right," she said.

I stepped around behind her chair and wheeled her out into the hallway. Sarah straightened herself as we left the room, holding her head up and nodding it slightly to residents we passed. I might not be much of a visitor, but what did they know?

The courtyard door stood open. We descended a concrete ramp and then followed a narrow walk to the bench where Mr. Cranny had dozed the day before. I parked Sarah next to one of the small evergreens that flanked the bench. The bench itself was warm to the touch. There was no real shade in the courtyard, except for a narrow strip of shadow along the eastern wall.

"Too hot for you?" I asked.

"No," Sarah said, holding her weathered face up to catch the sun. "I used to live for the summertime. I spent many a hotter day than this in my garden or working in the fields. Those were the stories your friend Michael liked. Stories about plowing behind a team of horses and cooking on a wood stove. Weaving cloth and canning vegetables. Stories about summers when I was a girl, when I'd visit my Uncle Jesse—he lived with his family in a houseboat on the Ohio River—and we'd swim and row all day and hunt for pearls."

"Pearls?" I asked, still on my guard against another whopper.

"Freshwater pearls," Sarah said with much dignity. "Little squiggly things like bits of hot wax dropped in cold water. My uncle would buy them from people up and down the river and sell them in Cincinnati. We children would crack mussels all day long just to find one pearl for him. He was a sweet man, my Uncle Jesse."

"That isn't the story that made Michael go away, is it?" asked Bulldog Keane, the relentless cross-examiner.

"No," Sarah said. "If I tell you that story, you might go away yourself and not come back."

"If you help me find Michael Crosley, I'll come back and bring him with me."

"Find him?" Sarah asked, her magnified eyes narrowing to something like normal size.

I remembered then that I hadn't told anyone at the home the truth about Michael Crosley. I owed it to Sarah. "Michael left St. Aelred's two weeks ago. We think he may have gone away for good. I'm trying to find out why he left."

"He found them, then."

"Found what?"

"The papers. My family papers." She gave me a curious, searching look. "I don't suppose you ever heard of John Keats."

"The poet?"

Sarah looked surprised. "Excuse me for putting it that way, but you didn't know about freshwater pearls..."

"And the schools aren't what they used to be," I said, quoting her observation from the day before.

"That's right. Anyway, the story I told Michael that made him leave me was about this Keats, the poet fellow. I'm kin of his."

I must have involuntarily raised my eyebrows, because Sarah said, "I know, I know. You think this is another wild story. You think I don't know day from night or up from down. I do, though. That game I played with you yesterday was just my way of taking my mind off things. A lot of the poor souls here play that game all the time, and they don't know they're doing it. I'm not one of that crowd. Not yet.

"When I tell you I'm kin to Keats, the poet fellow, I'm giving you God's truth. I could prove it in court, too, but Michael's run off with the proof. Run off with it and left me," she added bitterly.

"Keats never married," I said, thinking back to a course on the Romantic poets I'd taken at Boston. "He died of consumption. In Italy, not Indiana."

Sarah waved a hand at me impatiently. "He had family, didn't he? Brothers. His brother George was my great-great-grandfather. My grandmother, Ada Sprague, was his granddaughter. She remembered his widow. Georgiana Keats, her name was. And my mother had an old sampler that showed the family tree. George and Georgiana Keats were on the very top of the tree, I remember. That was on account of them coming over from the old country. The sampler's gone, too. One of my aunts took it when Mother died."

Sarah had quieted me with her talk of brothers and grandmothers and samplers, burying my doubts under a pile of reasonable details. But it was her manner, not her data, that was swaying me. She was serious and matter-of-fact, with none of the broad theatricality of the previous day.

"We did hang on to the family papers," she was saying. "And they were sure proof of what I'm telling you. Grandmother Sprague's things. The old family Bible. The homestead grant. And letters that George Keats had gotten from England, from his brother John."

The poet fellow, I almost added involuntarily. "You told Michael about the papers?"

"And didn't his eyes light up. Just the way yours were a moment ago, before you thought twice about it.

"Michael was going to solve all my troubles. He said the letters could be worth a lot of money. He wanted to help me, he said. He really just wanted to help himself."

She made the last statement without much conviction. I considered the charge against Crosley for a moment and rejected it. No one knew Michael Crosley very well, but everyone seemed to have a definite view of him, or at least an opinion of his limitations. Philip Swickard couldn't imagine him in love. Bill Koffman couldn't imagine him in a fight. I couldn't imagine him stealing from an old lady. Now I wondered if we might all three be wrong. The three unimaginable things might fit together to create one unpleasant truth.

"Do you really think Michael stole from you?"

Sarah shrugged asymmetrically, her right shoulder rising twice as high as her left. "I know he never came back."

"These Keats papers, have you seen them?"

"Years ago. When I was a girl. When Grandma Sprague was alive. I think I saw them." She seemed uncertain suddenly and disturbed by it. "Maybe I am forgetting things. Or remembering things that never happened. Sometimes I can barely tell the difference between a bit of a dream I had the night before and a memory from seventy years past. Maybe I'm slipping away from the world and don't know it."

"There's a way to find out about the papers. Tell me how to get to your farm."

"You're going after Michael?"

Sarah's question made me realize for the first time that the game had changed. I wasn't just after answers to Father Jerome's questions anymore. I wanted to find Crosley himself. "Yes," I said. "I'm going after him."

"Is he in bad trouble? For breaking his vows, I mean."

"He hasn't broken any vows. He hasn't taken any. Some seminarians study to become members of a religious order. They take vows. But others, like Michael, are studying to become parish priests. They're ordained by their local bishops when the time comes. Until then, they're just students."

Sarah wasn't interested in my hairsplitting dissertation. "He set out to be a priest and gave it up. Seems like that would be an awful thing."

I felt unreasonably embarrassed, perhaps for Crosley. "It is an awful thing," I said.

I looked away from Sarah and noted the wide figure of Nurse Wasson standing in the courtyard doorway. She was too far away for me to tell if her eyes were twinkling, but I suspected for some reason that they were not. She watched us for a moment and then disappeared inside.

Sarah had been chewing on Michael Crosley's situation. "I wouldn't want to get him in any deeper trouble," she said.

"I just want to talk with him. I want to make sure he's okay. And I want to make sure he isn't stealing from you." This last step in my program was less a goal of mine than an inducement to Sarah to go along with me.

It worked. "The farm is south of Ventor, way over on the other side of the county. Anybody in town can point you to it. Ask Josh McGriffith. He runs the feed store.

"Be sure to tell my nephew Frank that you've seen me. Tell him I'm going crazy for want of a friendly face to visit with. Tell him I'm dressing up outlandishly and forgetting my own name. Use your imagination."

"I'll think of something." I stood up, pulling at my shirt where it had stuck to my back. "I'd better get you inside where it's cooler."

"Suit yourself," Sarah said.

I wheeled her back inside the home, into a hallway that seemed as dark and cool as a cellar after the heat of the courtyard. As we entered her room, I said, "I'll be back with a report as soon as I've spoken with Frank."

Sarah didn't belive me. "I'll expect you when I see you," she said.

I parked her chair where I'd found it. I was almost out the door when Sarah stopped me with a single word: "Billy."

"What about him?"

"Billy was my boy. Died when he was twelve. Influenza."

I started to say that I was sorry, but didn't. It seemed silly and pointless somehow to console her for a death that had surely happened fifty years ago. Or had it been last night? I couldn't be sure. Perhaps Sarah wasn't sure herself.

"I'll see you soon," I said. Then I left her.

ELEVEN

UP UNTIL THAT MORNING in the nursing home, I'd kept the urge to play detective more or less in check. That temptation was never very far below the surface for me, like a rash that would flare up at the most casual, absentminded scratch. The urge was more than just the side effect of years spent reading paperbacks in which lone detectives quested after an answer. It was a view of the world, *my* view of the world. I saw life as a mystery whose meaning could be puzzled out, if only enough witnesses could be questioned, enough clues collected. I'd come to St. Aelred's in search of new witnesses and clues, naively thinking that I could spot the pattern in a mosaic that was incredibly old and endlessly complicated.

When I pulled out of the Good Fellows parking lot in my ersatz sports car, throwing gravel backward like a parting wisecrack, I wasn't stepping out of character. I was falling into it. I had a clue. I sensed the shadow of a real mystery, and I ran after it, feeling again the crazy hope that what I was really on the trail of was *the* mystery, *the* answer.

Ventor, when I finally found it, seemed like a major city after Evay, where Sarah Morell now waited for my report. Ventor had a row of shops, two filling stations, a bank, a Baptist church, and even a traffic light to irritate the truckers on State Road 64. It also had the feed store Sarah had promised me, McGriffith's, the front of which bore enameled metal signs advertising feed and fertilizer and seed.

The interior of the store was unfinished. I could see upward through the rafters to the corrugated steel of the roof.

Large fans in the back wall turned lazily. The bare concrete floor of the place was crowded with stacks of drums and piles of feed sacks arranged around a central counter. Behind the counter stood a big, red-haired man with mutton-chop side whiskers that were only a bare chin away from being a beard. The man was stroking a cat that shared both his counter and his weight problem. I noted several other cats spread out on feed sacks, dozing in the heat.

"Mr. McGriffith?" I asked as I stepped up to the counter.

The man nodded. "Let me guess," he said. "You want directions to the Morell farm." My confused expression gave him the answer he wanted. He laughed loudly, and the cat on the countertop shot him a reproving glance. "Sorry, son. Had to try that. I had a guy in here a month or so back. Hippie-looking city boy like yourself. He asked for the Morell place. I wondered all day what a greenhorn like that wanted with those hill jacks, so the thing stuck in my mind. When you came in just now, looking like the guy's skinny cousin, I had to try it. Damn if I wasn't right."

I didn't like being mistaken for Crosley's cousin, as it undercut the worldly, private-eye role I saw myself playing, but I tried not to show it. "What's a hill jack?" I asked.

"Where you from, boy? You sound like New York on a cold day."

"New Jersey," I said.

McGriffith nodded to show he'd heard of the place. "A hill jack is, you know, a hillbilly. Someone fresh from the hills of Kentucky."

Urbanity was a strange thing, I reflected. In New York City, they thought the people across the river in Jersey were hicks. Here in the wilds of southern Indiana, they looked down on people across the Ohio River in Kentucky. "Is that what the Morells are, hill jacks?"

"Frank Morell and his wife Agnes surely are. Curtis, their son, has been away to some college or other. No telling what he is now. Is that it? Are you a friend of Curtis?"

"No. I'm a friend of Sarah Morell, the owner of the farm."

"Is that right? I know Sarah. Nice lady, but a little crazy. All the Morells are a little touched. In the head, I mean."

I would have defended Sarah, had I not shared McGriffith's opinion. "How's the farm doing?"

McGriffith shook his head. "I don't know how they get by. They won't for long, I expect."

McGriffith then gave me about ten miles of directions, illustrating tricky points in the dust on the countertop. I thanked him and left.

It had been a productive stop, I decided as I headed west again on 64. For one thing, I'd learned that I was truly on Crosley's trail. That confirmed at least part of Sarah's story. She had sent Crosley on the same errand. It might still turn out to be a fool's errand, but I was optimistic. And McGriffith had supported another bit of Sarah's testimony, the part about her money troubles. The Morell farm was doing badly, and Sarah's situation was genuinely grim.

At an abandoned silo that rose from a field of weeds like the tower of a ruined castle, I left the state road and headed south. Shortly after turning off 64, I found myself on a narrow gravel track that ran through bits of forest and fields of corn. The corn was much taller than my car and planted close to the road, creating a green tunnel that reflected the noise of the Ghia's rear-mounted engine, giving me the uneasy feeling that I was being followed. The tunnel wound and turned, making me think of a maze from some formal English garden. The object of those decorative labyrinths was to find your way inside to some secret center, but I was more preoccupied now with the challenge of finding my way back out again.

Every mile or so, the wall of corn and trees was broken by a small cleared stretch containing a farmhouse. Sometimes the house was only a trailer sitting up on blocks, but more often it was a frame house set among barns and outbuildings. I passed one such house before I recognized it from the description McGriffith had given me of the Morell place. I had to drive half a mile away from the house before I found a dirt road I could use to turn around.

The house was a fairly large two-story with a steeply gabled roof. It didn't seem as old as Sarah's stories had led me to expect, despite its yellow paint having peeled away in places to expose the gray wood of the narrow board siding. On the right side of the house there was a tall brick chimney, the top third of which had been repaired at some time in the past. It was covered by an irregular cast of concrete and it rose at a slight angle, like a badly set bone.

The Morells' driveway consisted of a pair of wheel ruts separated by a median of weeds that ran past the house on their way to the barn behind it. The weeds brushed along the Ghia's flat bottom as I pulled in. My arrival set off a commotion in the local dog community, which seemed to be thriving. I could see only one dog, a liver-and-gray shorthaired hunting dog tied with rope to a front porch post, but I could hear several others joining in the alarm from somewhere behind the house.

The front porch dog was holding its rope taut as it leaned toward me, scratching at the ground. The dog made reaching the front door an impossibility, which was probably its goal in life. I stood in the heat of the yard, reconsidering the whole trip, until the screened front door opened and a man came out. He was something over six feet tall with black hair and a close-cropped black beard that merged very gradually with his dark red skin, showing no definite dividing line. The whites of his eyes looked very white against his ruddy face. He wore a work shirt and pants of identical dark blue, like those of a city garage mechanic. The pants had a formal crease, I was surprised to see, but they were soiled with dried mud from the calves down. His white socks were clean and he wore no shoes. I guessed his age as fifty.

"Mr. Morell?" I asked, with slightly more treble than I would have liked.

I relaxed somewhat when he smiled in greeting. "What can I do for you?"

"I'm a friend of your Aunt Sarah's," I said, repeating the exaggerated claim I'd made to McGriffith.

Morell responded with the standard Hoosier reply to any news: "Is that right?"

"Yes. I spoke with her this morning at the Good Fellows Home."

The sentry dog had continued to bark during this exchange. It stopped immediately when Morell said, "Quiet, Blue." He waved me up onto the porch. "Blue won't bother you."

The dog didn't interfere with my walk to the front steps, but it did come to me, running its pale nose down my left leg from my knee to my shoe and filing the information away: "Keane, Owen, seminarian, nervous as hell."

Morell shook my hand when I reached the porch. "We keep that old boy out front because he doesn't get along with the other dogs. Thinks he's people, is why."

Morell held the screen door open for me, and I stepped directly into the front room of the house, a living room or parlor.

"We were just having lunch," Morell said. "Come on out back."

"Out back" was the kitchen, a large white room fitted with antique appliances and cabinets that had glass fronts displaying the dishes and crockery within. Next to the open back door was a mat on which stood two pairs of muddy boots. The center of the room was filled by a long, narrow table. Two people were seated there eating lunch. I deduced their names before Morell had a chance to introduce them. Agnes Morell sat at one end of the table. She was dressed in a pink flowered housedress that resembled the one Sarah had worn that morning in the home. Her gray hair was drawn back into a bun, emphasizing the solid squareness of her face. My unannounced entrance seemed to embarrass her, but she smiled shyly. Across the table from me was Curtis, who appeared to be a mixture of the other two, with the dark hair and red skin of his father and the square jaw of his mother. He wore a plain, once-white T-shirt and jeans and he rose halfway out of his chair to squeeze my hand more firmly than was necessary.

"Take a chair," Frank said, indicating the one across from his son. "Join us for a sandwich and some slaw?" he asked as he reseated himself at the head of the table.

"No, thank you. I just had lunch." It was the second lie I'd told Frank Morell in as many minutes. I decided to throw in a little truth for variety. "I'm hoping you can help me. I'm trying to get a line on a student who recently dropped out of St. Aelred College. His name is Michael Crosley. He befriended your Aunt Sarah at the retirement home. She told me that she sent him out here to look over some family papers."

All three Morells were suddenly nodding. Curtis was the first to speak. "That's right. Must be almost three weeks ago he was here last. Tall guy, heavyset. Seminarian, isn't he?"

"He was."

"I wanted to talk with him about Nietzsche, to see what he thought about the idea of God being dead." Curtis shook his head. "I never got the chance. All he wanted to talk about was some letters."

"From John Keats," I said.

The trio nodded again. "He seemed to think there was money in it," Frank said.

"Did you know that you're related to Keats?" I asked.

Frank smiled down at his half-eaten ham and cheese. "To be honest with you, I'd never even heard of him. I wouldn't know a poet if I was to sit on one."

"What about the money?" Agnes asked me. "Is there any truth to that?"

Frank and Curtis gazed at her with identical looks of long-suffering embarrassment.

"There might be," I said. "I could try to find out for you."

"It doesn't matter, Mother," Curtis said patiently. "We haven't been able to find anything near that old or any mention of Keats."

"The money would be nice," his mother muttered.

"That's surely true," Frank said. "We could find uses for bags of money. We're grateful to Sarah for taking us on when we lost our own place, but that home she's in costs a lot. There isn't much left when those folks have been taken care of.

"But like I told this Michael fellow, I don't put much stock in Sarah's story. Aunt Sarah is a sweet person, but she can spin a tale. I suppose you've noticed that."

I nodded disloyally. "You said you haven't found any family papers. You have looked, though."

"Took the attic apart," Curtis said.

"Did Michael Crosley help?"

Curtis shook his head. "No. He came back a couple of times to see if we'd found anything. He finally gave up."

"Could he have found something on his own? Did he ever look around while he was here?"

The Morells exchanged inquiring glances. The consensus seemed to be negative.

"How about other family in the area? Could somebody else be looking after the family papers?"

"No," Frank said. "We're about all the family we know of, excepting Aunt Sarah herself. The thing you have to keep sight of is that Sarah is getting on. She doesn't remember so good anymore. She's maybe forgotten how well she cleaned house before she went into the home. Threw out a wagonload of things. That might be what happened to the letters she thought she had."

"And them worth money," Agnes said sadly.

I'd run out of questions for the moment. Curtis stepped in to fill the void. "What's your interest in this Crosley guy?" he asked me. He leaned across the narrow table to examine me, coming close enough for me to conclude that Agnes used too much vinegar in her slaw.

I gave him my standard answer, that I was looking into Michael's departure for the school.

"Are you a seminarian, too?" Curtis asked eagerly.

I understood his interest then. I might be someone else who would shag philosophical pop flies for him. I'd provided that service for others during my undergraduate days and found it tiring. It was hard to match some people's enthusiasm for radical, new, hundred-year-old ideas.

"So you don't think God is dead," Curtis said, confirming my worst fears.

"Curtis," his mother said sharply. "Mind that talk."

Curtis smiled and ignored her. "Where is God, then? What's happened to Him?"

I smiled back to him. "Why, had He been stopping by here, too?"

Curtis laughed. "Touché. You have to admit, though, that what's become of God is a more interesting question than what's become of Michael Crosley."

I could have countered that by admitting to Curtis that the two questions were one for me. Or rather, that I saw in Michael's sudden departure a possible clue to the larger mystery. But I didn't want to encourage him.

"Curtis has been to college," Frank said, his tone suggesting that it was a severe handicap. "They didn't teach him manners."

Curtis was unabashed. "I don't get much chance to discuss philosophy out here in the boonies."

"No problem," I said. To the table at large, I added, "Thanks for your time."

TWELVE

CURTIS STOOD UP to walk me to the front door. Before we'd left the kitchen, he suggested something that should have occurred to me. "You want us to call you if we hear from Crosley?"

I thanked him for thinking of that and gave him the phone number of my dormitory. He noted it on a pad that hung beside the wall phone.

Curtis led me as far as the parlor. The room was furnished in an unhappy combination of old and new pieces. A sofa represented the latter group. It was a Sears-quality Early American with pine trim and bright synthetic upholstery. Next to it stood a marble-topped antique table with intricately carved legs. The room's decorations continued this schizophrenic scheme. A large oval photograph of an old woman—she might have been Sarah's Grandma Sprague—shared a wall with a macramé owl.

Curtis paused short of the front door, leaning against a water-stained wall. "I bet you're wondering why I buried myself out here in the sticks, since I've been to college and all."

I hadn't been wondering, which seemed rude enough to keep me silent.

Curtis pulled a long piece of string from his pocket. While he talked, he wound the string around the thumb of his left hand. "The truth is, I've had a bellyful of this society. It's sick to the core; the people are disenfranchised, slaves to a military-industrial complex that sees them either as mindless consumers or cannon fodder. I came out here as a deliberate act, to get away from the corruption and manipulation. To find something simpler and better."

Curtis had been to college all right. He was fluent in the campus cant a whole generation had minored in, myself included. His defensiveness about his chosen lifestyle reminded me of the excuses I'd made to friends and family when I'd decided to come to Indiana and St. Aelred's. I didn't enjoy the reminder.

"See," Curtis said, gesturing toward the room behind me with the thumb he'd wrapped in string. "No television. No newspapers. No contamination. I even took my daughter out of school before they could brainwash her."

"Your daughter?"

"Krystal. Didn't Aunt Sarah tell you? I had Krystal while I was in high school." For a moment I thought Curtis was claiming to have accomplished this miracle alone. Then he said, "Her mother took off years ago. I'm trying to bring Krystal up clean of this world."

It was an odd idea, oddly worded. I gave Curtis a closer look. He was as tall as his father, but heavier. His dark hair was just short of shoulder length, and his eyes were small and deep-set. He must have been my age or perhaps a few years older, but he seemed much younger to me, the way a freshman looks to a jaded senior. Everyone knew that Curtis had gone to college, it seemed, but no one had mentioned his graduating. I wondered now if he ever had.

While I was thinking it over, Curtis roused himself from his relaxed position by the door. "Come back someday when you have time for a long talk."

I ended the visit as I'd begun it, untruthfully. "I'd like that," I said.

At least I thought that the exchange ended my visit. Blue, the dog that imagined he was people, certainly didn't dispute my departure. But there was a surprise waiting for me at the Ghia. When I was a few steps away from the car, a face appeared in the open passenger window. It belonged to a girl of eight or nine and it was dirty and framed by long, uncombed blond hair.

"Boo!" the girl said.

"Same to you. You must be Krystal."

"With a K." She drew the letter in the air for me. "Who are you?"

"Keane with a K. My first name's Owen."

"Owen," Krystal repeated, her Hoosier accent making it sound like an expression of mild pain. She opened the Ghia's door and climbed out. Her T-shirt and shorts looked like she'd worn them recently while burrowing. "Are you a friend of Mikey's?" she asked.

The nickname sounded all wrong for Crosley, even though it also seemed vaguely familiar. Beatrice Crosley had used it, I suddenly remembered. "Michael Crosley you mean?"

"Yep. He's my friend, but I haven't seen him in a long time."

"Neither have I."

"He's been talking with Paw about me going back to school."

"You want to go to school?"

"Yep. I like it." She nodded longer and more vigorously than seemed called for, perhaps because she enjoyed the feeling. "I want to be a doctor. You have to go to school to be a doctor, don't you?"

"It helps."

"When it was just me and Mamaw and Papaw, I went to school all the time." She made a face. "Then Paw came to live with us."

After a brief but fatal exposure to Nietzsche, I thought. I wasn't really interested in Curtis, though. "What did you and Michael talk about?"

"School mostly. Mikey's been to lots. Have you?"

"Wagonloads," I said. "Did Mikey ever mention going off on a trip somewhere?"

"Nope," Krystal replied without much thought.

"How about a girlfriend? Did he ever mention a special girl?"

Krystal didn't laugh at the idea. In fact, she seemed to take it very seriously. "I want to be his girlfriend, when I'm older," she said. She displayed her first shyness, looking down at her bare feet while she spoke. "We may get married, too." It took me a second or two to accept the obvious: she had a crush on Michael Crosley.

"Would you like to see my garden?" Krystal asked, perhaps to change the subject. "Mikey likes gardens."

That seemed unlikely, as gardening had been Martin Crosley's hobby and Michael had been his mirror opposite. I looked up to the house for parental approval, but Curtis had already gone back to his lunch. "Sure," I said.

She led me to a large patch in the side yard. I was expecting something similar to Beatrice Crosley's suburban garden of tomatoes and peppers. Instead, Krystal's was an eclectic collection of flowers and small shrubs.

"You must like flowers," I said.

Krystal nodded energetically and then pushed her hair back out of her face. "And herbs. I grow medicines."

"All these are for medicine?" I pointed to a plant whose spikes were nearly my height and covered with wrinkled leaves and large pink flowers. "That's hollyhock, isn't it?"

"Yep. If you cook the petals down and drink it in your tea, it'll cure a cough."

"How about the marigolds?" I indicated the golden flowers that bordered the garden with the toe of my shoe.

"You use them in case you sprain your ankle."

I started to ask her whether you swallowed the marigolds or rubbed them on, but Krystal was already pointing out another plant, one with small clusters of greenish flowers and star-shaped leaves. "That's a castor bean," she said. "You squeeze oil out of the seeds. It's good for..."

"I've heard of it. What's that one?"

"Sweet basil. It cures a bad stomach." She reached down and picked a leaf from a low, grayish-green plant. "Rub this on your teeth," she said.

"What?"

"This is sage. It makes your teeth white." She demonstrated, rubbing the leaf across her own very white teeth.

"What's that tall one with the violet flowers?"

"Oh, that's just rosemary. Mamaw uses it to cook with. It means something, though, if you give it to somebody. It means 'Remember me.'" She grew thoughtful for a moment, maybe wishing that she had given a sprig to Michael Crosley.

"That's rue," she said, pointing to a bluish-green plant with clusters of yellow flowers. "It means something, too, a word for being sorry."

"Repentance?"

"That's it. Repentance. It'll cure a stomachache and protect against snake bites. If you wear a piece around your neck, it'll guard you against the evil eye."

"Is that right?" I asked, smiling.

"Yep," she answered, nodding seriously. "That's right." Krystal regarded me critically, reminding me of her great-great-aunt. Perhaps like Sarah she was dubious about the quality of my education.

"Who taught you all this?" I asked.

"Mamaw. But I have to know a lot more if I want to be a doctor. That's why I have to get back to school. Will you tell Paw that?"

"Next time I stop by."

Krystal followed me back to my car. I said good-bye as I opened its door. "It was nice meeting you."

Krystal was examining her feet again. "Could you tell Mikey something for me?"

"If I see him."

"Tell him I'm waiting for him."

THIRTEEN

I PULLED SLOWLY out of the Morells' driveway, without the dramatic flourish I'd used when I'd departed the nursing home lot earlier in the day. I'd spun my tires then in my excitement over the Keats papers, thinking they were the best lead I'd had since Melissa Donahue. I still thought they were, but the Morells' polite lack of interest and calm denials had confused everything. If the family hadn't found any papers, how could Crosley have? I would have found the Morells angry, if Crosley had robbed them. They hadn't been worked up enough to interrupt their meal. And if Crosley had made no discovery, how could the Keats papers be related to his disappearance? Could one of the Morells—perhaps Curtis—have passed material to Crosley without telling the others? Could all three of them be working with Crosley against Sarah Morell's interests? I considered the possibilities as I drove out through the labyrinth of corn. I hadn't picked a favorite by the time I regained State Road 64.

The most obvious explanation—that there really was no Keats material—I didn't consider at all. The reason was the poem that Crosley had read at the Unstable. The poem had been bouncing around in the back of my mind ever since Sarah had mentioned Keats. I'd begun my investigation with the idea that Crosley had written the poem himself. I was suddenly sure that he had not, and that the true author was Sarah's long-lost relation. The poem had been unlike anything else read that night—a sonnet, according to Jim Carroll, as rare at a college poetry session as an ode to Richard Nixon. If the poem was really a sonnet by Keats, it upped the ante considerably. Letters in Keats's own hand would be valuable, but an autographed sonnet would be a major find.

Some objections to the poem being the work of Keats came to mind. I wasn't disturbed that I hadn't recognized it, and I was familiar with only a tiny part of Keats's output. The objections concerned Crosley's motives for reciting the poem at the Unstable. I'd been assuming that the performance was his public admission that he'd fallen in love. If the poem wasn't Crosley's own, inspired by his own love, why would he recite it at all? And why had his recitation been so heartfelt?

I decided that it was time to do some research on the life of Keats. That thought brought back a clue I'd forgotten, one that Crosley had stuck right under my nose. There was a biography of Keats in his room. In a room crowded with books, that volume sat singled out on his desktop. I'd focused on the bookmark Crosley had used, the slip of paper bearing Melissa Donahue's name and number, and forgotten the book itself. I found myself pressing harder on the Ghia's accelerator in my excitement. The presence of the book in his room surely proved that Crosley had been trying to substantiate Sarah's story. Perhaps he had even been trying to authenticate some material he had found.

As I drove, I reviewed what I could remember of John Keats from my undergraduate course on the Romantic poets. Keats was the most romantic of that group, at least in the view of the Victorian readers and critics who had rediscovered and immortalized him. Like Byron and Shelley, Keats had died young, but not as the result of a silly gesture, like Byron, or an accident, like Shelley. The Keats family had a history of tuberculosis, which had lent an urgency to Keats's life and had later given him the aura of one truly doomed. He had loved a woman named Fanny, to whom many of his poems were addressed, but he hadn't survived to marry her. He'd died, as I'd told Sarah, in Italy.

When I got back to St. Aelred's, I hurried to the old rectory. Katrinka Wilson, the landlady and future patron saint of the house, smiled when she opened the front door.

"No need to ring every time, Owen. We know you now. We almost never lock the door. Any news of Michael?"

I was fated to be at my most self-important and optimistic around Mrs. Wilson. "I'm on the trail of something pretty interesting now. Can I go up to Michael's room?"

"Sure," Mrs. Wilson said.

Crosley's room was shut up again and hotter than the inside of my Volkswagen had been. On my way across the room to open the window, I noticed something that made me stop dead in my tracks. The top of the small writing desk was empty; the Keats biography was gone. I looked around, trying to decide if anything else in the room had been disturbed. I had the impression that the stacks of books had been rearranged, but it was impossible to be sure.

I opened the window and began a systematic search of the room, concentrating on the bookshelves and their overflow piles. I flipped through each book, looking for stray pieces of paper. All I found were Crosley's colorless notes. There was no sign of the Keats study, but I did find two books of interest. They were both high school textbooks that had been published in the late thirties. One was a second-year Latin text. The other was a U.S. history. They were stamped with a school name, "Holy Cross High School, Evansville, Indiana." Inside the front cover of each was Martin Crosley's signature.

I sat in the heat at the small desk holding the two textbooks and wondering why Crosley would have them. They were odd mementos of a father who had reputedly hated books and academics. And why, if they were important to Crosley, had he left them behind?

My whys were mounting up faster than I could catalog them. I shut the room up again and descended the carpeted stairway to look for Mrs. Wilson.

I found her in a little room off the kitchen. It was outfitted with a love seat, a standing lamp, and an old console television. Mrs. Wilson waved me into the room, signaling at the same time for me to be silent. I squeezed in next to the standing lamp. The television's black and white picture was huge and grainy. I felt as though I'd wandered into the front row of a movie theater. Two people were on the screen. They were seated at a kitchen table, discussing someone else's divorce.

The scene faded to black and was replaced by a commercial for a laundry detergent that contained its own bleach. Mrs. Wilson leaned forward with a grunt and turned the sound down.

"Find something?" she asked.

"I didn't find something. There was a library book on Crosley's desk. It's gone now."

Mrs. Wilson put a hand over her mouth and said "Oh," or rather sang it, sustaining it for several seconds like the last note of a hymn. "The girl who does the cleaning for me. Paula. I forgot to tell her to skip Michael's room."

"Would she have taken the book?"

"Maybe. If it was due back."

"It was overdue."

"That sounds like Paula. A little too efficient, that one. A little nosy, too. She came yesterday, Thursday, her usual day. I was busy yesterday. I had a lady friend of mine over for tea. I didn't keep a good eye on Paula."

"Could you find out for me if Paula took the book?"

"I'll ask the next time I see her. Do you need this book? Because, if Paula took it away, it's probably back in the library right now."

I should have thought of that myself. I pretended that I had. "I was just on my way over there now."

St. Anselm Library was appropriately near the center of the campus, with the school's other buildings forming a protective ring around it. It was my favorite among St. Aelred's landmarks, a tall building—Gothic, of course—so narrow in relation to its height that it was almost a tower. The Keep was its campus nickname, the stronghold at the center of Castle St. Aelred's.

Brother Kevin, the head librarian, was on duty behind the main desk, a three-sided wooden affair that extended well into the main reading room. Each corner of the desk had a carved wooden post that rose upward to the ceiling, giving it the inappropriate appearance of an old-fashioned hotel bar. Brother Kevin had gotten to know me during my explorations of some obscure texts. "Still studying the Apocrypha, Owen?" he asked as I passed his station.

"Poetry today," I replied without breaking stride.

I made a quick stop at the card catalog and then ran up two flights of stairs to the Literature section, winding myself unnecessarily. Mrs. Wilson's story about Paula, the conscientious cleaning woman, had struck me as unlikely, and I was doubtful that I would find the book. It was yet another example of my intuition letting me down. Walter Jackson Bate's study of Keats was on the shelf exactly where it should have been, looking innocent and ordinary.

I carried the book to a study cubicle near a tall leaded glass window that had already been cranked full open. The cubicle had a frame of dark green metal, a rubberized desk top, and a small fluorescent light. It reminded me of the cubicles at Bapst Library on the Boston College campus, except that those had been etched with scatological graffiti. There was no such defamation here, which pleased me. I considered this old library to be well up on St. Aelred's list of sacred places.

I turned immediately to Bate's index, looking for the most easily verified fact that Sarah had given me: George, the name of her great-great-grandfather and John Keats's supposed brother. I found the name immediately, at the head of a long list of page references, "Keats, George (K's brother)." I scanned the list of subjects below his name until I found "to America." I noted the pages following this citation and then moved into the body of the text.

There I learned that George had decided to move to America because he was hard up for money. The problem must run in Sarah's family, I decided. On page 345, Bate told me that George and his wife first tried Illinois, lost most of the money they had, and then moved to Kentucky, finally ending up in Louisville, only fifty miles from where I now sat. Sarah was ringing true on every point. In Louisville, George eventually prospered. He died of tuberculosis, the same disease that had claimed his brother, on Christmas Eve in 1841. He was survived by his wife and seven children, two sons and five daughters.

A footnote on the bottom of the page told me that an article in a 1941 issue of the *Southern Literary Messenger* contained a list of George's descendants still living at that time, a list that should have included Sarah Morell. The footnote also gave me a more exciting bit of confirmation: George's widow had married again, to an engineer named John Jeffrey. Jeffrey had made copies of the papers George Keats had left behind and sent the copies to R. M. Milnes, John Keats's first biographer. These papers included letters and manuscript poems sent by John to his brother in America.

"Damn," I said aloud. Then I looked around quickly to see if anyone had heard me profane my sacred library.

Sarah had been telling the truth. There were Keats poems in America in Keats's own hand. Copies had been sent back to England and the originals kept, perhaps scattered through a family that had itself scattered. I had only to find a complete Keats and search it for the poem I had heard at the Unstable to complete my case. Thanks to Jim Carroll's memory, I had the poem's last two lines: "While doomed

to fall outside the promised land, / With fingers stretching
upward for thy hand.''

I hurried down to the card catalog to locate the book I
needed. On the way, I stopped briefly at the front desk to
put a question to Brother Kevin. "Have we the *Southern
Literary Messenger* for 1941?"

"We have not," the monk said, slightly amused by my
enthusiasm as he often seemed to be. He was thinner than
I was and sandy-haired, with rimless glasses as delicate as
Sarah's had been substantial. "Not from that long ago.
You might call the University of Evansville. Or you could
try Indiana University up in Bloomington."

"Thanks," I said. That little bit of additional documen-
tation would have to wait. It would be academic anyway
after I identified the poem.

"Would you like to check that out?" Brother Kevin
asked, pointing to the Keats biography that I still carried.

I handed him the book. "This recently came back overdue, did it not?"

"Yes," Brother Kevin said. "How did you know that?"

"Elementary," I replied, God help me. I was more than
a little high on deductions at that moment. I pointed to the
card that the librarian was carefully stamping with a new
due date. "I happen to know that it was just put back on
the shelf, but the last date on the card was a week ago."

Brother Kevin's amusement was threatening to break into
laughter. "As you say, elementary. Are you interested in the
book or in the seminarian who last borrowed it?"

The monk was letting me know that he was aware of the
assignment Father Jerome had given me. "I'm interested
in Michael Crosley and the book," I said. "Do you happen to know who returned it?"

"It was slipped into the night depository yesterday afternoon. I thought it was just a ploy by someone hoping to
avoid a late fee, until I found that Michael had checked it
out. I have no idea who brought it back."

He handed me the book. "Have you your magnifying glass? Perhaps you can deduce who it was."

"I'll let you know," I said, some of the pretension I'd used on Mrs. Wilson creeping into my voice. "In the meantime, can you tell me where to find a complete Keats?"

Brother Kevin nodded happily and pointed to the Bate book. "Within a foot or two of the spot where you found that, Mr. Holmes."

I climbed the stairs again, feeling only slightly chastened. Sure enough, on the shelf above the gap where the study of Keats had rested were a half-dozen different editions of his poems. I selected the Modern Library version and carried it to the cubicle where I'd interrogated Walter Jackson Bate. In my overconfidence, I started with the book's table of contents, thinking I might recognize the poem from its title. When that long shot didn't come in, I went through the volume page by page, checking the last two lines of each short poem I came to. There was no sign of the sonnet. I went through the book again more slowly, scanning even the longer works. Outside, the slow passage of the afternoon was marked by the sound of a mower being pushed back and forth across the quad beneath my window.

The mower and most of the afternoon were gone when I finally gave up and closed the book. Crosley's sonnet just wasn't there. That admission brought back the confusion I'd felt as I'd left the Morell farm earlier in the day with all my preconceived notions undone. I'd been sustained then by the memory of the sonnet. It had been the one truth around which I'd rearranged all my facts. It still was.

"A lost sonnet," I whispered to myself. That was surely the answer. A sonnet sent by Keats to his brother that hadn't been copied and returned with the others. An unknown sonnet in John Keats's own hand, a discovery far more valuable than any letter or autograph of a known poem.

Suddenly I seemed to have the key to another question that had troubled me earlier: why had Crosley given an emotional reading of someone else's love sonnet? The answer I came up with was a variation of my earlier theory that the reading had been Crosley's acknowledgment of his love for Melissa Donahue. The recitation had been a public announcement, I now decided, but not of newfound love. Crosley had been upset because he had chosen to throw over his vocation and steal the poem. The recitation had been his cryptic public confession.

FOURTEEN

IN THE PAPERBACKS I LOVED, tough private eyes kept their own counsel because they'd been made reticent by years of hard knocks and disappointments. I hadn't the benefit of that experience, and, for once, I ignored the wise example of my fictional role models. I had to tell someone, anyone, about my discovery. I would have told Brother Kevin before I left the Keep, but he'd gone off duty for the day. I was outside, running down the library's stone steps, before I thought of another audience, the perfect audience. Dr. Elizabeth Mott.

Dr. Mott was the head of the English Department of St. Aelred's liberal arts college. She was also something of a campus institution, as she had taught at the school for twenty years. Like Mrs. Wilson, she was the surviving member of a St. Aelred's couple, her late husband having been a professor of mathematics. Dr. Mott had befriended me because I'd been an English major at Boston and because we shared a common interest, the mystery novel. At least that's what I liked to think. It may be that I stood out for her in the crowd of seminarians for other, less flattering reasons.

It was after five o'clock and the Arts and Sciences Building, a relatively modern-looking limestone block, was all but deserted. I hurried up to the top floor where the English Department was hidden away. The departmental secretary was gone, but beyond her straightened desk and covered typewriter, the door to Dr. Mott's office was open.

The doctor herself was preparing to call it a week. She stood at the side of her desk, profile toward me. Her canvas bag was already hanging from her shoulder, and she was filing papers in a large leather briefcase. Dr. Mott had a classic profile, with a long, high-arched nose that would have flattered a Shakespearean actor. Her chin was less well defined, her jaw merging gradually with the lined softness of her neck. She wore her graying black hair long but brushed well back from her face.

I should have whistled or coughed as I approached her office. I startled her when I tapped on the door.

"Owen," she said, placing a hand theatrically to her heart. "I thought I was quite alone in here. I was just leaving for the day," she added pointedly.

Ordinarily I would have been responsive to the hint, but I was too full now of my own discoveries. "Do you have a moment?" I asked.

"As a matter of fact, you're standing between me and a gin and tonic, which is considered foolhardy by people in the know. Is this important?"

"Yes," I said. "It's about a mystery."

Dr. Mott's face brightened. "Don't tell me you've finally taken my advice and traded in Dashiell Hammett for Dorothy Sayers." We had a running debate on the relative merits of American private-eye novels and English whodunits.

"I finished Hammett years ago," I said. "I'm on Raymond Chandler now."

"A good writer," Dr. Mott conceded, "but rather inclined to shoot people. You really should expand your field of view. Have you ever heard of Margery Allingham?"

"No."

"There's someone to try. The clues in her books are more subtle than spent shell casings and nude photographs. Her detective once received a warning in the form of a bouquet of flowers and twigs. He had to know their traditional meanings to decipher it. That rhododendrons mean beware, for example, and a cypress sprig stands for mourning."

A detective after Krystal Morell's heart. "Sounds like an everyday experience to me," I said.

Dr. Mott's expression became professional and severe. "A very superficial standard of literary criticism, if you don't mind my saying so, Owen. What's true or false in a book has nothing to do with its being ordinary."

She was still standing with her bag on her shoulder, but I stubbornly refused to be shooed away. "The mystery I'm here about isn't a book. It's real."

Dr. Mott lowered her canvas bag toward the floor, letting it free-fall the last foot so it landed with a muted crash. "I thought I recognized a determined, private-eye look in your eye," she said resignedly. "Sit down and tell me about it."

I was talking before I'd settled in her leather visitor chair. "Do you know Michael Crosley."

"I've met him. He's in the graduate school, or at least he was. I've heard that he's left us."

"He has. Father Jerome asked me to find out why."

"Why would Father Jerome do that?"

I had to reach back through the clutter of the last few days to find the old priest's motive. "He said it was an exercise. He thought I might find out something about myself."

"Have you?"

"No," I admitted. "I haven't really worked that part out yet."

I'd only mentioned Crosley as a necessary preamble to my discoveries about the Keats poem. But Dr. Mott, now settled comfortably in her chair, would not be rushed. "What have you learned about Michael Crosley?"

"Mostly that he wasn't the most popular guy in the world. That he didn't really know himself. That he didn't have much time for human interaction or much talent for it. Except for..."

"Except for what."

"A girl named Melissa Donahue. I found her name and phone number in Crosley's room. I thought she might have been the reason he took off. But when I confronted her about it, she denied ever hearing of him."

"Then why did he have her phone number?"

"I don't know."

"Who told you that Crosley didn't know himself?"

"A psychologist I met at a halfway house in New Albany. Crosley was supposed to be counseling ex-drug users there. Seems like he might have been on the receiving end of the counseling. She also said that Crosley had low self-esteem."

"Who else have you spoken with?"

"Beatrice Crosley, Michael's mother. She told me that Michael never got along with his father, mainly because the father was an insensitive factory worker who thought books were for jerks. Mrs. Crosley felt that Michael might have come to St. Aelred's as an act of rebellion, because his father had laughed when Michael first mentioned the priesthood."

Dr. Mott shook her head at that picture but did not comment.

"Mr. Crosley died last spring," I said. "Michael may have lost his only real reason for being here when that happened."

"Then why didn't he leave in the spring? Why now?"

"I don't know. Something must have happened to bring things to a head. His landlady, Mrs. Wilson, told me he'd been acting strangely recently. Very moody. I thought it was because of Melissa Donahue. Now I've got another idea."

"Let's hear it," Dr. Mott said, smiling. She was well aware that her careful questioning had been holding me back from this announcement.

I held up the Keats biography. "It's this."

"Yes," Dr. Mott said. "I noticed that when you came in. Bate won the Pulitzer prize for it. It's really excellent."

"Two weeks ago, Michael Crosley read a poem at the Unstable's open-mike reading."

"A sonnet, wasn't it?" the professor asked.

"You know about that?"

Dr. Mott laughed slightly at my crestfallen expression. "Sorry, Owen. Everyone likes to play the role of the great detective and impress people with arcane knowledge. It's a cheap trick, really. I heard about the sonnet from Jim Carroll, the manager of the pub. He was up here the day after the reading, dropping that off." She pointed to an untidy manuscript on the corner of her desk. "He brings me endless doggerel to read. Jim really liked Crosley's poem. Did Michael imitate Keats?"

"I think he ripped him off," I said. I'd recovered a little of my enthusiasm, now that it was apparent Dr. Mott didn't know the poem's significance. I was primed to play the great detective again myself.

"Crosley was visiting a nursing home as part of his spiritual counseling. He met an old lady there who claimed to be a descendant of George Keats, the poet's brother. She told Crosley that George had ended up in Kentucky and that he'd saved the letters and poems sent to him by John."

I patted the book. "That's all borne out by Bate. He says that copies of the poems and letters were later sent to England, but the originals were kept here. Sarah, the old lady in the home, told Crosley that her family still had some of the papers. She sent him after them. I think the poem he read at the Unstable was from that Keats material."

"Have you identified the poem?"

"It can't be identified. It isn't in Keats's collected poems." Dr. Mott looked at me blankly. "Don't you see? It's a lost Keats sonnet. One that wasn't sent back to England for some reason. Michael Crosley found a lost sonnet of John Keats and took it away with him.''

Dr. Mott was a tough sell. "How could that have happened? How could the family not know how valuable the poem was?''

''It must have passed into a branch of the family that didn't know its significance. Some of the current generation haven't even heard of Keats. It's like 'The Musgrave Ritual.' The Musgraves passed the ritual down, but the meaning was lost.''

''That's fiction, Owen. Listen to yourself. You're trying to substantiate this theory of yours by citing Sherlock Holmes.''

I almost asked her if she knew a better authority, but I caught myself in time.

Dr. Mott was smiling happily at me, which was daunting. "You told me you'd finished with Dashiell Hammett, but I'm not so sure,'' she said. "Do you know what this reminds me of? *The Maltese Falcon.* You sound like Sam Spade on the trail of a fabulous statuette.''

The momentum I'd built up charging down the library steps was effectively countered by Dr. Mott's cheerful incredulity. "Don't you think this is exciting?'' I asked.

''Of course I do. It would make a great story, or perhaps an episode of that television show with the detective who dresses badly. What's his name?''

''Columbo,'' I said dejectedly.

''I'm sorry, Owen. I'm not trying to tease you. This is an interesting mystery. I'd love to know more about it. But the poem isn't going to lead you to Michael Crosley. If anything, it's leading you away.''

''What do you mean?''

''Look at what you're saying about him. For your story to be true, he has to be a thief. He has to rob an old woman in a nursing home. Do you believe he's capable of that?''

I remembered my own reaction to Sarah's charge that Crosley had robbed her. It had been disbelief. I'd lost track of my faith in Crosley sometime during the day, which bothered me now. "The sonnet would be very valuable," I said in my defense.

"Owen," Dr. Mott said patiently, "do you get less honest as the stakes go up? Aren't you inclined to be more scrupulous over big things than small ones?"

"Yes."

"I think the same would be true of Michael Crosley. Another person, someone older, more beaten up by the world, more disappointed, might be tempted by something like this poem, might see it as a last chance to grab the gold ring. But not a young man still on the threshold of his life. A young seminarian, Owen. I can't see you persuading Father Jerome of that."

Neither could I. "Where does that leave me?" I asked.

Dr. Mott stood up before answering. She handed me her briefcase and retrieved her shoulder bag from the floor. "It leaves you with Michael Crosley's personal problems. With this girl, whatever her name was, and Michael's relationship with his father. Those are your leads."

We walked out into the hallway together, Dr. Mott lecturing as we went. "Think of your private-eye novels. The shootings, the trailings, the physical evidence don't add up to a convincing mystery. It's the motives, the human passions and problems compellingly laid out, that make a great story."

She pressed the Down button of the faculty elevator and then reclaimed her briefcase. "I'd work on the father angle if I were you. He has to be at the center of this somehow."

FIFTEEN

OUTSIDE THE ARTS and Sciences Building, the standard muggy Indiana afternoon had given way to an ominous evening. The western sky was a slate gray backdrop against which white towers of cloud were forming. I ignored the warning and set off on a walk around the hilltop campus to think things out.

Dr. Mott had been right, of course. I'd let the attraction of the Keats mystery turn my head. I'd disregarded the little I knew of Crosley, and imagined him doing unimaginable things. I'd lost sight of the human being in my excitement over a mysterious poem.

Not that I now intended to forget the poem. Dr. Mott's blanket hadn't been wet enough to smother that flame. But I knew now that I had work ahead of me if I intended to fit the poem into Crosley's puzzle. If the Crosley I knew wouldn't steal, perhaps there was another Crosley, a truer one, whom I had yet to meet. Perhaps there was a motive that I had yet to uncover, a motive too compelling for anyone, even a seminarian, to resist.

In other words, while I resolved to tie up the loose ends of Crosley's story, as Dr. Mott had suggested, it wasn't because I shared her opinion that the Keats poem was a distraction. I was hoping to use one of those loose strands to draw the poem back into the mystery and settle Dr. Mott's skepticism.

The professor saw Crosley's father as the key, so I decided to learn more about him. There weren't many sources for that information. I'd already heard from Beatrice Crosley, and Michael's own views were unavailable. That left John Crosley, Michael's uncle who lived in Evansville. According to Mrs. Crosley, John had not seen his nephew since the funeral of Martin Crosley in the spring. But Michael had been to Evansville fairly recently, only two or three weeks before his departure. Philip Swickard had told me that Crosley borrowed his car for the trip. I'd carelessly passed over that point of difference between Swickard's testimony and Mrs. Crosley's in my fascination with Melissa Donahue.

The trail led me next to John Crosley, but I didn't hurry to follow it. I sat instead on a stone bench and opened the Keats study. I turned to the end of the book and read of the poet's last days in Rome, spent lying in a room papered in roses amid piles of borrowed books. Keats had slipped away, his lungs destroyed, thinking of himself as a failure, a forgotten man. Someone who had seen his dream and fallen short of it. I closed the book feeling depressed.

A roll of thunder shook me from my thoughts. The buildups I'd noted earlier on the horizon had snuck up and surrounded me. Overhead, the bottom of the overcast roiled with a strange animation, egg-shaped bumps jostling each other for space, joining and breaking apart again like a plain of giant soap bubbles held upside down above me.

I left my bench and stood staring upward, fascinated, until the first fat drops of rain began to fall. The drops felt like ice after the heat of my long day, and they hit me with the force of a finger poking incessantly at my shoulders. I slipped the Keats book inside my shirt and ran for my dormitory.

I was drenched by the time I reached St. Meinrad Hall, and the storm was just getting underway. I watched from the stone arch of the entrance for a time as the late afternoon light was choked off. Security lights came on in the quad before me, triggered by the darkness, but the rain was so heavy now that their lamps were only just visible. Then flashes of lightning began, almost synchronized with the thunder overhead. Each flash lit the quad for a second and then left it blacker than it had been before.

I decided that the lightning was a metaphor for my investigation. Each of my discoveries had briefly illuminated Crosley, before disappearing and leaving his mystery more obscure than ever. As I lingered in the doorway, it occurred to me that Michael Crosley had left St. Aelred's in a storm very like the one I was watching. I shivered in my wet clothes at the thought. It made his action seem both desperate and unnatural. And it made me despair of ever understanding him.

The dormitory's communal telephone stood on a shelf in the reception area. It was an ancient black desk model from the fifties with a thick cord and a metal dialing ring that would not be hurried. Once, when I'd been in a fanciful mood, I'd thought that the phone might be a gateway to an earlier time. As I'd dialed home that day, I'd imagined the phone connecting me with the Trenton, New Jersey, of ten years before. I'd pictured a younger Owen Keane answering my call, someone I could have coached. Or warned. Now I was actually trying to use the old phone to reach into the past. I approached John Crosley as I had his sister-in-law, Beatrice, by first calling Information. Then I wore out my index finger dialing the number the operator had given me.

A man answered the first ring: "Crosley."

"My name is Owen Keane. I'm calling from St. Aelred Seminary. We're trying to locate one of our students, your nephew, Michael Crosley." I spoke slowly, trying to sound offhand and official at the same time.

The combination must have been too ambitious to pull off. John Crosley wasn't impressed. "I don't have anything to say about my nephew. I don't know where he is. I haven't seen him for months."

I've found that it's easier to be tough over the phone. Almost too easy. I slipped into that act now, inspired perhaps by Dr. Mott's recent teasing about Sam Spade. "If you want to take that line with Michael's mother, it's jake with me," I said. "But I know better. Michael's been to see you in the last month."

This was all bluff, of course. I couldn't be certain that Crosley had visited his uncle in Evansville or even that he'd been truthful with Swickard when he'd told him that he'd gone to Evansville. I was in too deep now for second thoughts, however, so I dug my hole a little deeper. "If you'd rather explain it to your sister-in-law, that's fine with me. Either way, I'm going to find out."

Karen Koffman, the Green Streets codirector, would have loved my performance. She'd made me feel like a prison guard on the trail of an escapee, which was exactly what I sounded like now. I watched the water from my shoes puddle on the brown linoleum and listened to static echoes of the storm on the phone line.

Then Crosley said, "I'll be here tonight if you want to talk." He rattled off an address and hung up.

It took me an hour to shower, change my clothes, and grab my first meal since breakfast. Then I was driving southwest on State Road 62 toward Evansville. I began the drive in the premature darkness of the storm, which made it slow going. The Ghia's wipers had only one arthritic speed, and the wet blacktop before me soaked my headlights up like a black beach absorbing a wave. Around Boonville, I drove out from under the rain and into the purple light of a cool dusk.

Evansville was a big city by Indiana's standards, but like the other midwestern cities I'd seen, it seemed stubbornly dated somehow, a place that had skipped the sixties entirely and hadn't made up its mind about the seventies. John Crosley had given me a crumb of directions to go with his address. His road, Vanderburgh Avenue, was a mile north of 62 off Highway 41. That turned out to be all the help I needed. I drove to Vanderburgh Avenue, past a darkened downtown and its skyline of smokestacks and grain elevators, as if I'd been doing it all my life.

Crosley's house was a bungalow on a small, well-kept lot. There was a '69 Mustang in the driveway. I paused to admire the car on my walk to the house, stalling as I often did when the moment had come to act. The rain was still standing in beads on the car's blue paint. My Ghia, when I looked back to it, was already dry and dull.

When I'd changed out of my wet clothes, I'd put on my clericals. It was the outfit I visited the Crosley family in, I'd told myself at the time. Now, as I buttoned the high collar and slid the white tab into place, I wondered if my choice of attire wasn't an early symptom of the uneasiness I felt at the thought of dealing with John Crosley face to face.

Crosley opened the front door before I'd taken my finger from the bell, his sour expression quickly giving way to surprise. He was a big man, as tall as his nephew and heavier, broad from the shoulders down to the ground.

"I'm from St. Aelred's," I said. "I spoke with you earlier this evening."

"You're Keane?" He asked the question as though he hoped I'd deny it.

"I feel that way about it some days myself," I said.

Crosley shook his head. "I can't believe I let you bully me on the phone. What do you weigh in at, one fifty?"

"One fifty-two when I called you. I was soaking wet at the time."

Crosley turned my own wisecrack against me. "You're still all wet, as far as I'm concerned. I told you on the phone that I don't know where Michael is. He was here to see me a month ago, I admit, but I haven't seen him since. There's nothing I can tell you, even if I thought it was your business."

"I think Michael is in trouble," I said. "Serious trouble. I want to help him, which makes it my business. I need your help to find him."

Crosley stepped to the edge of his tiny front porch and gave me a hard, searching look. Then he said, "You'd better come in and sit down."

The bungalow's front room reminded me immediately of Michael Crosley's garret at St. Aelred's. For one thing, it was a bachelor's room, comfortable but untidy. It was furnished with an overstuffed sofa and an easy chair. A worn Oriental rug covered the center of the hardwood floor, and on the rug sat the strangest coffee table I'd ever seen. Its top was a slice of tree trunk, six inches thick and four feet across. It was heavily varnished, but the tree's rings were clearly visible. It reminded me of an exhibit I'd once seen in a natural history museum, a cross section of an old tree with its rings dated and tied to bits of history: 1776, Washington crosses the Delaware; 1927, Lindbergh flies the Atlantic.

"That's from a tree that grew on our old lot on Pershing Avenue," Crosley said. "Where Marty and I grew up. I made that table in shop class when I was in high school. Have a seat. I'll be right back."

While I waited, I finished my examination of the room. The feature that had made me think of Michael Crosley was a built-in bookcase that covered an entire wall. The few shelves that weren't crammed with books held a collection of miniature brass cannons from various eras.

Crosley returned carrying two glasses and a bottle of bourbon. "I need a shot," he said. "Join me?"

"Sure," I said, not feeling sure at all.

He poured a couple of fingers of whiskey in each glass, measuring with his own oversize fingers. Then he handed me mine. "Happy days," he said.

I took an ambitious swallow. My effort to choke down the ensuing cough was more embarrassing than the cough would have been.

"Tough guy," Crosley said. He dug a pack of cigarettes from his shirt pocket. "Smoke?"

I pulled out my own pack, but accepted Crosley's light. He lit his cigarette with the same match and settled back into his chair. "What kind of trouble are you in?" he asked.

"I said that Michael is in trouble."

"I know what you said," Crosley answered evenly. "I teach high school. History. I do guidance counseling on the side. Kids come to me all the time to tell me about other kids' troubles. It always ends up being about their own."

I took another sip of bourbon. It burned less going down this time. John Crosley's eyes were the same washed-out blue as his nephew's, but his expression had none of Michael's innocence. Oddly, John's long hair was more stylish than Michael's, a benefit, I decided, of spending his life in high school.

"Michael and I were both candidates for leaving the seminary," I said. "Or, in my case, being asked to leave. Now Michael's gone, and I'm supposed to find out why. The priest who asked me to find out said it might help me."

My host thought about that for a while. Then he refilled his glass. "Beatrice called to tell me Michael had skipped. I don't call that trouble. I call that a step in the right direction."

That wasn't the extent of Michael's troubles, I thought. But I hadn't come to Evansville to talk about a stolen sonnet. I'd come to learn about Martin Crosley. "You said on the porch that Michael's been to see you, but you told his mother that he hadn't. Why?"

"Michael asked me not to tell her."

"Why would he do that?"

Crosley took a long drag on the remains of his cigarette, drawing it down to a nub. "I can't explain that without giving you his life story."

"Why did Michael come to see you? Was it about his father?"

"What do you know about Marty?" Crosley asked, sounding genuinely curious.

"I know that he and Michael didn't get along. That he ran down the things Michael valued: school, books, the priesthood."

"Did Beatrice tell you that? She didn't know Marty." Crosley smiled at that odd statement in spite of his anger. "I should say she didn't know the Martin Crosley I knew. The one I grew up with.

"I've been thinking about it a lot since Marty's funeral. I tried to talk with Mike that day, but he was still so resentful of his father that I couldn't get through to him. So I asked him to come down here to see me. Finally, a month or so ago, he did."

Crosley looked at his empty glass and then at the bottle. Then he set the glass down on the floor. "I told Mike a lot the day he came to see me. Things he had a right to know. I'm not sure about your right to know."

"Give me an outline," I said.

Crosley shrugged. "I thought it was important that Mike know who his father really was. He wouldn't really know himself until he did. Mike had things screwed up for so long, thinking he was so superior to his dad, thinking that Marty was no relation to him somehow, that he was from a different planet almost. The truth is that Mike was as much like his father as any son's been since Jesus Christ. It made me tear up just to look at Mike when he was down here. It was just like having Marty back again, the way he was before the war."

Crosley turned in his chair and pulled a slender volume from the bookcase behind him. "I gave Mike some books that had belonged to his father. And I showed him this."

He handed me the book, open. I turned it over to check its cover. It was the 1941 yearbook for Holy Cross High School. Crosley had opened it to a page of smiling black and white photographs. I picked Martin Crosley's out without the aid of its caption. It was easy to do. His picture was almost a duplicate of the smiling portrait of Michael I'd seen at his mother's house. Below the picture was a list of Martin's accomplishments at the school. He'd been on the academic honor role regularly, been editor of the school paper and captain of the football team. His goal was "to be a teacher."

"You should have seen Mike looking at that book," Crosley said. "He was ten times more confused and surprised than you are now. There was the father he'd written off as an illiterate loser, smiling up at him off that page like a lost brother."

"What happened to Martin?"

"The war happened to him. World War II. He joined the marines and saw action in the Pacific. After the fighting was over, he landed in the mental ward of a navy hospital. Combat fatigue, they called it. I guess he lost it pretty bad. They ran him through the gamut of horrors, strait-jackets, shock treatments. When he came out, he was the Martin Crosley we buried last spring.

"It wasn't just the war, though. It was the girl, too. Her name was Lisa Logan." He pointed to the yearbook. "She's in there."

I leafed forward to the Ls and found her, a dark-haired girl with a broad, smiling face.

"They weren't engaged, not formally, but they were in love. Lisa got sick and died in the winter of forty-four. Pneumonia. Marty broke down just after that, like I told you. I've often thought that Marty never came back from the Pacific. Not really, not the brother I knew.''

Forgetting his earlier resolve, Crosley retrieved his glass from the floor and half filled it with whiskey. ''I'm the reason Mike left St. Aelred's. I don't know where he is now, and that's the truth, but wherever he's gone off to, I sent him there. Maybe I shouldn't have dropped that bomb in his lap. But he had to know the truth about his dad. Before he made decisions he couldn't undo, he had to know. I owed it to him. I owed it to Marty.''

Crosley's nose was red and his eyes were wet. I handed him the yearbook. He held it protectively against his chest.

I stood up. ''I'd better be getting back to St. Aelred's,'' I said.

''Are you sure about that?'' Crosley asked.

I understood that he had returned to the subject of Owen Keane's troubles. I also knew that there was no answer for me in his magic yearbook.

''Good night,'' I said.

IT WAS A HARD DRIVE back to the college. I was suddenly drowsy, and I chain-smoked and hung my head halfway out the Ghia's window to fight off sleep. I should have been sleepless with excitement. John Crosley had given me the key to the case, all the information I needed to explain why Crosley had run away. But I was unexcited and strangely uninterested. Perhaps it was because this was only the latest in a series of keys to Crosley, none of which had panned out.

To keep myself awake after my last cigarette was gone, I tried to list all the loose ends that the story of Martin Crosley tied up. It substantiated Karen Koffman's diagnosis that Michael had identity problems. He hadn't really known himself because he hadn't known his roots, his father. The story also explained why Michael had appeared dazed to Mrs. Wilson in the last weeks at St. Aelred's. The revelations had shaken everything he believed about his father and himself and the way he'd chosen to live his life.

John Crosley's tale also explained why Michael had asked his uncle to keep his visit to Evansville a secret. He didn't want Beatrice Crosley to know that he had learned of Lisa Logan, the woman who had preceded and possibly precluded her. He didn't want to hurt his mother's feelings.

The loose end that Martin's history couldn't explain was the lost Keats sonnet. Dr. Mott had probably been right about that, I conceded as I parked my car behind the old dairy. The Keats material had never been more than a passing interest of Crosley's. The revelations about his father had been his main concern.

I was too tired to argue with that echo of Dr. Mott's logic. I went straight back to St. Meinrad Hall, straight to my bed, and put the day behind me.

I WAS AWAKENED at four-thirty by Brother Dennis. He was standing in the doorway of my room in his bathrobe, the robe reminding me of my old surmise that he had once been a prizefighter. His hand was on the light switch, and the glare of the ceiling fixture was blinding me. But it was the monk's expression, more than the sudden harsh light, that shocked me fully awake. He looked scared to death.

"There's a sheriff's deputy downstairs," Brother Dennis whispered. "He's just come from Father Jerome. He wants to talk to you. A woman has been killed. Someone named Sarah Morell."

SIXTEEN

I'VE BEEN IN BIG-CITY police stations and small-town police stations, and I'll take the big-city ones every time. That's speaking as a suspect, of course. If I were in trouble and needed help, I'd opt for a small-town operation where nothing much is happening and every visitor is the center of attention. A suspect in a police investigation, on the other hand, appreciates a little anonymity. In a place like Boston, where I'd previously attracted the attention of the police, you can be waiting in a busy precinct to answer questions about an ax murder and, if you're quiet and don't spill things, everyone ignores you.

That was far from the case at the Huber County sheriff's office. From the moment I arrived there a little after six A.M., I was on center stage. It might have been a modern interrogation technique. The combined stares of a half-dozen deputies may have been taking the place of the bright lights and rubber hoses of the old days. It very nearly worked on me. After a couple hours of the treatment, I was close to asking for a stenographer.

On the plus side, the oppressive atmosphere of the sheriff's office kept me from thinking too much about Sarah Morell. If I'd been allowed to concentrate on her death, I could have worked up a paralyzing load of guilt, just when I most needed my dubious wits about me.

The deputy who had first questioned me back at St. Aelred's, a man named Springer, had been bad at his job. He'd looked the part—tall and well built in a uniform of navy blue pants, a white shirt with blue epaulets, and a straw cowboy hat—but he'd talked too much. He'd been both proud of his inside knowledge and nervous about having it. Instead of asking me questions and watching my reactions, Springer had given me a virtual briefing. Before we'd left the school together, I knew that Sarah had been suffocated by a pillow sometime between eight, when she'd been put to bed, and nine, when an aide had looked in and seen the pillow still in place. It had been raining in Evay around that time. Muddy footprints had been found near one of the fire doors. If the killer had come from outside the home, a pretty safe bet in my opinion, the prints were probably his. The Good Fellows staff had set the police on my trail and on Michael Crosley's.

After spilling all he knew, Spring had driven me to Randolph, the Huber County seat. The sheriff's offices were located in the basement of the courthouse, a delicate-looking building of white-painted brick that sat on a grassy square of ground at the center of town. One corner of the square was decorated by a Civil War cannon and another by a Sherman tank painted battleship gray. The basement waiting area where Springer had deposited me was itself a square, this one formed by a low wooden railing enclosing a few hard chairs. The enclosure was surrounded by desks manned by deputies who had nothing better to do than stare at me.

It might have been my clothes that interested them. When Brother Dennis had come knocking before dawn, my clericals had been draped over the chair near my bed, and I'd reached for them without thinking. More probably, I was the center of the deputies' attention because I had been Sarah Morell's last visitor, having spoken with her twice during her last two days on earth. I was also something of an authority on Michael Crosley. Springer knew, from a brief interview with Father Jerome, that Crosley was gone and I had been assigned to trace him. That was about all Springer had learned, but I didn't expect to get off that easily. Sure enough, at eight o'clock a gray-haired deputy named Clark took me aside for another questioning. I gave him an outline of my investigation into Crosley's departure, omitting details like the name John Keats. I also presented him with my airtight alibi, my trip to Evansville during the critical hours when Sarah had been killed. Clark took down John Crosley's name and promised to follow it up.

When Clark returned me to the fishbowl, he told me that Sheriff Roger Yeager would talk to me personally as soon as he arrived, and that he was expected "anytime now." A different deputy stopped by my chair every twenty minutes or so over the next two hours to repeat this promise.

Perhaps the long wait had created exaggerated expectations in me, but Sheriff Yeager, when he finally wandered in around ten, was a major disappointment. He was a short man who emphasized his lack of height by being very wide. The blue and white polyester uniform that had been intimidatingly official on Deputy Springer was comical on Yeager. His straw cowboy hat bent his ears down. The front of his white shirt showed gaps between its over-stressed buttons, and the belt of his holster was drawn too tight around his waist, creating a bulge above and below its black leather. I wondered if the belt's real function might have been to prevent Yeager's chest from sagging down into his shiny blue pants.

Something had recently winded the sheriff—the walk in from his car, I suspected. His face was red and he was perspiring generously. Wisps of gray hair were visible beneath the brim of his hat, and a grizzled beard fringed his fat cheeks, making him look like a country caricature of Henry VIII. He pointed a finger at me as he waddled past my chair. "Follow me, son," he said.

Yeager led me into a large, windowless office decorated with metal furniture, pictures of deer and fish, and dozens of commemorative plaques. Though short of breath, he talked on steadily. "Strange business this killing. Old lady who's not a threat to anyone. Hasn't any money or insurance. Only an old farm so mortgaged up you'd have to blackmail someone before he'd take it. Not a real easy one to figure out. No sir. Coffee sound good to you?''

I nodded yes, although I'd had a gallon already.

The sheriff yelled our order out to the world at large. Then he settled in behind his desk, grunting with relief as his wooden desk chair took up the strain. "Where you from, son?'' he asked me.

"Trenton, New Jersey.''

"You came all the way out here to study?'

"Yes," I said. "At St. Aelred's.''

Yeager nodded. He removed his hat and placed it on the desktop. His thinning hair lay wet across the top of his head. "Going to be a priest, are you? Help souls get across to a better place?''

"Something like that.''

Clark, the old deputy who had questioned me earlier, entered with two mugs of coffee. He also carried a typed sheet of paper, which he set before the sheriff. My statement, I decided.

"We heard from the Good Fellows Home again, Sheriff,'' Clark said. "They remembered someone calling up to ask about Sarah Morell three or four weeks back. An Indianapolis banker. We've got the name of the firm.''

"Probably chasing after a late payment,'' Yeager said. "Look into it anyway.''

Clark left, and the sheriff devoted his attention to my statement. He alternately blew on his coffee and sipped noisily as he read.

"Here's good news for you, son,'' Yeager said after five minutes of blowing and sipping and reading. "Your Evansville trip checked out. Now you and I can have a friendly chat. Suppose you start off by telling me why you visited John Crosley last night.''

"I went to talk with him about his nephew. As I told your deputy, Michael Crosley was a student at St. Aelred's. He left recently without telling anyone why."

"Did you think Mr. Crosley might be hiding his nephew out?"

There it was again, the suggestion that Michael had tunneled his way out under the wire. "I thought he might know where Michael's gone."

"Does he?"

"No. That is, he doesn't know where Michael is now. But John Crosley thinks he's responsible for Michael leaving St. Aelred's. He upset Michael with some stories about Michael's father, who passed away last spring." I wondered how I would explain the continuing interaction between Michael and his dead father to the sheriff. I needn't have worried. That ancient history didn't interest Yeager.

"So Michael Crosley was unstable."

"Off balance," I said. "Not unstable. Mixed up about his father's past and his own future."

"I'm sending somebody down to talk with John Crosley. We'll get the whole story from him. It interests me, though, to hear you call this Michael off balance."

"Why?"

"Let's talk for a minute about Sarah Morell. You went to see her because Crosley did, I gather. What was his interest in her?"

"He visited her as a charitable act. The retirement home was an assignment he'd drawn as part of his counseling at the school."

"Counseling for what?"

"Spiritual development."

Yeager grunted. "Seems like a priest trainee would need that about as much as a rabbit needs a marriage manual. You were saying that this Crosley visited Sarah Morell as a charity. Why did he latch on to her?"

"It was probably the other way around. Sarah was desperate for company. Michael became interested in Sarah's problems. She's hard up for money."

"Was hard up, you mean," Yeager corrected.

"Yes. Her family had been running her farm for her. But it was barely producing enough income to keep her in that home."

Yeager nodded as though the situation was familiar to him.

I took a sip of my cold coffee and went on. "Michael wanted to help Sarah with her money troubles."

"Says who?"

"Sarah. She told me yesterday."

"How was he going to do that? I thought you priests were supposed to be poor."

"Sarah had some old family papers at her farm that Michael thought might be valuable. Sarah sent Michael after them. He visited her family on the farm, but they couldn't find anything."

I stopped there, well short of any reference to John Keats and the lost sonnet. I could see where Yeager's interest in Crosley was leading, and I wanted no part of it. Before Dr. Mott's wet-blanket treatment, I had just about talked myself into believing that Crosley was a thief. But nothing, not a whole collection of lost poetry, could persuade me that he was a murderer. I had no intention of giving Yeager a motive.

As it turned out, I was wasting my dishonesty. Yeager already had his motive.

The sheriff's chair cracked and popped as he leaned backward. He raised his arms to form a headrest with his hands, revealing a series of concentric sweat stains of varying diameters under each arm. They reminded me of the rings on John Crosley's coffee table.

"Let's see if I've got this straight," Yeager began. "Michael Crosley is training to be a Catholic priest. He wants to help people find their way to God. He meets this lonely old lady in a nursing home. Sarah Morell. Sarah's got money troubles. Spiritual troubles, too, maybe. She's somebody this Michael wants to save. He tried to find some money for her in some old papers that turn out not to exist. Dead end there.

"Meanwhile, Crosley is having troubles of his own. Needs spiritual development, whatever that might be. His uncle tells him things about his daddy that disturb him. Their little talk mixes Michael up in the head. He leaves school to find himself. Maybe he gets better, maybe not. Maybe the idea that he's failed at the school rattles him a little more. Maybe he works himself into a big muddle of God and heaven and helping people. Maybe he decides to help that old lady waiting back at the nursing home."

"Wait a minute."

"Last night in the storm he comes back. He can't help this Sarah Morell with her money troubles. But he can help her escape them. Help send her to a better place. It would be a mercy, he thinks. The act of charity he was sent to do in the first place."

"That's crazy."

Yeager leaned forward, resting his forearms on the desk. "You're right there. But religion is a kind of craziness, if it's strong enough. A person with enough religion in him doesn't really think about this world. He thinks about heaven, streets of gold, pearly gates. A person who believes in that kind of thing, and I mean really believes, would be happy to send a lonely old lady off to a better place."

"A person who believes in that kind of thing wouldn't hurt a fly," I said.

"Oh, he didn't hurt her," Yeager replied. "Not hardly. Came up on her while she was sleeping, we think." He picked his cowboy hat up from the side of his desk to demonstrate. Holding it with a hand on each side of its wide brim, he set the hat down softly in the center of his blotter. "There was hardly any struggle."

SEVENTEEN

YEAGER SAT CONFIDENTLY behind his desk, rocking slightly in his noisy chair and enjoying the view of me sinking under the weight of his logic. Actually, his reasoning was mostly hot air, but two of the points he'd made had genuinely frightened me. One was the idea that Crosley might have lost his mind. It was just possible, given the pressure that Crosley was under at school and the double blow of his father's death and his uncle's revelations, that Michael had suffered a breakdown of some kind. That possibility undercut the only defense I had, my gut feeling that Crosley didn't have it in him to take a life.

The other part of Yeager's story that disturbed me was related to this possibility of madness. It was the picture Yeager had painted of Crosley coming to kill Sarah at the height of a storm. The night before, while watching the lightning outside my dorm, I'd thought of Crosley leaving St. Aelred's in just such a storm. It made the idea of his running away worse for me somehow, making the act seem unnatural, or more precisely, uncivilized. A primeval act, like taking the life of another. Those two thunderstorms might have been symbolic of some cataclysm inside Crosley, the madness Yeager had postulated that made all my reasoning worthless.

"Well, what do you think, son?"

Yeager was smiling happily at me, and his smile made me mad. Perhaps it was all the coffee I'd had with no breakfast to soak it up. Or it might have been Yeager's crazy ideas about the religious life. It was probably just that I had no rational counterargument at hand. Whatever the rea-

son, I went on the offensive, with no better goal than re-
moving the smug smile from Sheriff Yeager's face.

"I think you're way off base, Sheriff. If anyone's crazy
around here, it isn't Michael Crosley. You haven't a scrap
of physical evidence. All you have to go on is some muddy
footprints and a prejudice against religion. I'd hate to think
there's a jury that nonsense would impress."

"Well, thank you all to hell, Mr. Keane," Yeager said.
My primary objective had been achieved. The smile was
gone from his heavy lips. He leaned toward me, steadying
himself with his hands spread wide on his desktop. "Next
time I want some city kid who's greener than the corn in
June telling me how to do my job, I'll be sure to give you a
call."

I'd only just begun to make trouble for myself. "If this
case were about corn, I'm sure you'd be on top of it," I
said. "But it's not. It's about human beings. We know a
little about those in the city, and I'm telling you that Michael Crosley couldn't kill anyone."

Yeager's smile returned. "You could make pope someday, son, you really could. You've got the infallibility part
down already." He consulted the notes the old deputy had
given him. "Let's see. You were trying to find Crosley,
weren't you?"

"Yes."

"Who told you to do that?"

It would have been a good moment to withhold a little
more information. I'd done that for Crosley, but I wouldn't
do it for myself. "Father Loudermilk, my spiritual director, asked me to figure out why Crosley had left. As an exercise."

"Uh-huh. Was it for your, ah, what did you call it?
Spiritual development?"

I could have escaped Yeager's trap with a simple lie, but
I didn't. I was suddenly preoccupied by a mental image

successfully avoided all morning, the picture of Sarah Morell lying in bed with a pillow over her face.

"Yes," I said. "The exercise was part of my counseling."

"Shame you didn't do a better job of it," Yeager said. "With your wide knowledge of human beings and all. If you had, it might have helped you with your counseling. Might have helped Sarah Morell, too. She might be alive today."

Yeager's smile had disappeared again, but that was no signal of victory for me. The sheriff leaned to one side to have a clear view around me out the door. Then he hollered for Deputy Springer.

"I might have been wrong about your prospects, son," he said while we waited. "You may not be pope material. They might just have to stick with Italians for the time being. Seems like first to last you've been as useless as tits on a boar."

Springer entered the office and stood at attention beside me. "Frank Morell and his wife are outside, Sheriff," he said.

Yeager nodded. "I'll be right there. You can give this gentleman a ride home now. He's probably late for church."

I followed Springer out of the office. Frank and Agnes Morell were standing outside, awaiting their audience. Like me, they were dressed up for the occasion. Frank hadn't shaved his stubble beard, but he wore a blue suit and a brown tie and carried a brown felt hat. The hat and the tie may have been intended to complement Agnes's sleeveless brown dress. She glared at me with open hatred as I passed them. Her husband patted her on the shoulder and looked at me almost apologetically, shaking his head.

Springer and I had barely passed Frank and Agnes before Yeager came out of his office door, moving more briskly than I would have thought possible. He extended his arms as he approached the Morells, as though he intended to embrace them. "Sorry to keep you folks waiting," he said. "Terrible business. Just terrible."

"We've come about getting Sarah for burying," Morell said.

Yeager was already ushering them toward his office, his arm around Agnes's shoulder. "You just come in here and sit down," he said. "Can I get you some coffee?"

My escort and I watched this little scene from the railed waiting area. Then the deputy said, "I'll get the car and meet you out front by the cannon."

The cannon must have been a popular spot for rendezvous in Randolph. There was already someone waiting at it when I got there. Waiting on it, I should say. Krystal Morell sat astride the barrel. When I first saw her at a distance, I decided that she was playing. I was happy to think that Krystal was unaware of Sarah's death and the charge hanging over the head of her fiancé-to-be, Michael Crosley. That consolation was soon denied me. When I drew closer, I realized that Krystal was crying.

"Hello," I said when I was still a few steps away.

Krystal turned her head toward me without raising it, and her tangled hair hung down across her face, making her look like a pint-size Veronica Lake.

"What's the matter?" I asked.

An adult would have told me what a stupid question that was. Krystal merely answered it honestly. "Everything," she said.

Was she upset, I wondered, over the death of an old woman she probably hadn't know, or were the tears really for Crosley? Could she know that Crosley was in serious trouble over Sarah's death? Her grandmother seemed to. I had welts from the look Agnes had given me, Crosley's accomplice. If Agnes and Frank Morell knew, Krystal probably did, too.

"Mikey's going to be okay," I said, using Krystal's nickname for Crosley.

Krystal raised her head and pushed her hair back from her face. She hadn't cleaned up for the trip as her grandparents had. Her tears had left tiny streaks of erosion across her dirty cheeks. "It's you," she said.

It took me a second to realize that Krystal hadn't recognized me when I'd first walked up. I had just been an anonymous, solicitous adult.

I'd no sooner solved that mystery than Krystal presented me with a harder one. "You!" she said, her eyes wide with terror.

She moved away from me, sliding around until she hung beneath the cannon's barrel and then dropping to the ground on her back. Before I could move to help her up, she was on her feet, running splayfooted for the courthouse. "You, you, you, you, you!" she repeated as she ran.

Krystal's genuine fear of me was more unnerving than the long morning I'd spent with Yeager's staring deputies, and her one-word accusation cut deeper than the sheriff's questioning had. I couldn't answer her charges with my Evansville alibi, any more than I could quiet my own conscience with it. I'd gone to see Sarah, now she was dead. I couldn't see the connection yet, but I could feel it. As Krystal Morell did.

EIGHTEEN

I FOUND A MESSAGE taped to the door of my room when Deputy Springer dropped me at my dormitory just before eleven. The note was from my pen pal, Brother Dennis: "Please see Father Jerome as soon as possible." There was no signature or greeting or Scripture quotation. I wondered if I had slipped another notch in the monk's estimation. From amusing oddball to difficult probationer to what? A historical footnote maybe, like the reference to George Keats's descendants in Bate's book. Perhaps I had already moved into the past tense for Brother Dennis, as Sarah Morell had for me. I could hear him speaking of me to the returning seminarians in the fall: "Owen Keane, yes, a sad story."

I showered and shaved before reporting for Father Jerome, naively hoping to wash away the aura of the police station. As I was back on campus, I should have returned my clericals to their closet. I wore them instead, stubbornly. Or perhaps sentimentally.

Late on a Saturday morning, St. Bede Hall was quiet even by summer standards. The echo of my footsteps preceded me down the hallway, announcing me as effectively as any intercom system. Father Jerome called to me as I entered the reception area of the dean of theology's suite. "Is that you, Owen? Come in, come in, I've been waiting for you."

The dean didn't rise at my entrance to take his seat in front of the desk as he usually did. He didn't even look up at me for a moment. His long white head leaned to one side slightly, and he studied the empty center of his desk. I wondered if he'd been here waiting for me since Springer had roused the campus before dawn. The priest straightened himself with an effort as he raised his eyes to mine.

"Sit, Owen, sit. This is a terrible business," he said, unconsciously repeating Sheriff Yeager's comment to the Morells. "An old woman, killed like that. Were you able to help the police?"

"I eliminated one suspect for them. Me."

"Owen." The old priest was shocked. "Surely they didn't think that anyone at St. Aelred's..." He had been shaking one long, thin hand at me, shooing the idea out of his office. Now his hand suddenly froze in the air. "Michael Crosley. That policeman asked about him, too. Do they suspect him?"

"I think he's at the top of their list."

"And Michael not here to defend himself," Father Jerome said, as though Crosley's extended absence was just an unfortunate coincidence. "How could they think that? What is their reasoning?"

"I don't know if reason has anything to do with it. The sheriff of Huber County, Roger Yeager, holds an unflattering view of the religious life." I searched for an inoffensive way to convey Yeager's theory to the dean and decided there wasn't one. "The sheriff seems to think that seminarian is another word for religious fanatic. He thinks that Crosley may have completely lost his grip recently, because of pressure here at school and his father's death."

"Gone mad, you mean?" the priest asked, giving the condition a Victorian sound.

"Yes. Yeager thinks he killed Sarah Morell as an insane act of charity."

Father Jerome's pendulous ear lobes swung aggressively as he shook his head. "The whole idea is insane. To think we're living in the seventies with notions like that. It's enough to make you question human progress. Do you think this evil thing is possible, Owen?"

"I think it's possible that Crosley had more coming at him than he could handle," I said.

"You've learned something, then."

"I confirmed the insight you sent me off with. That Crosley came to St. Aelred's to escape a bad situation at home. He was defying his father, or at least he thought he was."

"What do you mean?"

"He was defying a person who didn't really exist. I think Michael left St. Aelred's when he realized that."

"Explain, please."

"Michael grew up believing that his father, Martin Crosley, was an anti-intellectual factory worker. He learned recently that Martin was a damaged person, a fragment of a young man who went off to war in 1941. The prewar Martin Crosley was very like Michael, a good student who wanted to go on to college. Michael found out the truth about his father from John Crosley, Martin's brother. Michael went to see him about a month ago."

"Two weeks before he left us," Father Jerome said. "You've spoken with John Crosley?"

"Last night. He told me that Michael and young Martin were as alike as brothers. Except that Martin had once been in love. Really in love. The girl died while he was in the service. John thought that her death hurt his brother more than the war."

"Did the uncle tell Michael about this lost love?"

"Yes. Michael had never heard about this girl, Lisa Logan, before."

Father Jerome pushed his chair back from his desk and away from me. I leaned forward involuntarily to close the distance between us.

"I think then, Owen, that you're wrong about the reason Michael left," the old priest said. "Or at least you haven't worked out the whole reason. It wasn't just that his father had an unsuspected intellectual side. It must also have been because Martin Crosley had once loved."

"I don't follow you, Father."

In spite of his fatigue and the shocks of the morning, Father Jerome managed a kind smile. "Don't you, Owen? Don't you see that Michael's real problem is an inability to love? To reach out to another human being? That was the harmful legacy he brought with him from home."

The priest pointed to me. "Sitting in that very chair, Michael told me that he resented his father's indifference to Beatrice Crosley, his mother. That was the father's great sin in his son's eyes. Unfortunately, we often follow our parents in their sins as well as their strengths. Michael grew up believing that it was possible to live without love, because he thought his father had done so. He thought it preferable to live without loving, because his mother had suffered when her abundant love had not been returned by her husband. Michael lived with his guard up always against human love."

Father Jerome's gentle demeanor didn't hide the fact that he was very disappointed in the job I'd done. I was disappointed myself. I'd had all the information I needed to fit Martin Crosley's lost love into Michael's mystery. I'd seen the hurt and disappointment in Beatrice Crosley's eyes. Karen Koffman had told me that Michael described his parents' marriage as loveless. I'd had the clues, but I hadn't worked them out. I'd been too busy with mysterious girlfriends and lost sonnets."

I thought of telling Father Jerome about the Keats angle, as a way of countering his disappointment in me. But the priest was already moving on.

"And the revelations of the uncle, Owen. You misread them entirely. Michael wasn't shocked to learn that his father had been a good student. Saddened maybe, that he had misjudged him now that it was too late to make it right. Saddened but not shocked. What shocked him to his roots was the idea that his father had loved. Loved, Owen. Michael's whole plan for his life was undermined by that knowledge. His plan to be a pious, chaste, unloving priest.''

He stood up. ''Come, Owen. I've been sitting here all morning waiting for you to return. Let's stretch our legs while we talk this out.''

We walked side by side in silence until we were out of the building. Then Father Jerome looked around him, evaluating the day. ''Last night's rain helped. The humidity isn't quite what it's been. Let's walk toward the library, Owen. It's a shady path.''

I thought again of broaching the subject of the Keats poem. Father Jerome had other mysteries in mind.

''Why do you think I asked you to look into Michael's history?''

Dr. Mott had recently stumped me with that same question. I found an answer now in my growing depression. ''You said it was to help me with hurdles I was facing. Questions about leaving St. Aelred's, I guess you meant. Was I supposed to decide that Crosley had found the right answer? My answer?''

''Owen.'' The priest put a hand on my shoulder. ''Perhaps I shouldn't have given you the exercise. I shouldn't have most definitely, since it has involved you with the police and this sad death. It was supposed to be an experiment, the exercise I gave you. I wanted to see if you'd arrive at a certain insight concerning the priesthood. One I've found very valuable.

''I came across this idea recently in a book by Bishop Fulton Sheen. It has to do with the dual nature of the priesthood, which stems from the dual role of Christ as priest. He was the celebrant of His great sacrifice and He was also its victim. Priest and Paschal Lamb. It is the same for His priest. We are representatives of both Christ the celebrant and Christ the victim. Dual roles, hard to reconcile.

"Think of it this way. Every priest has a spiritual, cere-
monial role to perform. But he also has a calling to victimhood. We sacrifice ourselves, dedicate our lives to our
vocations, but it's more than that. We're called upon to
identify with the victims of this world, because Christ was
a victim. We are outside this world as celebrants and deeply
immersed in it as victims, responsible for both the spiritual
welfare of our flock and its temporal well-being. With me
so far?"

"Yes, Father."

"It's a balance that is difficult to maintain. When I was
a young man, priests commonly erred by leaning too
heavily on the celebrant side of the equation. We produced
many pious young men, possessed of great faith, but out of
touch with the world. Out of touch with the people they
served."

"Michael Crosleys," I said.

"Yes. Michael was on his way to becoming just such a
priest. A holy, pious man, but only half a priest.

"That was the old tendency. Lately I've noticed that the
pendulum has swung the other way. We're living in the
great age of social conscience. Priests marching for civil
rights or against the war. Priests who see social justice as
the real goal of their work, perhaps because they aren't
certain any more that there are other, higher goals. These
are men who love people greatly, who want to help them
greatly, which is all to the good. But the balance between
the celebrant and the victim must be maintained. A great
social conscience cannot make up for a shaky faith, Owen.
The celebrant must still inspire his people to strive for God.
He can never merely be concerned with untangling their
temporal difficulties."

"You're speaking of me now," I said.

"I've been speaking of you and Michael. I've come to see
you as opposite sides of this balance. As two men who have
come to St. Aelred's on different paths. A calling to the

priesthood can seem as real to a person who has a great love of mankind as it does to one who has a great love of God. And the two loves can be mutually exclusive, which is where the problems arise. One love without the other may be enough to make a decent person, but not a good priest.''

We had reached the center of the campus. Without speaking, Father Jerome took a left turning of the path that led us back toward St. Bede Hall.

The priest's silence made me uncomfortable. ''You gave Michael Crosley his service projects at the halfway house and the nursing home so he would be exposed to the temporal part of his job?''

''So he would be exposed to people, Owen. People. It's too easy to bury yourself here in books, meeting only other seminarians who—let's face it—are not representative of the world at large. I wanted Michael to brush up against people, people in need. I wanted him to test himself. To honestly answer the question 'Can I serve God's people all my life?'

''I was hoping, too, that the exposure would thaw him out somehow.'' He waved his hand impatiently, as though embarrassed by that hope. The nervous hand ended its flight on the sleeve of my black shirt. ''I asked Michael not to wear clerical garb so he wouldn't have even that thin barrier between himself and the world.''

''What about my assignment?''

''Ah well, that was more subtle. Too subtle, I suppose. I'd hoped that you would get to know Michael Crosley. To see his strengths as well as his weaknesses. To recognize that they were the opposite of your own.

''And something else. I'd hoped that you would recognize the hopelessness of solving the mystery of even a single human life. That you'd recognize the unsolvable mystery at the center of every person and come to some peace with the great, unsolvable mysteries of this existence.

"Are you familiar with the *Nosce Te ipsum* of St. Bernard of Clairvaux, Owen?"

"No," I said.

"It's an interesting work. In it, he says that the obstacle to real faith isn't a conventional sin. Not lust or sloth or impiety. The one critical stumbling block to faith, according to St. Bernard, is curiosity. The desire to know all the answers. The fallacious belief that we can figure out the causes of things. That we can untangle the unsolvable mysteries, like the soul of Michael Crosley. Something for you to consider."

The old priest stopped walking and turned to face me on the path. He put his hands on my shoulders, and I felt his weight as he leaned on me slightly. "You've had a hard day, Owen, and the bells are just now ringing the noon hour. We both have had hard days. Now is not the time for this talk. I've said enough for one morning.

"The exercise I gave you is over. Put Michael Crosley out of your mind. There is something else I want you to do for me now. I'd almost forgotten to mention it, we've ranged so far."

"What is it, Father?"

"I want you to go and see Elizabeth Mott."

"Now? It's Saturday. Will she be in?"

"She'll be in. I asked her to be. Go and see her now." He released his hold on my shoulders. "And think about what I've said. We'll talk again later."

NINETEEN

I LEFT FATHER JEROME and cut across the lawn that lay between me and the Arts and Sciences Building. On my way, I passed a statue of the Virgin Mary surrounded by a well-tended bed of brilliant white geraniums bordered by blue ageratum. The flowers reminded me of Krystal Morell's garden, and I wondered if they had any folksy medicinal uses. I needed an elixir that could cure a defeated spirit or a charm that was proof against the evil eye of reality. When I reached the steps of the building, I looked back across the quad. Father Jerome was standing where I'd left him, his white hair as bright in the full sun as the Virgin's flowers. Without thinking, I waved to him. He waved back, encouragingly.

The Arts and Sciences Building felt cool after my high-noon walk. At least it did until I began to climb the three flights of stairs to the English Department. By the time I reached the top, I was breathing faster. That might not have been because of the climb. It might have been a side effect of walking blind into an unknown situation. I couldn't imagine why Father Jerome had asked Dr. Mott to be here waiting for me or why he wanted me to talk with her. Perhaps the two of them had discussed my situation and decided that I should drop theology and pursue a graduate degree in detective fiction, someplace far, far away from St. Aelred's.

In my current state of mind, I couldn't help feeling threatened by the mystery, a feeling that grew when I discovered that Dr. Mott was not alone. I heard her speaking to someone while I was still in the hallway. She was describing a trip she and her husband had once made to New England. I waited outside the reception area doorway for a time, hoping to hear her visitor's voice, but Dr. Mott rambled on without a break.

The secretary's desk was still tidied for the weekend, as I'd last seen it. Dr. Mott's office door was partially open. I could see her, but not her audience. Remembering how I'd scared her on my last visit, I knocked on the top of the secretary's desk as I passed it.

"Owen, come in," Dr. Mott said. "I've someone here who's come a long way to see you."

I pushed her door open slowly. Before looking around it, I spoke the shortest prayer of my life. "Mary?"

And it was true. In the leather visitor chair sat Mary Fitzgerald, the girl I'd left behind. The woman, I should say. Seeing her without warning here at St. Aelred's gave me a small taste of Michael Crosley's recent disorientation. The tiny world of the college was shifted off balance by this nudge from the larger universe. *I* was shifted off balance. I held on tightly to the doorknob for support.

She'd cut her honey-colored hair short. It should have made her look younger, but instead it gave her a grown-up elegance, emphasizing her delicate profile and the length of her neck. She lowered her head slightly as I examined her, her blue eyes giving me a familiar up-from-under look through long lashes. Her mouth was small and given to one-sided smiles expressing skepticism. At the moment, the smile was symmetrical but tentative. As I watched, her lightly tanned complexion began to darken.

"You're staring, Owen," Dr. Mott said.

"Sorry," I said, addressing Mary. "You took me by surprise."

"People who don't return phone calls deserve to be surprised," Mary said. "I called three times." She was teasing me for Dr. Mott's benefit, but I could tell that my silence had hurt and puzzled her. Her voice was husky and hesitant.

"Three times?" I asked.

"I called from the Louisville airport this morning."

"I have a good excuse for missing that one."

"We know," Dr. Mott said. "Brother Dennis took Mary's call. He drove to Louisville to fetch her. Father Jerome asked me to come in and chaperone until you got back."

"Thank you," I said.

"Oh, I was happy to do it." The professor was dressed for a Saturday. Her straight, sleeveless dress glowed with an irregular yellow and white pattern, as bright as a van Gogh sky. Mary's outfit was sedate in comparison: a long-sleeved white blouse with a wide collar under a blue paisley vest. Her navy blue bell bottoms were secured by a wide belt of golden links.

"Female conversation is hard to come by at St. Aelred's," Dr. Mott was saying. "We've been drinking tea and discussing you, Owen."

It was my turn to blush. "The little I heard was about New England."

"Yes. We'd just about exhausted the Owen Keane file. Although I must say, Mary has told me some amazing stories. I have a whole new picture of you now."

A picture of a nutty amateur detective, I thought.

Dr. Mott promptly confirmed this guess. "I should never have recommended new branches of crime fiction to you. You need a drastic change, a new genre entirely. Louis L'Amour may be called for."

Mary jumped in to change the focus of conversation. "Elizabeth was telling me that she recently applied for a teaching position at Boston College."

"You'd leave St. Aelred's?" I asked.

"Everyone does, sooner or later, Owen. Even hoary old campus institutions like myself." Her banter sounded as forced now as Mary's earlier teasing. I took time off from covertly admiring Mary to examine the professor more closely. Like Father Jerome, she looked wearied by the events of the morning. There were dark half-moons under her eyes, and she leaned heavily on one arm of her chair.

Dr. Mott met my eye and read my thoughts. "A bad day, Owen. Has there really been a murder?"

"Yes. Sarah Morell, the old woman I told you about. The one who sent Michael after the Keats material."

"The police can't suspect you." Mary spoke with a confidence that I appreciated greatly.

"Not anymore. They're after Michael Crosley now."

"The seminarian you've been looking for?" Mary asked. "Elizabeth told me about him."

Hearing her call Dr. Mott "Elizabeth" reinforced the feeling I had that Mary had grown up while I'd been frozen in time at the seminary. I felt like a truant child standing at attention before examining adults.

"Why would the police suspect Michael?" Dr. Mott demanded. "You surely didn't fill their heads with that fantasy of yours about the Keats poem."

"The poem isn't a fantasy," I said.

"What poem are you talking about?" Mary asked.

"A lost sonnet by John Keats," Dr. Mott said. "I forgot to mention it. Owen thinks Michael Crosley stumbled across one here in southern Indiana. Happens all the time."

"The sonnet must be connected with the murder if Michael Crosley is," I said. "It's the only link between his disappearance and Sarah Morell's death."

"Is that what the police think?" Dr. Mott asked.

"I didn't tell them about it."

"Then they must feel there is another link between Michael and this Sarah Morell or they wouldn't be interested in him."

She had me there. "Yes," I admitted. "Sheriff Yeager thinks that Michael's religion is the link. He thinks Michael visited her as a charity and then killed her as a charity."

That idea silenced all three of us for a time.

Then Dr. Mott said, "There's nothing in this world so hard to understand as another person's goodness. We empathize with weaknesses easily enough, because we all have them. If you had told this Sheriff Yeager about your poem idea, Owen, he would have understood it immediately, even though he's probably never heard of Keats. He'd understand because he's felt the same temptation to steal that all of us have at one time or another.

"But Michael Crosley's piety and simplicity are so unusual that they make him an alien in his own home state. Those qualities even made him stand out here in a seminary. That's the only thing Michael is guilty of, standing apart from the crowd. God help us all."

She straightened herself in her chair. "Father Jerome told me that he's canceling your investigation, Owen. Is that true?"

"Yes," I said. "It's true."

"Good," Dr. Mott said. She might have sounded less pleased if she had noted Mary's one-sided smile and interpreted it correctly. Mary knew me too well to take my acquiescence at face value.

"Since you're done with that mystery," the professor continued, "perhaps you'll take on one for me. I confess it has me stumped."

"I'll try."

"It seems there is this seminarian. He comes into an office—this one, say—and he's surprised by an old friend. Does he rush up and hug her in greeting? No. Of course, there is a third party in the room. Still, he might discreetly shake her hand. Does he? No. He stands rooted in his shoes like an overgrown doorstop."

"It does sound strange," Mary said, her eyes laughing at me.

Mary's remark drew Dr. Mott's attention to her. "Then there's the girl. She's flown all the way in from New York City to see the seminarian, not even knowing if he'll be around to see. She's a confident, self-assured young woman, working for a big company. But when she's face-to-face with this young man, she's suddenly as fey as a high school freshman at her first dance."

Mary's eyes continued to laugh, at herself now.

"Any thoughts on this puzzle, Sherlock? Do you think you can unravel it?"

"Yes," I said. I released my death grip on the door and took the two fateful steps to Mary's outstretched hand. It was warm and dry and soft.

"That's better," Dr. Mott said. "Now I'm going home to read in my garden. I'd ask you two along, but it's a small garden. Take good care of her, Owen."

"I will," I said.

TWENTY

WE LEFT DR. MOTT at her desk. When we reached the stairwell, I turned and faced Mary. I had a strong impulse to kiss her, which she preempted by kissing me first, lightly on the cheek.

"Sorry I arrived unannounced," she said. "I should have guessed that you were mixed up in some mystery when you didn't call me back."

"Just plain mixed up," I said. "As always. I'm glad you came." I *was* glad. Mary's visit was exactly what I needed: a reminder that there was a world outside of St. Aelred's, a world where I still had roots.

I held Mary's hand until we reached the front door of the building. Then Mary reclaimed it with a small parting squeeze.

The awkwardness I'd felt in Dr. Mott's office returned when we stepped out into the light of day. We walked around the campus for a time like two people who had just been introduced. I named the buildings we passed, and Mary asked general questions about the school. Then, by degrees, the discussion became more personal.

"Sorry I wasn't at the airport to meet you," I said as we passed the Keep for the second time.

"Don't be. Brother Dennis was very nice." As an afterthought, Mary said, "Okie. I can't believe that I never thought of that nickname for you."

"I'll always be grateful. Brother Dennis is a good man," I added.

"He told me about being wounded in the war."

"Vietnam?"

"No. Korea. His best friend died in his arms. That changed his life, made him decide to enter the monastery."

It was typical of Mary to have found that out. While I'd been weaving imaginary pasts for the damaged monk, she'd learned his real one. Not by asking him, I was sure. Just by being her interested self.

The subject of Brother Dennis's vocation reminded Mary of my own. "I didn't expect to see the same old Owen Keane when I came out here," Mary said. "I thought you'd be different somehow."

"I don't remember wearing this much black in Boston."

"I don't mean your clothes; I mean you. You haven't changed."

"Were you expecting a halo?"

"No, never," she said quickly. Then she turned and examined my head as though giving the possibility serious thought. Her inspection ended in a smile. "I thought they might have asked you to get your hair cut at least."

"You're thinking of the marines." I started to reach up to touch what remained of Mary's hair but thought better of it. Instead I said, "While we're on the subject, I like your hair short."

"Liar," Mary said. "You couldn't stop staring at it back in the office."

"That might have been a compliment. Did you save me a lock?"

Mary ignored the question. "It's easier to fix for work this way. Harry's wearing his hair shorter now," she said, referring to my old Boston College roommate and our mutual friend. "He says it's the style in law school."

"I hope he saved some locks for himself. He's going to need them someday."

"Owen."

"I should have known that Harry's art-versus-music debate would be settled in favor of law school. His father has always called the shots."

"Harry just waited too long," Mary said. "He couldn't decide whether he wanted to be a Bohemian painter or a jazz musician."

"They say talent is a curse."

"While he was vacillating, his dad persuaded him to try law school. It's only an experiment. Don't be too hard on Harry."

"I won't be. I can't blame him for hesitating over a decision that could screw up his entire life."

"You don't believe that, do you, Owen? No one decision can spoil your entire life."

That was typical Mary optimism, but it was tinged with genuine concern.

"I hope not," I said.

We walked in silence for a while. Mary slipped her arm through mine from old habit. I should have told her then of my doubts about the priesthood and the priesthood's doubts about me. It was the perfect moment. Too perfect. I hated to spoil it.

"When did you see Harry and his short hair?" I asked after a time.

"At B.C.'s homecoming game last fall. I almost didn't recognize him. He's shaved his moustache off, too. He told me he'd written to you a couple of times, but you'd stopped writing back. I knew that, of course, from my own experience."

"Sorry," I said. "Not much happens in Indiana."

"I was hoping you might come East this summer. Don't seminarians get a summer vacation?"

I thought of feeding her the line I'd used on my family, that I'd stayed over to take some extra classes, but I'd long since proven to myself that it was impossible for me to lie to Mary. "I decided it would be better if I didn't get back into the old routine."

Mary slid her arm out from under mine, and I felt like apologizing again. "Let's talk about you for a while," I said. "What's new in your life?"

She hesitated over that question for a time. Then she said, "Just my job, I guess."

"Tell me about it."

"I'm a typewriter salesperson. That's the bottom line, as my boss is fond of saying. It's fun. Or at least it was at first. Buying clothes, dressing up every day. Working in the city. Lately it's seemed like a lot of time spent doing things I don't really care about. I am the United Way coordinator for my office, though."

I smiled at that, thinking that she surely also ran the coffee fund and collected money for flowers when somebody's grandmother died. That thought reminded me of Sarah Morell, unfortunately. I reached up to my shirt pocket for the pack of cigarettes that wasn't there.

Mary observed the motion. "Still smoking?" she asked.

"I'm supposed to be the detective. Yes, to answer your question. But I ran out last night."

"You really should quit, Owen. It's bad for you. Remember that Humphrey Bogart poster you bought at the Harvard Co-op? It was blown up so big, you could read the brand of cigarettes he was smoking."

"Old Golds. Filterless. I remember."

"You ran right out and bought a pack and tried to smoke them. Harry had to hang you out the window when you got sick."

"It's great talking over old times."

"Your body was trying to tell you something then."

"Yes, that I'm no Humphrey Bogart. I've kept it in mind ever since." Our discussion of cigarettes had given me a genuine craving for one. I picked the best available substitute. "Have you had lunch? I missed breakfast this morning."

The cafeteria had closed early for lack of business, but the adjoining snack shop was still serving cold sandwiches. It was manned by Jim Carroll, the Unstable's bartender and manager. He slid two turkey sandwiches across the counter to us while looking sidelong at Mary. When she turned to find a table, Carroll gave me a discreet thumbs up.

The snack shop's tables were glass topped and tiny and flanked by wrought iron chairs painted white. "This is like an old movie set," Mary said as she sat down. "Do they make root beer floats?"

"And malteds. They'll even flavor your Coke."

"It's like a time machine. Indiana, I mean."

"Yes. I'm always conscious of the past out here. It's like the undertow in the ocean, subtle but steady. Always pulling you back."

"Are you thinking of your lost sonnet?"

I'd actually been thinking of Mary and wondering why I'd put so much distance between us, but the sonnet seemed like a safer subject.

"Dr. Mott's wrong about the poem," I said. "It's real."

"Tell me about it. And about Michael Crosley."

It seemed as though I'd made that report over and over in the last twenty-four hours, first to Dr. Mott, then to Sheriff Yeager, and most recently to Father Jerome. Each telling had been sketchy, though. Sketchy by design in Yeager's case.

I began at the beginning and told Mary everything. I listed all my clues, all the little bits of string I'd carefully collected and tangled together. Michael Crosley's poetry reading. His moodiness and his mysterious black eye. His departure in the storm in a raincoat that was too small for him. The Melissa Donahue dead end. Mrs. Crosley's testimony about a father and son who hadn't gotten along because they were so different and her self-delusions about Michael coming back to her. The Koffmans of the halfway house and Ronnie, the resident who'd reacted more strongly than anyone else to the news of Crosley's departure. Sarah Morell and the tale of her ancestor, George Keats. The American Gothic Morells, Frank and Agnes. Curtis, the nihilist, and Krystal, the herb doctor. The missing book on Keats that had turned up back in the library and its footnote that confirmed Sarah's story. Dr. Mott's insistence that the key to the mystery was Crosley's father and not the poem. John Crosley's revelation about a father and son enough alike to be brothers. Sarah's murder. My interview with Sheriff Yeager, talent scout for the papacy. I ended with Father Jerome's belief that Crosley's entire world had been undone by the idea that his father had once loved.

The storytelling seemed to relax us both. We sat for an hour while I talked and Mary chewed each bite of her sandwich twenty-five times.

When I was finished, Mary asked, "Do you really think that the cleaning woman took the book back to the library?"

"It's possible. Do you have another candidate?"

"Yes," she said. "Michael Crosley. He might have slipped back onto campus and returned the book to eliminate a connection between him and the Keats material. That would mean he's still in the area."

"It would mean more than that. It would mean that he intended to steal the poem. I don't want to believe that anymore."

"Because it makes him a legitimate suspect in Sarah Morell's murder? Or because you've started to identify with Crosley?"

I couldn't lie to Mary or even hide my thoughts from her very well. I had begun to pull for Crosley, almost without realizing it. Sheriff Yeager's crazy antireligion theories may have shoved me over into Crosley's corner. Or perhaps it had been Father Jerome's admission that he saw Crosley and me as two fragments that together could make a complete priest. It suddenly seemed very important to find Crosley and clear him. To save him and myself.

I couldn't tell Mary all that without also telling her about the trouble I was in at St. Aelred's. I cracked wise instead, paraphrasing Sam Spade, the patron saint of my investigation. "When one of your organization is accused of a killing, it's bad business to let the real killer get away with it. It's bad all around. Bad for St. Aelred's. Bad for every seminary everywhere."

Mary let me know that she understood my joke by topping it. "Just don't end up taking the fall for him," she said.

TWENTY-ONE

MARY HAD LEFT HER SUITCASE with Brother Dennis for safekeeping. After lunch, we set out together to find the monk and the bag. Neither were in St. Meinrad Hall. I left Mary to cool her heels in the first-floor common room while I went upstairs to change into what Father Jerome called street clothes. As I had no intention of following my spiritual director's instruction to drop Crosley's case, I had no right to pass myself off as an agent of St. Aelred's.

When I reappeared in jeans and a Boston College T-shirt, Mary shook her head. "Indiana *is* a time machine," she said.

We next looked for Brother Dennis at the pottery. It was a long shedlike building on the edge of the campus that had once been used to house chickens. Brother Dennis's white Rambler sedan was parked outside.

Inside the building, the monk was carefully packing pieces of his eccentric pottery into a large carton. "Okie, Mary," he said in greeting. "You two finally got together. Good."

He was holding a blue jam pot whose lid sat at a jaunty angle like a yachtsman's cap. He handed the pot to Mary. "A souvenir of your visit," he said. "I'm taking some pieces over to a convent in Oldenburg. The sisters sell it for me. How did it go with the police this morning, Okie? Not too bad?"

"Not too bad."

"And you saw Father Jerome, I hear."

I noted that the monk hadn't asked me how that meeting had gone. He didn't have to. "Yes, I saw him."

"Good. So what have you two been up to?"

Mary fielded that question. "Owen's been showing me around the campus," she said. "It's a beautiful place."

"Yes," Brother Dennis said. "Beautiful but cloistered. Not the real world. Not the whole world anyway. There are plenty of things outside it. Good things."

This last observation was addressed to Owen Keane. I refused delivery. "We're looking for Mary's suitcase. Do you have it?"

The monk touched his forehead lightly with the flower pot he was holding. "I forgot all about it. It's still in my trunk." He pulled a ring of keys from his pocket and tossed them to me. "Just lay them under the front seat when you're finished. And Okie, leave the trunk open. I'll be carrying this stuff out in a minute."

I twirled the key ring on my finger as Mary and I walked out to the car. The keys reminded me of a stray detail I'd forgotten. I told Mary about it as we rescued her bag from the Rambler.

"Remember me telling you that Crosley took another seminarian's raincoat the night he left?"

"Philip Swickard, wasn't that the name?"

"Very good."

"That's part of the IBM sales training. We never forget a name. What about the coat?"

"Swickard kept his car keys in the pocket. He was in a lather when he realized that the keys were gone. Crosley had borrowed the car regularly. Swickard checked and found that the car hadn't been moved. Another resident of the rectory found the keys later. They were in the street in front of the house, lying in the gutter."

"You didn't find anything when you searched the car?"

I was leaning through the open door of the Rambler when Mary asked that. I froze in the motion of hiding the keys under the seat.

"You didn't search the car," Mary said.

I slowly extracted myself from the Rambler. "No. We know Crosley didn't take it when he went away."

"But he'd used it before. He probably used it when he went out to the Morell farm to look for the Keats letters. Maybe he didn't drop the keys by accident. Maybe he was trying to leave a message."

"I'm not quite with you."

"That's because you've made up your mind that Michael Crosley is innocent. Suppose for a moment that he's guilty. Guilty people often do things that give them away. It's their way of asking for help."

"Pretty comprehensive, this IBM training." As much as I didn't like it, I had to admit that Mary was right. "We'll search the car."

First we checked Mary in at Guest House, the small hotel maintained by the college for visiting parents and friends. Then we set out together for the old rectory. On the way, I proposed a change of program.

"We don't have to do this today," I said. "You didn't come all this way to play detective with me."

I was offering Mary the chance to tell me why she had come. She didn't take it. "This is fine with me. I was always jealous when you and Harry went off sleuthing at B.C. Besides, you won't be able to think of anything else until this is cleared up."

"Well, let me know when you've had enough."

On my last visit to the old rectory, Katrinka Wilson had invited me to enter without knocking. We did that now, as the front door was unlocked.

"You'd better wait down here," I told Mary. For some reason, I was whispering. "We don't want to scare him."

"Right," Mary whispered back. "Save that for a last resort."

Mrs. Wilson had mentioned Swickard's room number on my first visit, but I'd forgotten it. I located his name on one of the mailboxes in the entryway. "Two-B," I read aloud.

"Or not to be," Mary whispered back. Then she giggled nervously.

The old house was very quiet. So quiet that I heard Swickard's radio before I'd reached the second floor. It was tuned to a classical station. A Chopin polonaise was building to a breakneck climax. I waited outside Swickard's door until the piece ended. Then I knocked.

The door opened so quickly that I was sure Swickard had been listening on the other side. He was dressed formally, as he had been at our last meeting, in dark dress trousers and a white shirt. At close range he seemed thinner and shorter than I remembered. And less friendly.

"What do you want?" he demanded.

"The keys to your car. I want to search it."

"You've got to be kidding."

I was conscious of Mary's presence at the bottom of the stairs, well within earshot of Swickard's haughty voice. "I'm not kidding," I said calmly. "We think Crosley might have left something in the car."

"Who's we?"

"Michael Crosley's sister and I. She's downstairs now," I added in a slightly louder voice. "She's come to get Michael's things."

Swickard hesitated. "I didn't know he had a sister."

"I'll be happy to introduce you. Or, if you want, you can give Father Jerome a call."

If Swickard had called that bluff, I would have been on my way back to New Jersey before the sun set. He folded instead.

"I'll come with you," he said.

Mary had suppressed her giggling and looked appropriately somber when Swickard and I got downstairs. I don't know what Swickard had been expecting—Michael Crosley in drag, perhaps—but he was clearly impressed by Mary. He smiled sincerely for the first time in our brief acquaintance and extended his hand.

"Nice to meet you," he said to Mary. "I hope your brother's okay."

"So do I," Mary said.

The old rectory offered other privileges beside private rooms. There was an alleyway behind the house where the residents were allowed to park their cars. On our way to the back door, Mary asked Swickard to tell her the story of the lost raincoat and the prodigal keys. I understood that she was giving me the chance to double-check the seminarian's story. Swickard's second telling was consistent with the first, except that he made light of the loss of the coat and omitted his earlier complaint about the bugs Crosley had left on his windshield.

He made these changes, I knew, out of consideration for Mary, for whom he held open the back door of the house. He walked beside her to the car, stealing an occasional upward glance. I followed along behind, forgotten.

Swickard's blue Chevy Nova looked as though it had just been washed, despite the rain of the previous evening. Swickard unlocked the passenger door and got in to roll the windows down.

I leaned over to address Mary sotto voce: "Another Fitzgerald conquest."

Mary pretended to examine a passing cloud as she answered. "Celibates don't count."

When Swickard climbed out of the car, Mary asked him where he was from.

"Fort Wayne," he said. He then began to reel off trivia about the city like a proud Rotarian. I stood by puzzled until Mary caught my eye and nodded toward the car. Then I realized that she was distracting its owner to give me a clear field of action.

I started with the glove compartment. It held only the owner's manual, the car's registration, and a box of spare fuses. The ashtray was pristine and empty. All I found under the front seat was a plastic ice scraper and a flashlight. There was no space under the back seat to hide anything.

Swickard was describing his undergraduate work at a no-name state college when I got out of the car empty-handed. I was ungracious enough to interrupt him. "Mind opening the trunk?"

He did mind, of course. "There's nothing in there."

"Just a quick look," Mary said.

That made it all right with Swickard. He walked Mary around to the back of the car and unlocked the shallow trunk. It was empty and as clean as the ashtray had been.

I leaned over to raise the panel that formed the false floor of the trunk.

"That's just the spare tire well," Swickard said, exasperated.

Mary quickly cut in. "Your car looks brand new. How do you do it?"

That got Swickard off on a paste wax tangent. I set the floor panel aside and examined the well. The spare tire lay flat within the depression and filled it completely. A threaded metal rod extended upward from the bottom of the trunk through the center of the spare's rim and the base of the jack. A large wing nut held the jack base firmly against the rim, securing the tire in place.

I backed the wing nug off while Swickard lectured Mary on the evils of dealer-supplied rustproofing. Then I derailed his train of thought by lifting the spare from the well and setting it on the pavement.

"Keane, this is too much," he said. "I told you there's nothing in there."

"There is, though," Mary said.

She had stepped forward and was now looking down into the trunk. Swickard and I jostled each other as we took up positions on either side of her. I don't know what my fellow seminarian was expecting to see. His missing raincoat, perhaps. I was expecting a manuscript, fragile and brown with age, bearing some lost glory of English literature.

What I saw was a plastic bag about the size of a lunch sack. Its top was gathered and fastened with a rubber band. The bag was full to bursting with green/brown fragments of dried leaves.

"Pot, by God," Swickard said. Then he stammered, "I mean, is it?"

I extracted the bag and undid the rubber band. The aroma from the open bag was strong and unmistakable.

"Marijuana," Mary said. "What on earth can that mean?"

"First things first," I said. I held the bag up for Swickard's inspection. "Is your story that you've never seen this before?"

Philip Swickard had somehow managed to get through most of an Indiana summer without a tan. At the moment, he looked very pale indeed. "It's not a story. It's the truth. Look, Owen, would I have let you search my car if I'd known that was in there?" He addressed an additional appeal to Mary: "Would I?"

"How did it get there, then?" I asked.

"Crosley," Swickard said. "Michael Crosley. He took my raincoat. Now he's done this to me."

I wasn't that fond of Swickard, but I couldn't buy his persecution theory. He seemed to be having second thoughts about it himself. "You know how strangely Crosley was acting this summer," he said. "This could explain that."

Crosley's "sister" reluctantly agreed. "You know, it could explain a lot, Owen."

It didn't sound right. The bag I held was the answer, but we hadn't matched it to the right question. I did a little thinking out loud.

"Suppose Crosley was smoking pot as a way of getting past his father's death or the pressure he was under here at school. Why would he leave this behind? This has to be a month's supply.''

"He dropped the keys," Swickard said. In his eagerness to convey his point, he grabbed my arm and pulled me around to face him. "We know he dropped the keys. Suppose he couldn't find them in the dark. He would have had to leave this behind.''

That would have been plausible, except for the detail of where the keys were found. "Where was the car parked the night Crosley went away?" I asked.

"Right where it is now.''

That wasn't helpful. Why, I wondered, would Crosley be in the street in front of the house when his secret stash was in a car behind the house. While I was pondering this, Mary came up with another mystery.

"Is there anything else in there?" she asked as she shifted pieces of the jack that lay in the bottom of the well.

"No," I said. "Why? What are you looking for?"

"The newspapers call it paraphernalia. You know, cigarette paper, pipes. Something to smoke this stuff with.''

Her casual knowledge seemed to alarm Swickard. He took a step back from her.

"Did you find anything like that in his room?" Mary asked me.

"No. Not so much as a match.''

"He took it away with him," Swickard said.

"No," Mary countered. "He would have kept it all together.''

Swickard had gotten over his initial shock, and his natural bad humor was returning. "Of course he was smoking it. Why else would he have it?''

An answer finally came to me. "He took it away from somebody.''

Swickard and Mary said "What?" in unison.

"I'll tell you on the way," I said to Mary. To Swickard I added, "We're taking the pot with us. I'll keep your name out of this if I can." I made that useless promise in exchange for something I wanted. "Don't you tell anyone about this."

Swickard was already struggling to lift his spare tire. "See if anyone ever borrows my car again," he said.

TWENTY-TWO

MARY AND I MADE our way to the parking lot behind the old dairy. I affected a nonchalant air toward the bag of marijuana, carrying it under one arm with my hands in my pockets.

"Where are we off to so suddenly?" Mary asked when we were some distance from the rectory.

"Green Streets, the halfway house for drug users that Crosley visited."

"You think Crosley took the pot from someone at the home?"

"That's the latest in my long series of amazing hypotheses."

"Why would he do it?"

"To prevent a resident who was backsliding from being thrown back into jail."

Mary kicked stones on the path while she thought it over. "That could explain his black eye, I guess."

I was more enthusiastic than my old love. "It could also explain the anger I saw in Ronnie, the Green Streeter I told you about. Crosley takes his pot, lectures him about it probably, and then runs off with it. That has to make Ronnie feel like a sucker and a half."

Mary expressed her lingering doubt in a left-handed compliment. "Sometimes your reasoning is almost too brilliant to follow."

When we arrived at the Ghia, Mary patted its rounded nose affectionately. "Hello again," she said.

I unlocked her door. "You're on window detail," I said. "The crank's in the usual place."

"What detail are you on?"

"Marijuana concealment." I opened the driver's door and reached inside to pull the release for the Ghia's trunk, which was in front where the engine should have been. The spare tire sat almost upright in a slot at the front of the trunk. I lifted the tire, slipped the bag of pot behind it, and then let the tire fall back into place. Only Michael Crosley would think to look for it there.

By the time I'd finished, Mary had both windows down and the rear vents open. She was sitting in the passenger seat, looking like old times incarnate.

Mary must have felt the same way. "Want to drive over to Fenway and watch the Sox play?" she asked.

"It would be nice," I said.

Instead, we headed for New Albany, Indiana. We spent the hour the drive lasted not talking much and feeling self-conscious about it. At least I felt that way. The inside of the little car seemed too intimate a space for us now. Mary must have been uncomfortable, too. When we left the highway and descended into the quiet Saturday streets of New Albany, she suddenly launched into some animated and pointless stories about her coworkers. The gossip stopped abruptly when I pulled the Ghia up in front of the Green Streets lot.

There were no signs of life on the manicured lawn or the deep front porch. In the drive to the left of the house, two young men were shooting baskets. They were shirtless and glistening with sweat.

I pointed one of the shooters out to Mary as we climbed the front walk. "The guy in the blue shorts is Ronnie."

I rang the bell. A minute or so later, Karen Koffman appeared on the opposite side of the screen door. She was in jeans today and an oversized T-shirt that may have belonged to her husband. Her long hair was drawn back in an anachronistic ponytail.

"Father Keane, back again? You should have phoned first and saved yourself a trip. We haven't heard from Michael Crosley."

"We have," I said. "In a manner of speaking. I'm hoping you can help us interpret the message."

"Us?"

Mary had been silent, waiting to hear whether she was still Crosley's sister or someone entirely new. I didn't like our chances of pulling any wool over Karen Koffman's eyes.

"This is an old friend of mine from back East who's visiting for the weekend," I said. "Mary Fitzgerald."

Koffman pushed open the screen door to shake Mary's hand. "Come on in," she said.

The inside of the house presented an interesting contrast to the shining exterior. The green carpeting in the hallway was stained and worn down to the mat in spots. There were holes in the white plaster of the hallway walls. The living room we passed had peeling wallpaper. One strip was gone entirely. The center of the bare spot was covered by a poster advertising an Iron Butterfly concert.

Koffman led us out into a sun porch that was set up as an office, with a folding table serving as a desk. It was backed by a row of mismatched filing cabinets, the tops of which were crowded with potted plants, including some eccentric-looking cacti.

Our host took the swivel chair behind the desk. Mary and I sat in metal folding chairs facing her.

"Bill isn't here today," Koffman said. "He took some of the boys boating on the river." She made it sound like a breach of duty, probably because her husband had left her alone to deal with me. "You say you've heard from Michael?"

"I should have said we've found something he left behind. Before we get to that, did Michael ever mention a Sarah Morell to you?"

She thought it over. "No. Who is she?" Koffman paused long enough to look Mary up and down. "Another old friend? You seminarians do okay."

"Yesterday Sarah was a resident of a nursing home in Evay. Today she's an ex-resident. Someone entered the home last night and killed her."

If I thought I could shock some information out of Karen Koffman, I was wasting my time. She never batted an eye. "What has that to do with Michael?"

"He visited the nursing home, just like he visited Green Streets. He often talked with Sarah. He may have tried to help her with some money troubles she had. The Huber County sheriff is looking for Michael now."

"No," Koffman said. "No." She underscored these words by slapping the top of her desk. "I don't see that at all. There's no way Crosley would hurt anyone. Not even to save his own life."

I was glad to hear her say it, even though she seemed to regard me as the source of the error. She leaned forward and fixed me with the kind of look a mongoose gives a snake. "You said you found something Michael left behind. What exactly?"

"A bag of marijuana. I think he may have taken it from one of your residents."

"Taken it?"

"To protect someone. I'm assuming that anyone caught smoking pot here would be in serious trouble."

"You're assuming wrong," Koffman said. "As usual, I suspect."

She swiveled her chair around and opened the lowest drawer of the filing cabinet directly behind her. With her back still to us, she began to take items from the drawer and toss them onto the desk. These included two plastic bags of pot, each less than a tenth of what we had found, packs of cigarette paper, and an assortment of pipes, including one with a bowl carved in the shape of a dragon's head.

Karen swiveled back to face us. She picked up one of the bags and weighed it in her hand. "A little light, I think. My husband must be raiding the pantry in the wee small hours."

Mary straightened in her chair. "Your husband smokes marijuana?" she asked.

"Occasionally. I tell him he's gunking up his lungs, but he's not what you'd call a health freak."

Her casual attitude didn't mollify Mary. "But he's in charge of a home for former drug users."

"This is 1973," Koffman said. "The *Reefer Madness* mentality is over thirty years out of date. Occasional pot smoking is no worse than an evening cocktail."

"You work with kids who have messed up their lives with drugs and you believe that?" Mary asked.

"The kids we get aren't drug users. They're drug abusers. They had problems in their lives that made them turn to drugs the way an alcoholic turns to booze. The drugs didn't create the problems. We try to address causes here, not the results. It's naive to think that a kid will be insulated from drugs when we send him back into the world. Our only chance is to work on the problems that made him think drugs were the only way out."

I knew that Mary was far from satisfied by Koffman's answer. I decided to cut in before their debate got out of hand. "You're saying that being caught with marijuana in this house wouldn't be a serious offense?"

"Exactly. We'd confiscate it, of course. That's how we collect this stuff. But we wouldn't send a boy to jail because of it. They're safer from drugs on the streets than back in jail."

I wouldn't give up my theory without a fight. "Would Crosley have known that?"

"You mean he might have taken the pot thinking he was doing somebody a favor? Sorry, but that's out, too. He and

I had a long discussion on marijuana. He was very curious on the subject. I told him pretty much what I've told you."

"When was this?"

"The last time he was here, I think."

The phone on the folding table desk rang. "Excuse me," Koffman said. She answered the phone with the name of the home and listened for a while. Then she said, "He's not here right now. He went out on the river. Do you want me to have him call you? Wait a minute."

She dug around in the papers on her desk until she found a notepad. A pink notepad. She wrote a phone number on the top sheet. "Okay, I'll have him call you."

Koffman hung up the phone. "Sorry about that. I really should be getting back to work. Was there anything else?"

"Two things," I said. "I saw Ronnie outside as we came in. Do you mind if we talk to him?"

"You can if you want to, but he won't know anything about any marijuana. Ronnie's a boy after your own heart," she said to Mary. "A real bluenose on the subject of drugs. He has good reason to be. He messed with things a lot more dangerous than pot. Came really close to killing himself."

"I'd still like to talk with him."

"You said there were two things. What was the other?"

"I'd like a sheet from that notepad."

That puzzled her. She tore off the top two sheets and handed me the blank one. "Need a pen?"

"No, thanks." I slipped the piece of paper into my pocket. "Thanks for your time."

Mary and I showed ourselves out. When we reached the front porch, Mary asked, "What was the business with the pad all about?"

"It was a lucky break for the home team, I hope."

I took the blank piece of paper from my pocket and handed it to Mary. Then I dug out my wallet and extracted from it a piece of physical evidence, the slip of paper from

Crosley's room that had sent me out after Melissa Donahue.

Mary held the two samples side by side. "They're identical. What can that mean?"

"It means I've been barking up the wrong conclusion."

"What?"

"Stick close."

I led Mary off the porch and over to the driveway basketball court. His opponent was gone, but Ronnie was still
there. He was sitting on the basketball in the center of the
drive with his arms on his knees and his head down.

"Tough game?" I asked as we came up to him.

Ronnie scrambled to his feet. Then he recognized me.
"Padre," he said. "What do you want?"

The question was addressed to me, but his dark eyes were
on Mary. "I want to return something that belongs to
you," I said. I held up the Melissa Donahue note.

Ronnie snatched it from my hand before I could react.
"Where did you get this?"

"From Crosley's room. What's the story?"

Ronnie said nothing.

"Okay. I'll tell you one. Crosley was supposed to call
Melissa Donahue for you. She's your girl. Isn't that right?
Isn't that why you were so mad when I told you that Cros-
ley had gone away?"

During my speech, Ronnie's eyes had moved from me
back to Mary. They remained on her now as he answered.
"Yes. Crosley promised he'd call Melissa. Her old man
won't let her talk to me. He hated me even before I went to
jail. Because I came from the wrong part of Indy. Because
I wasn't good enough for his daughter. I'm not good
enough. Not now."

"What were you in jail for?" Mary asked.

"Stealing to support a habit. I was some big man then.
A tough guy. I met Melissa at a concert. We were in love
that same night. In love forever."

Mary had taken over my part of the interview. "How long has it been since you've seen her?"

"A year. I've tried to call her, but I couldn't get past her old man. I wrote to her, but she stopped writing back. Her father stole my letters. I know he did."

From the little I'd seen of Melissa, I thought it likely that forever had just dragged on too long for her. That suggestion wasn't going to get me in solid with Ronnie, though, so I changed the subject.

"You told me that Crosley had asked you some naive questions about drug use."

"That's right."

"Was that recently?"

"Last time he was here. The day I gave him this." Ronnie held up the scrap of pink paper.

"Did he ask about a specific kind of drug?"

"Yes. Marijuana. He'd been talking with the lady of the house." He nodded toward Karen Koffman's office. "She'd told him how harmless it is."

"What did you tell him?"

Ronnie shrugged. "That I started with pot. That it made me think I was a tough guy. Made me think I could handle anything. I was wrong about that." Ronnie picked up the basketball and studied it, turning it over in his hands like the globe of a dead world.

"Did Crosley tell you why he wanted to know about pot?" I asked.

"He said he had to make a decision. I guess he made it. He's not here anymore."

TWENTY-THREE

DURING OUR DRIVE BACK to St. Aelred's, Mary tuned and retuned the Ghia's radio, trying to find a song that fit our current mood. It would have been an interesting piece of music, had she found it, something slow and sad about two people who'd found that love wasn't the answer after all.

After several circuits of the AM band, Mary gave up the search. "Now what?" she asked.

"I wish I knew," I said. "I've never been down so many dead-end streets before in my life."

Mary found the silver lining, as usual. "At least you eliminated the Melissa Donahue angle."

"Yes, I did that." I was surprised to find that my modest accomplishment made me sad. I already missed Melissa, perhaps because, of all the crazy scenarios I'd imagined for Crosley, she figured in the only happy one. Or perhaps my sadness had nothing to do with Crosley or even with Melissa Donahue. I might have been nostalgic for the idea that a romance could save a desperate seminarian.

I shook the sadness off. "The pot's the key," I said. "I know it is. Crosley had to get it somewhere. If not Green Streets, then somewhere else."

"I assume there's pot smoking at St. Aelred's," Mary said.

"You do?"

"Yes. You told me there's a campus pub, so they're not against intoxication on principle."

"Mild intoxication."

"Right. So the odd joint probably isn't more scandalous than the occasional beer. Not, to quote Karen Koffman, in 1973."

"You're forgetting that one is against the law," I said.

"Meaning that the official position is no marijuana. What's the unofficial position?"

An eighteen-wheeler blasted past us on the narrow two-lane highway, shaking the car and causing its wipers to fluctuate wildly like needles on a seismic scale.

"You should be the one in law school, not Harry," I said. "There is marijuana smoking at St. Aelred's, but it's pretty underground."

"So Michael Crosley could have taken that pot away from another seminarian."

I didn't see it that way. For one thing, Crosley had hidden the pot in Swickard's car, which suggested that he'd gotten it off campus. And there was also Father Jerome's intuition, which I trusted. He seemed to think that the truth of Crosley's mystery lay outside the seminary. Mary's idea looked like one more tour down a blind alley. But if I systematically eliminated all the dead ends, like a real detective, the road that remained might lead me to Crosley.

"We'll check it out," I said. "I know who to ask." Mary had suggested a source by mentioning the campus pub. Jim Carroll, flower child turned bartender, would know the ins and outs of St. Aelred's drug culture if anyone did.

It was four o'clock when we pulled in behind the old dairy. Before leaving the Ghia, I reclaimed the bag of marijuana from the trunk. It was too large to fit inside Mary's shoulder bag, so I bundled it up in an oily towel I used to keep my jack from rattling.

We tried the snack shop where Carroll had served us a sandwich earlier in the afternoon, but it was locked up tight. The Unstable wouldn't open for hours, but we went there anyway. I was encouraged by the idea that Crosley's tangled trail was leading us back to the spot where the case had begun for me, even though I could see no link as yet between the marijuana and the sonnet.

The Unstable's door was locked. Mary and I took turns knocking for the next few minutes. During my shift, the door opened to the width of Carroll's bearded face. His eyes were angry and half shut, a strange combination that told me he'd been asleep.

"We're closed," Carroll said. "Come back at six."

"I don't want a beer," I said. "I want some information."

I'd brought the bag of marijuana along for just this situation, figuring that it would interest Carroll enough to get me an interview. It turned out that I'd brought something else that worked as well or better. Someone else, actually. Mary Fitzgerald.

"Is your, ah, friend with you?" Carroll asked, pushing his head out through the doorway a little farther and blinking in the sunlight. When he finally spotted Mary, he smiled too broadly, like a three-year-old posing for a photograph. "Come on in," he said.

The inside of the bar was too dark by half after the sunny afternoon. Mary and I waited by the door while Carroll drew back the heavy curtains on a single window, creating a shaft of dusty sunlight. The three of us sat at a table on the knife-edge border between darkness and light.

"Did you find the hand?" Carroll asked as I sat down.

"The hand?"

"From the sonnet. The woman, I mean. Did you find her?"

"Not exactly," I said, thinking of Fanny, Keats's unrequited love. "Do you remember anything else about the poem?"

"You-men-a-days," Carroll said. "Or something that sounded like that. I've been meaning to look it up."

"Could it have been Eumenidies?" Mary asked. "They were characters from Greek mythology. The three Furies, demonic female spirits sent after someone for revenge."

Carroll's admiration grew. "There were furies mentioned in the next line," he said. "'Thy furies sent to torture and something.'"

"Beguile," I said. "'Torture and beguile.'"

Instead of congratulating me on my small contribution, Carroll shot me a look that made me feel like a man cutting in on a dance floor. Then he remembered something I was good for. "Got a cigarette?"

"No. Sorry."

"That's okay," Carroll said, thoroughly fed up with me now. "What is it you want? You didn't come banging on my door to talk about that poem, I hope."

"No," I said. "I want to talk about marijuana."

Carroll's sleepy eyes had never gotten fully open. Now they began to narrow again. "What about it?"

"I want to know about marijuana smoking at St. Aelred's."

"Is this a new assignment from Father Jerome?"

"No. The old one. Michael Crosley's disappearance may have something to do with pot smoking here at the school."

Carroll shook his head. "Are you telling me that you've never been at a party on campus where grass was being smoked?"

"No. I'm not telling you that."

He held up a hand to reclaim the floor. "How about a little rap session in a dorm room with some of the boys? You're sitting around talking about transubstantiation or the girls you took to the senior prom." He leered in Mary's direction. "You telling me that no one ever produced a joint and passed it around just to be sociable?"

"What's your point?"

"That smoking a little grass is no big deal and no big secret. I'd be surprised if even Michael Crosley didn't know it was going on. I'd be shocked to find out that he gave a damn. Excuse me," he said to Mary.

I'd held the bag of marijuana out of view in my lap. I put it on the table now, unwrapping the oily towel at the same time. "Then where did Crosley get this?" I asked.

Carroll finally looked wide awake. He picked up the bag and weighed it in his hand. Then he undid the rubber band and opened the bag. After sniffing the contents, he spilled some out in his hand and turned to examine it in the light from the window behind him.

When he turned back to me, Carroll was wearing a smug look that took me by surprise. "Let me get this straight," he said. "You think Crosley bought this on campus?"

"I think he took it away from someone. Possibly here at St. Aelred's."

"Well, you're nuts," Carroll said. "This stuff isn't from St. Aelred's."

Mary leaned across the table. "How could you know that?" she asked.

"Because it's Indiana weed. Grown right here in Hoosier-land. It's garbage, in other words. Low-grade, bug-eaten garbage." He twisted the top of the bag closed and tossed it back to me.

"I've had occasion to examine the grass distributed at St. Aelred's," Carroll said coyly. "And it's the best. Colombian mostly, and always first rate. Nobody here would touch this ditch weed."

I shifted my chair toward the light streaming in behind Carroll. "Back up a minute," I said. "You're telling me that marijuana is grown in Indiana?"

"Quick, isn't he?" Carroll said to Mary.

"I thought marijuana was grown in the tropics."

Carroll stood up. "A pretty good description of Indiana in the summertime." He crossed the room to the bar, addressing us over his shoulder. "You East Coast guys slay me. You think you live at the center of the damn universe.

There's a big wide world out here you don't know the first thing about."

He returned, carrying a pack of cigarettes. His first, maybe. "Got a light?" he asked as he sat down.

I leaned across the table with my lighter to do the honors. "Tell me about it."

Carroll took a deep drag and blew smoke in my face. "Notebooks ready, kiddies? We first travel back in time to the dark days of World War II. Uncle Sam needs hemp for rope, but the Philippines, where you get hemp, is suddenly Japanese territory. So Sammy asks farmers in beautiful Indiana to grow an alternative source."

"Marijuana," Mary said.

"Hemp, in forties slang," I said, drawing on a memory from some dated paperback.

"You're catching on." Carroll pushed his pack of cigarettes across to me. Mary gave me permission to light up by ignoring the transaction.

"I don't know how the rope-making went," Carroll said. "But the marijuana-growing went fine. So well, in fact, that when the war was over and the farmers went back to soybeans, the grass carried on all by itself. It still grows wild in northern Indiana, millions of plants every year. Ditch weed, they call it up there, because it grows in roadside ditches mostly and other unused bits of land.

"Now for a pop quiz. What state leads the nation in domestic marijuana plants destroyed?"

I played along. "Indiana?"

"That's correct. It's mostly the wild stuff up north they get. The feds try to kill it off. The farmers plow it under. But it still comes back every year. Mother Nature's bounty. Kids drive down from Chicago or up from Indy to harvest it 'long about this time of year. Not that it's worth the effort. It's weak as the punch at a Baptist wedding, but it's free. And it's fun to find, like hidden treasure. There's even an underground market in maps showing the best places to look. Treasure maps.''

"You think this is ditch weed?" I asked.

"Could be. It's rank enough. But I think this comes from someplace a lot closer to home. That wild grass is just one part of the story. Now we move up in time to the seventies. Marijuana is a booming commodity, even in sleepy Indiana. Some farmers, mostly down south here where things are more laid back, start growing it as a cash crop. Farming's a business where cash is always short. A little cushion against the mortgage man is a welcome thing.''

"What about the police?" I asked.

"There are always ways of getting past the cops. Say you plant corn in a field. You've done it every year. This year you plant the corn again, but you add a patch or two of grass. At the center of the field. The corn grows up and provides a natural screen.''

"No one will know it's there," Mary said.

"Exactly. There's a problem, though. Grass grows faster than corn. And taller. A stalk can grow to ten feet or more. So you have to be smart. You have to work something out.''

Without closing my eyes, I pictured Curtis Morell playing with a bit of string while he talked of Nietzsche. "You tie the tops of the plants down," I said. "You pull them over and stake them down.''

Carroll and Mary both stared at me. "Right," Carroll said. "That's how you do it.''

He settled back in his chair and examined the burning stub of his cigarette contentedly. "It's not much different than the moonshining of forty, fifty years ago," he said. "The government says it's evil, but the farmers know better.''

"What's the point of growing it at all if it's so inferior?" Mary asked. "You said yourself you wouldn't touch it.''

"That's because I know better and I can afford better. Kids just starting out, they smoke it. It's plenty good enough for them."

Mary turned back to me. "Kids just starting out. Michael Crosley went to ask Ronnie about that."

"Who's Ronnie?" Carroll asked.

"He used to be one of those kids," I said.

TWENTY-FOUR

MARY COULD BARELY contain herself until we were outside of Jim Carroll's lair and alone in the drowsy quiet of the campus.

"We've solved it," she said as soon as the Unstable's door had locked behind us. She stood on tiptoe to meet me eye to eye, her hands squeezing my arms.

"Have we?"

"Yes! Michael Crosley went out to the farm looking for the Keats letters. Instead he found the marijuana."

Mary's blue eyes were brighter than the late afternoon sun, lit from within by an addicting rush I knew well, the excitement of solving a mystery.

"He found the Keats material," I said. "I heard him read the sonnet, remember?"

"Okay. He found the sonnet and the marijuana farm both. What difference does it make?"

It added slightly to the list of questions Jim Carroll's lecture wouldn't answer. They paraded through my head as I stood a foot from Mary. How had Crosley gotten anything—poem or pot—if the Morells hadn't let him search the farm? Had the sonnet been a payoff for his silence? Was that the meaning of his tearful recitation at the Unstable? If not, why had he kept the pot but told no one about it? And where was he now?

My questions faded away, bleached out against the bright blue background of Mary's eyes. I realized then that I was holding her close to me. Closer than I'd held her in a long time.

I saw her eyes darken an instant before she gently pushed me away. "Sorry," she said. "I'll have to behave myself. The locals might misconstrue."

That group included me, I understood.

"What do we do now?" Mary asked.

I bent down to pick up the marijuana, which had fallen at our feet. It reminded me of my earlier resolve to be systematic. "I find out if the pot actually came from the farm. I get some proof."

"Isn't that a job for the police?"

"I don't trust Roger Yeager, the local sheriff. He treated the Morells like old friends."

"Do you think he knows about the farm?"

"He could. I know he thinks I'm a greenhorn who couldn't find Indiana in the dictionary. I'll need evidence if I'm going to convince him. More than I have now."

"What's your plan?"

I didn't have one, so I extemporized as we walked down the hill toward the old dairy. "I go back to the farm right now. Find growing marijuana if there is any. Bring some out with me."

"With us, you mean," Mary said. "I'm going, too."

"No way."

"I told you how jealous I was when you and Harry played Hardy Boys back at Boston. I'm not missing my big chance."

I turned her toward me so I could look into her eyes. It was a mistake. My arguments danced a jig in my head. "Mary," I said, speaking slowly to steady myself. "We're not playing now. We know what happened to Sarah Morell. It has to be connected to that farm. Someone there is very dangerous. It may even be Michael Crosley. I can't let you near that place."

She didn't answer. She might have made light of the danger or threatened to tell Father Jerome or the police if I didn't let her go along. Instead, she just stood there, looking at me very seriously. It was a technique I knew all too well. Mary never argued with me. She waited me out, confident that I'd eventually second-guess myself around to her position.

"I promised Dr. Mott I'd take care of you," I said.

She smiled at the feebleness of that objection. "Who's going to take care of you, Owen? Who's going to run for the cavalry when something goes wrong?"

"Nothing will go wrong," I said.

It would have required a gullible person new to Owen Keane to have believed that. Mary was neither. "I won't set foot on the farm. I'll drive the getaway car. Please, Owen. I want to keep an eye on you."

"You can't drive a standard shift," I said, my reasoning becoming specific and desperate.

"I'll learn on the way. Come on, Owen. We'll miss Mary Tyler Moore if we don't hurry. Seriously, we have to get going, or it'll be dark before we get there."

She was right about that. The perfect moment for the search was fast approaching: the lazy, soft Indiana dusk. Then a quick getaway as darkness fell. It was even the perfect day, Saturday, if marijuana farmers observed conventions like weekends. I let this apparent alignment of the planets convince me.

That and the excitement of the moment. It was shining again in Mary's April-blue eyes as they urged me on. Not that I needed much urging. A sweet old woman was dead, my career at the seminary was in shambles, and I was excited because the solution to a mystery might lie in a cornfield in a far corner of the county. The solution to a mystery and perhaps *the* mystery. I must have been feeling awfully lucky.

We almost ran the last hundred downhill yards to the Ghia. En route I outlined an expanded plan to Mary. "A quarter of a mile past the farmhouse is a dirt road. I used it to turn around yesterday. You drop me off there. Then you go back to the main road. Drive away from the farm-house.''

"How far?"

"My odometer's broken. You'll have to time it. Drive for twenty minutes.''

"Twenty minutes," Mary said, the giggle she'd suppressed at the old rectory threatening a return.

"Right. Then turn around and drive back. When you get close to twenty minutes on the return trip, start looking for the dirt road. And for me.''

We were at the car then, looking at each other over the chalky paint of its roof. "If I'm not there..."

From force of habit, Mary reached up to smooth the long hair she no longer had. "You'll be there," she said.

The drive to Ventor was hard on the Ghia. By the time we passed Josh McGriffith's store, Mary had carved her initials into my clutch plate. The feed store was locked up tight, which I took as a promising sign. We didn't pass a single car or truck or combine on our way into the green maze that led to the Morell farm. It was as though the way were being cleared for us, a thought that made me uneasy.

My unease was heightened by the green wall of corn that lined both sides of the road. Any field we passed might be hiding marijuana. They could be hiding anything. The ramshackle houses and house trailers suddenly seemed as secretive and ominous as the fields. I remembered an observation Sherlock Holmes had once made about the country being more dangerous than the city because of its isolation. I paraphrased him absentmindedly. "Think of the deeds of hellish cruelty that may go on year after year out here and none the wiser.''

"It's too late to scare me into staying behind," Mary said.

"Sorry. I was just getting homesick for Trenton. Speed up a little through here. We're about to pass the Morells' house.''

"Is that a good idea? Shouldn't we be sneaking in the back way?"

"This is the only way I know."

"I forgot you were a greenhorn. Hold on, then."

We were past the fields of weeds that was the Morell front yard in two seconds flat. I scanned the house as we passed, seeing no one but Blue, the front porch guard dog. He never raised his head.

"The pickup truck wasn't in the drive," I said. "We may have lucked out. Here's the dirt road."

Mary actually downshifted as she slowed to make the turn. "Nothing to this," she said.

The dirt track wound away from the main road and topped a small rise. Mary stopped the car at its apex. There was corn on both sides of the lane. Up close, it looked less healthy than the fields we'd passed on our drive in, uneven in height and a yellower green. Before us, the dirt lane descended to a wooded creek, where it ended.

"Be careful," Mary said, her high spirits suddenly gone. She grabbed the sleeve of my shirt and pulled me closer for a kiss that was both familiar and strange. "For luck," she said.

I took a pocket knife from the Ghia's glove compartment. "See you in forty minutes."

I climbed out and shut the car door quietly behind me. I watched Mary back away until she disappeared around the bend in the lane. Then I stepped into the field of corn that lay between the dirt track and the house.

I hadn't gotten very far before it occurred to me that what I really needed was a compass. The corn was thickly planted and blocked my view on all sides. It was also drier than I'd expected. I was certain that the rustling noise I made as I pushed my way through the stalks could be heard for miles. In reality, I was probably effectively drowned out by the noise of the field itself. What I'd taken for silence when I'd left the car was really a steady white noise like a waterfall. It was made up of the buzzing and droning and chirping of countless insects, the day and evening shifts all going at once now as dusk faded into night. The living sound made my skin crawl.

I'd gone perhaps fifty yards into the field when I found the first of the marijuana. Moving from the cornfield into the hidden patch was like stepping into a make-believe garden realized in plastic at some amusement park. That feeling was due in part to the color of the plants, an unexpected emerald green still bright in the fading light. The stalks were tall and lush and unworldly against the commonplace background of the corn, like plants sown by a passing comet. Contributing to the sense of unreality was the way the taller plants were drawn down and tied to stakes, as I'd guessed at the Unstable under Jim Carroll's prompting. These plants were bowed and taut like catapults waiting to fire. I thought again of a fairy-tale garden with Munchkin-size pathways under incredibly green arbors.

I selected a plant almost my own height that hadn't been tied down, pulling it over and cutting off the top foot or so with my knife. Then I checked my watch. Barely ten minutes had passed. I moved farther into the field, turning to my left now, away from the distant sound of barking dogs that marked the location of the farmhouse.

Twenty yards from the first marijuana patch, I found a second. I cut off another sample, for luck. I stuck my two pieces of evidence through my belt and headed on. The barking was continuous now. I decided that it could mean the Morells had returned, not that the possibility worried me. It was almost time for me to start back to the dirt road anyway. I passed a third secret patch without pausing to examine it or to collect souvenirs.

Then I saw the tops of some trees above the corn. I emerged from the field at the edge of the tree-lined creek I'd seen from the Ghia. If I followed it to my left, the creek would lead me back to the dirt road and Mary. But I didn't head for the road. Looking to my right, I saw that the fringe of trees along the creek widened into a small forest. Through the growing darkness and the trees, I thought I saw a house.

I checked my watch and decided there was just enough time to investigate. I started off through knee-deep weeds at the edge of the field, hurrying now but making less noise than I had in the corn. My goal was becoming less clear as the light failed. I could only tell that the house was two stories tall and that the trees grew close around it.

The steady barking of the dogs rose in a crescendo that made me think I'd somehow wandered too close to the Morells' farmhouse. That mistaken notion passed quickly, as I realized that the barking was drawing closer to me. Closer by the second.

I turned and started to run back along the creek the way I'd come, covering two or three of my own footmarks in the weeds with every stride as I got up to speed. It occurred to me that I should run through the creek itself, to throw the dogs off my trail. I'd no sooner had that bright thought than the first dog broke through the wall of corn twenty yards behind me. I looked back long enough to confirm that the time for stratagems had passed. It was Blue bounding after me, with half a dozen of his near relations. I selected a tree and ran for it.

The tree I'd picked was an ancient ash whose trunk broke into several spreading arms close to the ground. I grabbed at a heavy branch that grew sideways for a few feet before turning upward for the light. I swung myself up into the crook of the branch seconds before Blue arrived at the base of the tree. He stood with his forepaws on the trunk, not barking or even growling, just staring up at me intently. I remembered then Frank Morell's remark that Blue thought he was a person. He looked like one now, a dour police inspector from some old English movie.

I interpreted the look in those pale eyes. "What's all this, then?" I asked. My dry voice struggled with that simple line.

Additional dialogue was provided by Blue's posse, which arrived now to bark up at me happily. To laugh at me, if dogs can laugh. I thought of climbing higher in the tree, in the forlorn hope that the dogs would lose interest in me in the growing darkness. I was looking upward, picking my route, when the beam of a flashlight hit me.

From near the corn, a voice called out, "Mr. Keane, is that you? It's me, Curtis Morell." He turned the flashlight on himself, displaying his swarthy, smiling face. The beam revealed something else as it swung back toward me, the barrel of a shotgun.

"I thought they'd treed a raccoon," Curtis said. "You ever hunt raccoon? All you have to do is tree one and shine a light on it. The light dazzles it, you know, makes it freeze in place. It just sits there waiting to be shot."

With an effort, I looked away from the beam of light. "Sounds pretty sporting," I said.

"Passes the time," Curtis replied cheerfully. "You can come down now, by the way. The dogs won't bother you with me here."

I swung around on the branch and dropped to the ground. Curtis stepped closer. "Whatever were you doing out here anyway?"

His question gave me a second's foolish hope. I started to word a story about Michael Crosley and the lost sonnet.

Then Curtis pointed to my waist with his flashlight beam. "What's that you got?"

I looked down innocently. One of the marijuana stalks must have fallen out during the chase. The other was still there, sticking through my belt like a shaggy green sword.

At the edge of my vision, Curtis made a rapid movement. Before I could look up, the lights went out. All the lights in the world.

TWENTY-FIVE

I AWOKE FROM A NIGHTMARE of Keats being murdered in Italy to find myself face to face with Agnes Morell. There was a searing pain in my left temple that stiffened the whole side of my face, making my skin feel as rigid and fragile as an autumn leaf. Mrs. Morell's square face bobbed about in the shadowy half light a few feet from my own. I was seated on the floor, my untied legs stretched out before me. My hands were bound behind me. Ropes around my chest secured me to something solid against which my back rested.

I wasn't granted the blessing of a disoriented moment during which I was unaware of my situation. I knew immediately who had me and why. The where took some working out. What light there was flickered unsteadily. It was accompanied by a faint rushing noise, like the wind blowing through a crack in the wall. Ignoring the flaring pain in my head, I followed both the light and the sound to a single source, an old lantern hanging above Mrs. Morell. I could make out a heavy timber above the lantern. Based on that scant evidence, I concluded that I was in the barn behind the house. There, and in big trouble.

Then I remembered Mary. She had been right about my needing someone to look after me, someone to run for the cavalry. She was surely doing that right now, if she had been able to find her way out of the green maze that surrounded me. If she'd been able to find her way out in the dark with only the Ghia's yellowed headlights to guide her. I put those doubts out of my mind. Mary had found the way out. She was hurrying back now with the police.

That happy thought gave me the courage to look Agnes in the eye for the first time. She responded by leaning forward and examining my head, her blunt fingers poking at the epicenter of my pain.

"I'll say this for you, boy," Agnes grunted. "You're tougher than you look."

"Everyone's tougher than he looks," a voice behind me said. It was Mary's voice.

I pulled against the ropes that bound me and tried to turn toward her voice, the movement making my head light up with pain.

"Take it easy," Mary said. "You're squeezing the life out of me. I'm tied to the other side of the post."

My contribution to the conversation was Mary's name, which I repeated over and over again in time with the throbbing in my head.

To quiet me, Mary continued speaking in a calm, ordinary voice. "A man was waiting at the end of the dirt road when I backed out. He had a gun. When I tried to get away, I stalled the Ghia. Sorry."

My skin was suddenly cold and damp. The pain in my head was being overtaken by a vertigo that made the massive timber behind me feel like a swaying reed.

"Use the bucket, boy," Agnes said. With the toe of her shoe, she tapped a steel pail that sat next to me. I bent my head toward it gratefully.

"Are you all right, Owen?" Mary asked as my retching died out in painful dryness.

Agnes answered for me. "He will be in a minute." She bent to pick up some straw from the floor of the barn and used it to wipe my chin.

"What are you going to do with us?" I asked.

Agnes declined to answer the question directly. "We're waiting for Morell to come back. He went looking for a drink this afternoon. He'll be a while yet, I expect."

"Let Mary go," I said. "Before it's too late."

Agnes shook her head. "It's long since too late, boy."

She turned toward a sound outside the barn. "That'll be Curtis," she said, with an echo of my own fear in her voice. "Keep a civil tongue in your head, and we'll all be better off." She stood up and stepped backward into the darkness, leaving center stage to her son.

Curtis entered the circle of light. His cap was sitting well back on his head, the brim reaching upward toward the lantern and casting a shadow over his face. In one hand, he carried a burning marijuana cigarette. In the other, the bag of marijuana that had brought us to the farm.

"Here we are again, Mr. Keane. Got time, do you think, for our discussion of Neitzsche?"

He took a drag from the joint and then bent to examine my head. After a moment, he exhaled the smoke into my face and straightened himself. "Barely broke the skin," he said. "You really have to know how hard to hit a man's skull. Especially with something as heavy as a gun butt. A little too hard, and you just bust everything to hell. I've got it down to an art."

"Lucky for me," I said.

Curtis chuckled and moved to one side of the post toward Mary. "Comfy back there?" he asked.

"I'm fine," Mary said shortly.

"Sorry about the dark," Curtis said to her. "If you feel anything biting at your ankles, just say 'Shoo!' real loud."

I felt like using the bucket again. Instead, I straightened with an effort and leaned my head back against the post. To draw Curtis away from Mary, I repeated the question I'd asked his mother. "Just what do you intend to do with us?"

He came back into the light and sat down on the crate Agnes had occupied, setting the bag of marijuana down beside him. "That's a tough nut, for sure. I have my own ideas on the subject, but Paw will have to be consulted.

He's very sensitive about being left out of the decision-making process."

"If we're not back soon, the police will come looking for us."

"Using what, a Ouija board?"

"I left a note on the desk in my room, telling about the marijuana and where we were going. If we're not back, the letter will be found and read."

"Your dorm room, did you say? Room 217 at St. Meinrad Hall, isn't it?"

"How do you know that?"

"You gave me your phone number, remember? I called it that day while you were out in the yard talking with Krystal. You seminarians have a soft spot in your heart for little girls, that's for sure. Some stiff answered the phone at your dorm. I asked him for your address. Told him I wanted to mail you something. He handed it right over."

"Why did you do that?"

"I thought it might come in handy. I'm getting to know that campus of yours pretty well. It'd be no job at all for me to retrieve your letter, if it turns out you really left one."

"They'll come looking for us with or without a letter."

"Looking isn't finding," Curtis said. "You should know that, if anyone does. You found Michael Crosley yet?"

My head was sagging again. I forced it upright. "Where are you holding him?"

"Nice try, Mr. Keane, but the truth is, we're not holding him. He's joined us, so to speak." Curtis laughed. "Become one of the family, in fact. He wanted to be family from the start. Wanted to tell me how to raise my daughter. Even Maw and Paw don't do that. I had to blacken Crosley's eye for it. But we don't have any disagreements now. Like I said, he's one of the clan."

He took another drag from his joint. "Care for some?" he asked, drawing in air with each word.

"I could use a cigarette," I said.

Curtis responded by losing his temper for the first time. "A cigarette! Man, if you want to poison yourself, do it somewhere else. I can't believe you'd put one of those to your lips in this day and age. Haven't you read the Surgeon General's report? Are you guys walled in in that seminary of yours? They ought to call it a cemetery," he added, regaining some of his good humor. "You're all brain dead.

"Take your buddy Crosley. It wasn't enough for him to tell me how to raise my own daughter. He was going to muscle in on our farm."

"Muscle in how?"

"By stealing from us." He picked up the bag of marijuana. "Thanks for bringing this back. I found it in that funny little car of yours.

"Speaking of your car, it's way too noisy for the job of sneaking up on folks. I heard that little doodlebug go by this evening, and I wasn't even in the front of the house. Wasn't expecting company at all. I had to really hustle to catch your lady friend back there. She didn't tell me where you were, by the way. I worked that out by myself."

"Congratulations," I said.

"Oh, I know," Curtis said. "You think you're the only one with any brains. Crosley was the same way. He thought he was way ahead of us poor hicks, but he wasn't. We got a call one night from some kind soul who let us know that Crosley had ripped us off and that he intended to cut himself in and us out. We had to stand up for our rights."

"Who called you?"

"I don't know. The patron saint of pot growers, maybe. That gimcrack Church of yours probably has one. Anyway, we went to talk with Crosley, Paw and I. Ended up inviting him back here for a visit. It was one ugly night. Rained harder than a cow pissing on a flat rock.

"By and by, we came to an agreement with Mr. Crosley. He decided if he couldn't beat us, he'd have to join us."

I didn't believe the punch line, but Curtis's crazy story seemed to offer a way out. "If what you say is true, we won't make any trouble for you. We're not interested in the farm. I only want to find Crosley."

Curtis laughed heartily. "A pretty smooth line for a man with blood in his hair and straw on his chin. I really have to hand it to you. Not that I'm buying it. You're locked into a medieval value system, totally brainwashed by it. I'm evil, right? And you're good. What a joke."

He scratched his chin noisily while he savored the humor. "That's why I talked Paw into this kind of farming in the first place. It's a way of breaking free of all the old hypocrisies. And a way of freeing other people. Of spreading the revolution. That's what I am really, a revolutionary. But to you, I'm just a dope peddler, a corrupter of schoolchildren.

"So you'd have to turn me in, if you ever got the chance. Otherwise, you're just a fraud. I guess we should explore that possibility. Are you a fraud, Mr. Keane? An imposter? Go ahead. Tell me you don't really believe in this Jesus crap. Renounce the whole business and maybe I'll let you go. It's worth a try."

I strained to read his eyes through the shadow that covered his face, trying to gauge his offer. They were two pockets of blackness.

Before I could speak, Mary called out, "Don't give him the satisfaction, Owen. He won't let us go."

"There's a woman with the courage of her convictions," Curtis said. "She's the one to discuss philosophy with, if time permits."

He stood up and looked at his watch. "If Paw isn't home soon, he'll be too liquored up to be of any use."

His joint was just an ember in his fingers. Curtis dropped it and ground it out with his boot. "Time to reload. I'll be back directly. Before I go, here's some of your stuff. Seems only right to return it as you brought back my produce."

He dug in his pocket and produced my lighter and keys. He dropped the lighter at his feet and jingled the keys thoughtfully. "Better keep these. Paw will be after me to dump your car somewhere. Maybe I'll run it back to St. Aelred's when I go after that letter of yours. That would be a nice touch. Oh yeah, there's one more thing."

He reached into another pocket and came out with my knife. "Here's something I'm sure you've been missing." He opened the knife and held it by the blade. "I used to be good at this." He flicked the knife downward with a quick movement of his wrist. It stuck in the dirt floor at the edge of the circle of light.

"That's it, I guess, unless you have any questions."

I had a question, although it seemed frivolous in the context of the Morell barn. I asked it anyway. "Where did you find the Keats sonnet?"

Curtis came very close to losing his temper again. "Keats sonnet? Are you still worried about some fucking poem? Do you think any of this had anything to do with a poem? A fluffy piece of nothing?" He bent toward me and spit his words in my face. I could see his eyes clearly now. They were empty pinpoints. "Poetry. Do you think anything in the world happens because of nursery rhymes like that? A thing happens because a man with guts decides to do it.

"Aunt Sarah wouldn't let go of that. She had to keep sending you yokels out here looking for that stuff. Her pot of gold. She won't do it anymore. None of you will bother us anymore."

He straightened up and walked toward the door, pausing there to address us from the darkness. "The funny thing is, you'll end up forgiving me. You will, you know. It's really amazing. There's no reasoning that out."

TWENTY-SIX

AS THE BARN DOOR CLOSED, Mary whispered, "You told me to say when I'd had enough of playing detective. I've had enough."

Agnes Morell emerged from the shadows. She was looking off in the direction Curtis had gone, but she addressed me. "You did okay, boy. Won't pay you to rile Curtis up."

"Is that what your aunt did?" I asked.

Agnes answered me in her indirect way by distancing herself from the dead woman. "She was Morell's aunt, not mine."

I summoned up my reserves for one more try at acting tough. "Either way, she's dead now. That will happen to us unless you do something. You'll be as guilty as Curtis."

Agnes turned her face toward me. Her eyes were still looking elsewhere. "He's blood of mine. You're not," she said.

She looked around the barn as though dazed, her glance coming very close to the spot where my knife stuck out of the dirt floor. To distract her, I tossed questions into the light of the hissing lantern.

"Where is Michael Crosley, Mrs. Morell?"

"I don't know."

"What's happened to him?"

"I don't know."

I understood that she meant she didn't want to know. That it wasn't safe for her to know. She would be answering questions about Mary and me the same way soon. If anyone came by to ask.

I tried an easier subject. "I saw a house back in the woods. Does that belong to the farm?"

Agnes shook her head at my curiosity. "That's the homestead. The first house built around here."

"The original house on the farm?"

She didn't answer me. She was distracted by the noise of dogs barking near the barn. "That could be Morell now," she said.

Her eyes strayed to my knife again, but she made no move to retrieve it. The barking of the dogs had risen to a furious pitch. "Something's spooking those dogs," Agnes said. "Why don't Curtis do something?"

She started for the door of the barn. At the edge of the circle of light, she paused and looked down at the knife. I wondered whether she was hesitating because she wanted to help us or because Curtis had put the knife there and she dared not counter even his whims. For whatever reason, she left it in the dirt and walked out of the barn.

"Give me as much slack as you can," I told Mary. "I'm going to try to reach the knife."

I swung my legs to my left and stretched them out, struggling downward in the ropes that held my chest to gain an extra inch or two of reach.

While I struggled, Mary talked to keep our spirits up. Her voice came out in gasps as I pulled the ropes against her. "We should actually have left a letter behind. 'To whom it may concern. We are walking into something we don't really understand.'"

"I should leave that note every time I go out."

"Asking for a cigarette was a good idea. You were going to burn through the ropes, right?"

"No. I just wanted one."

I made one last effort to reach the knife with the toe of my shoe, my head swimming. "It's too far. I'm sorry, Mary."

"You tried your best."

I moved my head around, searching for a position that would ease the pain. I settled for resting it against the post. "I mean I'm sorry I landed you here."

"Never mind that. I'm waiting for you to tell me that you've gotten out of tighter places than this."

"Not since the birth canal."

Mary rewarded that effort with a strained laugh. "Curtis didn't hit you hard enough," she said.

As my head cleared, another idea entered it, inspired by Mary's remark about the cigarette.

She groaned as I pulled against our bonds again. "I thought you were giving up."

"Plan B. I'm going for the lighter." I placed my left heel on it as I answered her. I drew my leg up until the lighter was even with my right thigh. Then I rested my leg on top of the lighter and tried to inch it toward my hands by first dragging my legs backward, then throwing them forward and beginning again.

Mary grunted and sighed with each cycle. I said, "Why don't you use some of that air to tell me why you came to Indiana."

"Maybe I came to ask you the same question," Mary replied. When I didn't answer, she said, "I came to see how you were doing. To talk with you."

The lighter was moving backward by half-inches. I was almost sitting on it. "To talk about what?"

"Life. The future. The Detroit Tigers. How are you doing?"

"Almost there." I used my legs to raise myself off the ground and reached for the lighter with my bound hands. I put one finger on it, then two. Then I was drawing it back to the small space between me and the post.

"Do you have it?"

I didn't answer right away. The lighter felt wrong to me. I flipped the top open to confirm my fears. "It's just the case. Curtis took the works out."

"The bastard," Mary said.

A moment passed in silence. Then Mary said, "I don't think I ever called anyone that before."

"You saved it for the right occasion."

"How's your head?"

It was a good opening. Mixed up, I should have said. Filled with half-baked ideas about life, the priesthood, my vocation, my dreams. Half-thought-out ideas that had carried me halfway to my goal but couldn't go the distance. I should have told Mary all that. It's what she'd come to Indiana to hear. While I was at it, I could have mentioned that I still loved her.

Instead, I answered her question literally. "It's better."

She wasn't listening. "Owen," she said softly. There was more fear in that one word than I'd heard from her since I'd come to. "There's something moving over there in the shadows. It's coming this way."

"Don't be afraid, lady," a small voice said. A voice I knew.

"Krystal," I whispered. "Is that you?"

"Yep. It's me, all right." She crawled into the circle of light on her hands and knees. Her long blond hair hung almost to the ground. There were dark smudges on her cheeks. "I want you to take me away from here."

"Get my knife and cut these ropes. It's there in the dirt."

"Will you take me? Promise?"

"I promise. Hurry up, before your father comes back."

"He'll be busy for a while," Krystal said. "I set the tractor shed afire."

That announcement took my breath away. I watched in amazement as she retrieved the knife and went to work on the ropes that held us to the post. The bonds around our chests were loops of a single rope. They all went slack when Krystal cut through one. I heard Mary moan with relief behind me.

Krystal next worked on the cord that bound my hands. "You sure don't keep this knife very sharp," she said.

"It's had a rough evening," I said. Then I was free. I took the knife from Krystal and crawled around to where Mary waited in the darkness. I knelt behind her and began to saw away at her bonds, the feeling slowly returning to my hands in the form of a dull pain. Krystal crouched beside me, listening intently.

I listened, too. In addition to dogs barking, I thought I could hear the fire now. Then I heard something very definite: Curtis cursing madly in the distance.

"We best get going," Krystal said.

Mary's ropes finally parted. She turned and put her arms around me. I could feel her hot tears against my cheek.

"Hurry now," Krystal said.

"Where's my car?"

"Behind the barn. Follow me."

I retrieved the lantern first. Krystal led us through a corridor formed by bales of hay and into a stall where a horse or cow had once been kept. Against the outside wall was a feeding trough, a roughly made basket of two-by-fours open at the top. Krystal hopped inside.

"This way," she said. "There's a hole in the wall."

I held the lantern up. The boards at the back of the manger were rotted away. The hole had been patched from the outside with a rusted sheet of tin. Krystal pushed this up and out of the way with her shoulder and rolled out into the darkness. Then she held the flap open for us. "Come on," she whispered.

Mary was into the manger before I could help her. She crawled through the hole on her hands and knees. I left the lantern on the floor of the stall and followed her.

A weird light was playing about the barnyard, a huge flickering bonfire light cast by the burning shed. The Ghia sat in the barn's shadow five yards away from us, looking better than the day I bought it. Krystal was through the car's open window before I'd staggered to my feet. Mary and I crossed the grassy space more slowly, supporting one another. "I'll drive," I said.

"Are you sure you can?"

"I'm sure I can shift."

Mary suddenly stopped, squeezing my arm at the same time. "We don't have the keys."

"We don't need them. There's a flashlight under the passenger seat. Get it and meet me up front."

I reached in through the driver's window, rattled the gear shift lever for luck, and pulled the release for the forward baggage compartment where I'd previously hidden the marijuana. Then I raised the hood and pulled down the cardboard flap that provided access to the inside of the dashboard.

Mary appeared on the other side of the car and shone her light into the compartment, revealing the backs of the radio and instruments and switches. I reached for the wires attached to the ignition switch and yanked them out.

"Nice to know all your reading hasn't been wasted," Mary said.

"These two green ones are the ignition wires." I twisted them together. "This black one's the starter."

I paused with the black wire in my hand, remembering Curtis's crack about my noisy car. "Is there a back way out of here, Krystal?"

She was hanging out the window, watching the operation. She shook her head with her usual enthusiasm, her hair slapping the side of the car. "Just the way by the house."

"Get ready to duck, then." To Mary I added, "Get in on your side and pump the gas."

I touched the starter wire to the knot that connected the ignition wires. At the first contact, the engine began to turn over. When it caught a second later, I pulled the hot wire away.

"Never sell this car," Mary said as I climbed in beside her.

I backed the Ghia from behind the barn and turned it toward the house. As soon as we cleared the barn's shadow, the inside of the car was lit by the burning shed.

I hesitated for a second at the sight of that spectacle. The shed had disappeared in a tower of flames that rose higher than the house, the heat making the stars shimmer. In front of the fire, a silhouetted figure ran back and forth, hopping in anger or helplessness or stoned glee. It was Curtis Morell. Agnes Morell stood by watching, her arms folded. Together mother and son made me think of a priest and priestess presiding over some ancient dance of sacrifice, some lost ritual of a forgotten time coming to life again by chance in this dark corner of Indiana.

"Go," Mary said, waking me from my vision.

I slammed the car into gear and floored the accelerator. I was in third by the time we drew even with the burning shed. I saw Agnes turn toward us, her face immobile, her arms still folded. Then Curtis appeared in the corner of the windshield. His dark face was streaming with sweat and his lips were drawn back in a manic grin. I followed the tire-track drive, unable to turn for Curtis but unwilling to swerve away. At the last second, he drew back and disappeared into the darkness.

We flew into the gap between the house and Krystal's garden and out into the blackness of the front yard. I switched on the headlights and took the turn onto the gravel road too fast, running both right-side tires into a grassy ditch. Our momentum carried us up and onto the road. As the car steadied, I saw two bloodred eyes sweep past.

"Good-bye, Blue," Krystal said. Then she began to cry.

TWENTY-SEVEN

WE DROVE WITHOUT SPEAKING until I successfully negoti-
ated the twists and turnings that brought us out to State
Road 64. Krystal cried on with the easy pace of a mara-
thoner, while Mary tried to comfort her as best she could
from the front seat. I concentrated on steering and shifting with one hand while I held my head steady with the
other. I also watched for the Morell pickup truck on its in-
bound trip from whatever bar Frank Morell favored. I
hoped he was still out enjoying himself. He would have one
hell of a hangover in the morning if I had anything to say
about it.

When we were safely on the highway, Mary looked up
from our passenger. "Are you going straight to the sheriff's office?" she asked.

"No."

"You still don't trust him?"

"I don't trust him more than ever. You heard Curtis say
that someone had called to warn them about Crosley."

"You think that was Sheriff Yeager?"

"Or one of his men. It would have been the most natural thing in the world for Crosley to have gone to Yeager
with that marijuana. The sheriff or a deputy could have put
him off with some promise of action and then called the
Morells."

Mary sounded tired of my endless guesses. "Curtis didn't
seem to know who had called them. If the sheriff or some
deputy were on his side, Curtis would have bragged about
it. Besides, if Crosley had gone to the police, they would
have taken the marijuana as evidence, or in your scenario,

to give it back to the Morells. Michael Crosley wouldn't have kept it."

They were her usual solid objections. I chewed on them for a few miles. Perhaps Crosley had phoned his information to the sheriff. Then the pot wouldn't have changed hands. I didn't think enough of the idea to run it by Mary. Then, too, I wanted to give her a rest. Her voice had been flat and rough-edged as she'd batted down my latest idea. I stole a glance at her in the light of a passing car and saw that she had wrapped her arms tightly around herself, comforting herself now that Krystal had quieted down.

"Sorry," I said.

"What for this time?"

"Making you miss Mary Tyler Moore."

I couldn't tell in the darkness if she smiled, but her voice sounded lighter and softer. "It was a repeat anyway. Where are we going if not to the sheriff?"

"The state police, but I don't know where to find them. When we're far enough from the farm to feel safe, we can stop and call them."

"We'll be in Ohio before I'll feel safe," Mary said. "Let's call from St. Aelred's."

"All right."

The thought that even now Curtis and his father might be barreling after us through the darkness made me urge the car on a little faster. It would have made more sense to drive anywhere but St. Aelred's. Anywhere Curtis wouldn't think to look for us. To New Albany and the sane, sterile Green Streets house. To Evansville and Michael's Uncle John. To Elizabeth Mott's quiet garden.

It didn't make sense to return to St. Aelred's, but like Mary, I felt drawn to the place. In the isolation of the Indiana night, the old school seemed to promise an island of light and peace. A sanctuary from Curtis Morell. From all the Curtis Morells of the world. At that moment, I saw the school as a place I had undervalued stupidly, a precious thing I'd wasted.

The campus was wonderfully ordinary at eleven o'clock on a Saturday night. The handful of students walking the lighted pathways ignored us as we violated school regulations by driving a car up campus hill. I'd taken us back to the one place on earth where the Morells could find us. Now I drove us to the very spot they would first look, the address Curtis had taunted me with, St. Meinrad Hall. I parked illegally at the curb before the front door and reached for the ignition key that wasn't there.

"We made it, thank God," Mary said.

The car clattered on faithfully as we climbed out. While Mary helped Krystal out of the back seat, I opened the hood and pulled the ignition wires apart. The resulting silence was immense.

Brother Dennis met us at the front door, drawn by our noisy arrival. His appearance reminded me of my brief meeting with Earl Donahue, Melissa's angry father. Brother Dennis was dressed less formally—in an undershirt, dark pants, and sandals—but like Donahue he carried a newspaper.

"Okie? Mary? What on earth happened to you two?"

I turned to examine Mary in the entryway light. Her white blouse and paisley vest bore dark marks from the ropes and her bell bottoms were the same soiled color as Krystal's entire outfit. The two also shared dirty, tear-streaked faces. Together they looked like a mother and daughter who had survived a train wreck.

I could tell from the concern in Mary's eyes that I looked worse. She started to reach up to touch the bump on my head, but I winced in anticipation, and she drew back.

"What happened to you?" Brother Dennis repeated.

"The same thing that happened to Michael Crosley," I said. "We spent the evening with the people who kidnapped him. This is Krystal. She helped us get away."

"Someone kidnapped Michael? Who?"

"I'll explain later. Where's the nearest state police post?"

"In Jasper, I think. I'll look it up in the book." He started for the phone.

"There's one other thing," I said. "The ones who took Michael. They may be coming after us."

"I hope to God they do," the monk said. "I'd like to get my hands on them. Take these two to my room. They can clean up there."

I'd never seen the inside of the housemaster's apartment. The main room was unadorned, except for a crucifix over the bed and a San Francisco Giants pennant over the door to the bath. The room was softly lit by a standing lamp next to a bentwood rocking chair.

Mary squeezed my hand in parting at the doorway. "We'll be fine," she said.

Brother Dennis was on the phone in the common room. "I've got the state police, Okie. And I've called Brother Kevin. He's on his way over now with some of his boys. I'll roust ours out now."

A librarian, a potter, and some unarmed seminarians. Their number would have to be enough to scare the Morells off.

The state trooper on the phone was a sergeant named Hubbard. He listened patiently as I described the marijuana farm and how Mary and I had been held there. I gave my report in my usual backward fashion, ending it with the Morells' most serious crimes, the kidnapping of Michael Crosley and the murder of Sarah.

"You think this Crosley is still being held?" Hubbard asked.

I didn't want to muddy the waters with Curtis's story about Crosley joining them. I didn't want to believe it myself. "I hope they're still holding him," I said.

"Understood," Hubbard said. "I've got a car on the way to you now. I'll send another if there's someone who can guide us to the farm. We may need help finding it."

I could have given him directions or told him to follow the burning tractor shed, but I wanted one more visit to the Morell homestead. "I'll be ready," I said.

A group of bewildered seminarians had gathered on the front steps of the hall. Their happy chatter died suddenly when I paused at the door, pale and bloodied, like Banquo's ghost from some summer stock *Macbeth*.

Mary and Krystal had cleaned up a little. They sat together on the side of Brother Dennis's bed, Mary trying to force a brush through Krystal's tangled hair.

I dragged the rocking chair over to the bed and sat down in front of Krystal. "How are you doing?"

"I'm okay," she said. "You still got blood on your face.'

"I know," I said.

"Brother Dennis promised me he'd take care of that," Mary said.

"Thanks for the warning."

"I'd make you a poultice if I had my medicines," Krystal said. "I wish I could." She had gotten over her crying, but she still wasn't the friendly girl who had once shown me her herb garden. The fear I'd seen in her the day we'd met on the courthouse square in Randolph was still there. Something had happened to her between our first two meetings.

"I'd like you to do something else for me, Krystal."

"What's that?"

"Tell me what happened to Michael Crosley."

"Owen," Mary said. "Not now."

I explained it to both of them. "I'm going back to the farm in a little while. With the police. I want to find Michael Crosley and help him if he's there."

Krystal just stared at me, more frightened than she'd been in the barn with the sound of the fire and her father's rage coming in to us. Mary put her arm around the little girl.

At that moment, Brother Dennis entered the room. "Okie, there you are. Just sit still while I fix you up." He carried a tray that held towels, a basin of water, and some bottles.

"I've got aspirin and peroxide," he said as he set his equipment down on the bureau. He dragged the reading lamp closer and stared into each of my eyes in turn. "Looks okay. Now I'm going to clean up that wound of yours. This may hurt a little."

His first attempt hurt a lot. When the stinging died down enough for me to open my eyes, Krystal, the doctor-to-be, was standing beside me. "I can do it better," she said. "Let me."

"You can if you'll tell me about Michael Crosley."

"All right," Krystal said. Brother Dennis handed her the moistened towel. She held it out from her with one hand while she dug in the pocket of her cutoffs with the other. She drew out a square of paper about the size of a match-book. It was surprisingly white, and there was black printing across it.

Krystal handed the white square to me. "Mikey gave me that." I unfolded the stiff paper as the little girl began to gently pat my temple. It was a holy card. The front bore a picture of the Sacred Heart of Jesus that was similar to the old print in Crosley's garret. On the back was printed: "Jesus, meek and humble of heart, make my heart like unto thine. In loving memory of Martin P. Crosley." Below Crosley's name were the dates of his birth and death and the name of an Indianapolis funeral home. The card had probably been given out at his viewing.

I handed it back to Krystal. She was examining my scalp carefully. "Mikey tried to help me get back to school," she said. "He told me to pray to Jesus."

"Mikey asked your father about school, didn't he?"

"Yep. Paw knocked him down. But Mikey didn't blame me. It was after that he gave me this Jesus picture."

"How often did Mikey come to see you?"

"Two or three times."

"Good job, Krystal," Brother Dennis said. "Now put this bandage on him."

As Krystal stepped back to admire her handiwork, I asked, "You gave Mikey something in exchange for the holy card, didn't you?"

She drew back against Mary. "How do you know?"

"Was it some old papers you'd found? A poem?"

"A poem?" Krystal repeated, her confusion a small echo of her father's exasperation with the same subject. "No. It was a bag of Paw's grass. I shouldn't have done it. I wish I hadn't." Her bony shoulders began to rise and fall a second before her crying started again. Sobs spaced her next few words. "I just wanted to get back to school."

Mary gathered Krystal in. "That's enough," she said.

It was all the misery I had time to inflict. A seminarian appeared in the doorway. "There's a state police car outside," he said, "and another coming through the main gate."

Brother Dennis slapped the side of his scarred brow. "And I haven't called Father Jerome yet."

I stood up, unsteadily. "Call him after I've gone."

The monk put a hand on my shoulder. "All right, Okie."

Krystal, still sniffing rhythmically, stepped forward to hand me something. The holy card. "You be safe," she said.

Mary left Krystal in Brother Dennis's charge and walked me to the front door. "You shouldn't go back," she said.

"I'll have half the police in the state along to keep me out of trouble."

"That may not be enough."

I held her for a moment by the front door, ignoring the gaping seminarians. "I have to go back," I said. "I haven't forgiven Curtis yet."

TWENTY-EIGHT

THE TWO STATE POLICEMEN who drove me to Ventor were taciturn in the extreme. I'd entered the back seat of the cruiser worried that I'd be asked to repeat everything I'd already told Sergeant Hubbard. But after a few miles of silence, I began to feel neglected. It was a cruel lesson I should have learned from my beloved paperbacks. A private eye is the hero of his story until he calls in the cops. After that, he's just a pain in some official ass.

It was almost one o'clock on Sunday morning when we pulled up in front of a deserted store in Ventor. It was Josh McGriffith's feed store, appropriately enough. The store was closed, but the parking lot was doing a great business. There were two other state police cars there already. Beside them were two black-and-whites from the Huber County Sheriff's Department. That surprised me more than somewhat, as I'd mentioned my suspicions regarding the sheriff to Sergeant Hubbard.

A bigger surprise awaited me when I stepped into the humid night air. Sheriff Yeager himself was waiting to greet me.

"We meet again, eh, Mr. Keane? I almost didn't recognize you in your civvies. And you've solved my murder case, I hear. Must be true what they say. Even a blind hog finds an occasional acorn."

"You're welcome," I said.

"You're still sore at me for riding you so hard, I guess, since you took your business to the competition. This here is Lieutenant Kidwell of the Indiana State Police. He specializes in these drug busts."

Kidwell was Abbot to Yeager's Costello, tall and thin with an angular nose, a receding jaw, and eyes that were very alert considering the early hour. He examined my bandage, but didn't comment on it.

"I'm glad I was nearby when your call came in," Kidwell said. "We'll be ready to move in shortly. There was a problem with our search warrant, but it should be on the way now. We're covering the roads in and out of the farm. We'll get them if they're still there to get."

"We should go in now," I said. "A seminarian named Michael Crosley may be in danger."

Kidwell took his cue from the lack of conviction in my voice. "Did you see Crosley there?" he asked.

"No," I said.

"Did the Morells say they were holding him?"

"They said they weren't, but they admitted taking him from the school by force."

"When was this?"

"Three weeks ago."

Kidwell blew air out of his thin cheeks. "Another hour isn't likely to matter. We'll wait for the warrant."

Yeager was shifting his weight from one foot to the other. "My guess is they've flown the coop anyway," he said.

Kidwell remained stoic. "If they have, the all-points bulletin will reel them in. For the moment, everything back there is nice and quiet."

"Didn't any of the neighbors report the fire?" I asked.

Yeager laughed softly. "If what you say about the Morells is true, their neighbors will know better than to stick their noses in, even to help them out."

The sheriff had had his fill of standing. He started for his car. "Wake me when the fiddle player gets here," he said.

After he'd gone, I took a step closer to Kidwell. "How well do you know Sheriff Yeager?" I asked.

In the light from the feed store sign, I saw Kidwell's sharp eyes draw a bead on me. "Quite well. He's done more to get his county free of drugs than any sheriff in this part of the state. Sergeant Hubbard passed on your, ah, reservations. They're unwarranted. You can take my word for that. It would be a disservice to a good officer if this story of yours went any further."

"I understand," I said. I should have by then. My finely honed intuition was running true to form.

Kidwell lost interest in me after that. It didn't hurt my feelings. A few minutes afterward, a call brought the collected car radios to life. The last cruiser was in position. I bummed cigarettes and paced the lot in the moonlight while we waited. It was the better part of an hour later when an unmarked blue sedan pulled up carrying a special delivery from a judge back in Randolph. Kidwell's warrant.

The lieutenant gave a short speech that confirmed my status as an outsider. "You all know what to do," he said. "Now let's do it."

Having no idea what to do, I waited in the center of the lot until Kidwell waved me into the back seat of his car. I directed the expedition from there, saying "left" and "right" and otherwise keeping my mouth shut. We passed a one-car roadblock on the gravel road leading to the farm. I slowed us down to a walker's pace shortly after that, so we wouldn't miss the house in the darkness.

There were no lights anywhere in sight. The house blocked our view of the tractor shed, but I could smell the smoke of the fire through the open window of the car.

Once we were safely established on the driveway, the trooper behind the wheel accelerated sharply. We came to a sliding stop on the grass a few feet from the front porch. The other cars pulled up on either side of us, lighting the front of the house with their headlights.

"Stay here," Kidwell said to me. To the man behind the wheel, he added, "Keep an eye on him."

One of the troopers was already banging away on the front door. There was no answer. He tried the door and found it open. Kidwell and another officer disappeared inside. The others were fanning out around the house. In a moment, it seemed, my keeper and I were alone in the quiet night.

It was far too quiet. The aspirins Brother Dennis had given me were wearing off, and I thought I could actually hear the throbbing in my head. I certainly heard crickets and the drone of an airplane passing high overhead. Of the sound I would always associate with the farm, the barking of dogs, there wasn't a trace.

The trooper in the front seat was less absorbed by the atmosphere of the farm than I. Without turning his head, he said, "So you're studying to be a priest."

"Yes," I said.

"How do you know?" he asked the windshield.

"Pardon me?"

"That you have a calling, I mean. How do you know?"

The throbbing in my temple picked up its beat. I wanted the trooper to turn and face me. I almost asked him to. Then I was suddenly frightened by the wild idea that he would turn and reveal the smiling face of Curtis Morell. He'd outsmarted everyone, I thought, and trapped me here alone. Or worse, Kidwell and Yeager had put him here to finish me off. I grabbed the seat in front of me to steady myself.

The trooper continued speaking in an ordinary voice. "I mean, you can't even be sure there is a God. So how can you be sure about anything in this life? How can you really be sure?"

I reached for the door handles, but there were none in the back seat. "Trapped," I said aloud.

I was making a drunken move for the open window, when a face appeared in it. There was enough moonlight for me to recognize the newcomer as Deputy Springer, Yeager's athletic errand boy.

"You all right?" he asked.

"I need some air."

"I guess you do. You're white as a sheet." He helped me out of the car. "I thought you were smoking too much back at the lot. What with your head being banged up and all. The sheriff wants you to come around back. Feel up to it?"

"Yes," I said.

With Springer as backup, I felt secure enough to look in the window at my driver. The face that looked back at me wasn't Curtis Morell's or any other I'd ever seen before. It was a plain, clean-shaven, ordinary face. A face I could expect to meet over and over again. The trooper smiled at me. "Good luck," he said.

TWENTY-NINE

SPRINGER LED ME AROUND the side of the house, past Krystal's medicinal garden. "Something terrible happened back here," he said. "I'd dearly love to catch the person who did it."

There was still a glowing red pile at the heart of the ruined shed. In its faint light, I could see a half-dozen dark forms on the grass. Springer played his flashlight over them, revealing the solution to the mystery of the dogs that didn't bark in the night. They were all dead. I again had the feeling that some pagan sacrifice had been reenacted here without anyone's conscious intent. The thought that Mary and I might have been its victims made me sway on my feet.

"Shot," Springer said. "Do you believe it?"

I examined the bodies more carefully. Blue, the dog that thought he was people, wasn't there. I was glad of that for Krystal's sake.

Yeager waddled out of the darkness and looked down at the dead animals. "I'll believe the worst thing you want to tell me about the Morells now," he said. "They're long gone, the lot of them. Got clean away. We've checked all the outbuildings."

"There's an old house back in the woods," I said. "Agnes Morell called it the homestead. Has anyone searched there?"

Yeager turned to Springer. "Borrow that state trooper fellow over there and have a look. Keep your wits about you."

"I'd like to go, too," I said.

"Still looking for that seminarian friend of yours? I'll say this for you, Mr. Keane. For a city boy, you're a sticker. Let's let them check the place first, then you and I can go sightseeing."

After Springer had left us, I showed Yeager where Mary and I had been held in the barn. Our ropes were still lying around the post.

Yeager played his flashlight beam over them. "One close shave, youngster," he said.

Kidwell joined us outside the barn. His teeth glinted in a stray movement of Yeager's light. "There's an old tobacco curing shed on the other side of the house," the lieutenant said. "There must be thirty or forty marijuana plants drying inside."

His loudspeaker delivery made my head ring. My own voice sounded far away. "There's something else you should be looking for. Family papers. They're the key to Sarah Morell's murder. She sent Michael Crosley and me out here to find them."

Kidwell wasn't interested. "Sounds like we'll need another warrant," he said. "In the meantime, can you point me to the field where you found the marijuana growing?"

I reluctantly performed my last official function, pointing the cornfield out with the aid of Yeager's flashlight. Kidwell went off happily into the darkness.

"Best wait till dawn," Yeager called after him. To me, he added, "I've heard that some of the pot farmers are booby-trapping their fields now. We know they've moved into the Hoosier National Forest, planting the stuff back where you have to be a Boy Scout to reach it. Places I'll never see."

Just the thought of a trek through a forest seemed to wear the sheriff out. He sat down on a wooden bench and leaned back against the barn, exhaling loudly. "We've been thinking about starting aerial searches. They're trying that over in Spencer County. Might not hold up in the courts, though.''

I sat down beside him. "How bad is the growing?"

"Not as bad as it's going to be. I went to a seminar in Indianapolis last winter. They were predicting an era of new hybrid plants, as potent as anything from south of the border. A single plant with a street value of a thousand dollars. Think of that. This pissant operation here won't be anything compared to the growing we'll have if that ever comes to pass. Please God, I'll be retired by then and fishing for blue gill. If not, you'll have to come back and straighten it all out for me.''

I couldn't tell in the darkness if he was laughing at me. "I wasn't kidding about those family papers," I said. "They're important.''

"I haven't forgotten them," Yeager replied. "I just thought you might have had enough brain work for one day. I'll have my boys collect every scrap of paper on the place. You can come by my office after you've had a rest and tell a poor country sheriff what this murder business was all about.

"By the way, I owe you an apology for that tirade on religion I treated you to yesterday. I lost my wife a year or so ago, by which I mean she up and left me. She found religion in a big way a while back. Got holier and holier until I could barely recognize her as the girl I married. Then one day she just kind of floated off. Left me with a feeling for religion that I should really keep to myself. That's enough true confessions.''

He then talked about fishing and hunting and a cabin he had on a lake. The place sounded so peaceful that I fell asleep staring at its blue water.

I was awakened by the return of Springer and the trooper. "There's a house back there all right," the deputy said. "Someone's been there recently, but it's deserted now.''

"Satisfied?" Yeager asked me. "Or do you want to put your fingers in the wounds?"

"I'd like to see it."

"Lead on then, Springer," Yeager said as he struggled to his feet. "Just don't set any speed records."

The four of us walked back into the woods, paced by the wheezing sheriff. The night had rushed past like a familiar journey. Already, I could see individual trees in the predawn light.

I could also see the homestead. It was a small, two-story building with chips of white paint on its board siding and shark's tooth fragments of glass in its windows. We were approaching the front of the house. The black hole where the front door should have been was in the very center of the wall we faced. To our right was a one-story addition with a sloping roof. There was a remnant of a chimney on the end of the addition and another on the opposite end of the house. The gabled roof of the main structure had as many holes as wooden shingles.

The homestead was nothing to look at, but I couldn't take my weary eyes off it. I felt as though every step I'd taken since I'd set out to find Michael Crosley had led me to it. Every person I'd spoken with—Mrs. Crosley, the Koffmans, Ronnie, Sarah, John Crosley, Jim Carroll—had been directing me to this one forlorn spot, even though most of them hadn't known that the house existed.

Yeager caught the mood of the moment. "Seem like the end of the trail to you, son?"

"Could be," I said.

"I bet a dollar there's a log cabin under here somewhere," Yeager said. "That was the pattern in those days. Build a cabin to start with, then add on and gussy it up until you have a nice little house. Here, Springer, pull on that siding there."

The deputy handed me his flashlight and pulled at the loose boards Yeager had indicated. They came away easily in his hands. I shone the light on the exposed timber, which was gray and massive.

"What did I tell you? Hand hewn and a foot square. Lordy, I'd like to have these old logs for my cabin."

The cabin/house was a survivor from a time when George Keats was still remembered as the patriarch of a family. It was a bit of solid foundation for Sarah's story, more convincing somehow than the footnote I'd found in Bate's book. I could easily imagine an old chest, forgotten in some corner of the homestead, filled with bits of homespun cloth, metal plates and utensils tarnished black, and yellowed pages written by a doomed poet.

I started for the door, flashlight in hand.

"There's nothing in there," Springer said.

"Let him look," Yeager said. "He won't rest otherwise."

I was already inside the lower story, shining my light around. The interior smelled like a forest after a rain. The floor was indistinguishable from the ground outside, a tangle of weeds and vines growing from a carpet of dead leaves. The main room was perhaps twelve by twenty, with a fireplace in the wall to my left and a doorway to my right. The interior walls had lost most of their plaster, but here and there a fragment remained, one of which still held a piece of colorless wallpaper. Light for the growing carpet was provided by large holes in the low, beamed ceiling. Shining my light upward, I was able to see all the way through to the skeleton of the roof.

I went through the doorway to my right and found a slightly smaller room in a similar state of decay. Beyond it, the room that had probably been the kitchen was choked off by the fallen fragments of its chimney. There was no sign anywhere of a treasure chest or a place to hide one.

I shone my light on a stairway that rose against one wall of the second room. Most of its steps were missing or broken through.

"Skinny as you are, that won't hold your weight," a voice behind me said. It was Deputy Springer. He squinted and smiled in the beam of my light. "Even if you could get upstairs, there's no place solid enough to stand on."

I felt a little of the dizzy panic that had overtaken me earlier in the state police car. I wondered if the clean bill of health Lieutenant Kidwell had given to Sheriff Yeager extended to his deputies. Springer would have been in a position to intercept Crosley's call and warn the Morells.

"You said there were signs that someone had been here," I said.

"Right," Springer said. "Back here in the main room. In the fireplace. Somebody burned something."

We crossed to the fireplace, Springer leading the way. "It was cloth, I think," he said. "They must have used gasoline to get it alight." He picked up a stick from the hearth and poked at the black fragments. "There's a zipper, though. A real long one. See? What do you supposed that was from?"

"A raincoat," I said. If I'd been in the mood to impress Springer, I could have given him the make of the coat— London Fog—and the name of its rightful owner—Philip Swickard. Instead, I turned and left the house.

Outside, Sheriff Yeager had switched off his light. "Find anything?" he asked.

"Michael Crosley was here," I said. "He's not here now."

The sheriff grunted. "I'm beginning to wonder if there is such a person."

Yeager was turning to leave when he noticed the state trooper examining something in the woods a few yards from the house. "What've you got?"

"Just some old headstones is all," the trooper replied.

Yeager and I crossed to the spot, the sheriff discoursing on the way. "Family burial plot. All these old farms have them. They're often all that's left to mark an old homestead. Many's the time I came across one in the woods when I was hunting. Always gave me a sad feeling to think that everything these souls worked for was gone except for a piece of old stone poking up out of the ground.''

These stones were ancient and discolored, their inscriptions long since worn away. There were six headstones of varying sizes. They leaned at random angles, some almost touching and others slanting away as though they were distancing themselves from the group. The graves they marked were decorated by dead leaves and a soft fringe of ferns.

In one corner of the plot, the ground had been disturbed recently. A tall plant with clover-shaped leaves and yellow flowers rose from the middle of the fresh earth. It was a plant I'd seen before.

"That's an herb my old granny used to grow," Yeager said, following my gaze. "Rue."

"It means repentance," I said, remembering the lecture Krystal had given me.

I remembered something else then: Curtis Morell's happy taunt that Michael Crosley had become one of the family. My hand went to the folded holy card in my pocket.

I felt the old graves moving beneath my feet and grabbed Yeager's shoulder to steady myself. I thought, disjointedly, of the fictional detective Elizabeth Mott had told me about, the one who found clues in the secret meanings of flowers. I owed her an apology for laughing at that idea. I had just become that kind of detective myself.

"We're going to need a shovel," I said to Yeager. I had finally found Michael Crosley.

THIRTY

THE EXCITEMENT had died down at St. Aelred's by the time the state police returned me at nine o'clock on Sunday morning. The cordon of seminarians around St. Meinrad Hall had dispersed, but the two state troopers were still on duty outside. My safe return marked the end of their shift. I watched as their car and the one that had carried me back rolled out the main gate in tandem. When they were out of sight, the campus looked impossibly normal. The only sign that the night's adventures had ever happened was my old car, still parked illegally at the steps of the dorm. I patted its hood on my way inside.

As I entered the dorm, I spotted Mary and Brother Dennis, asleep in facing lounge chairs in the common room. Their heads came up simultaneously when the front door closed behind me.

"Owen," Mary said. "Thank God."

It was the kind of entrance a detective might dream of making, with a beautiful woman to greet him and an audience to hear the solution of his mystery. At that moment, I was ungratefully wishing that I'd found the lounge empty.

"Did you get them, Okie?" Brother Dennis asked. "The ones who tied you up?"

"Not yet. They're halfway to the Ozarks by now. Our police protection has called it a day."

The monk was dressed as I'd last seen him, in an undershirt, trousers, and slippers, and he needed a shave. "Did you skip matins?" I asked him.

"They never miss me. I only move my lips anyway. How about Michael Crosley? Did you find him?"

I sat down heavily on the arm of Mary's chair.

She took my hand. "You did find him," she said.

"Yes. He's dead. He's been dead for a while."

Brother Dennis made the sign of the cross. Mary, who had never met Crosley, began to cry for him softly. Mary's would be most of the tears Crosley got, outside of his mother's. Melissa Donahue, whom I'd imagined to be Crosley's great love, would never even hear that he'd been found in a shallow grave on a tiny Indiana farm.

Mary was drying her eyes before I remembered another sure mourner, Crosley's would-be fiancée. "Where's Krystal?"

"Asleep in my room," Brother Dennis said. "You two should try to get some sleep, too. I can find an empty room for you here, Mary, if you'd feel safer."

"I'll be fine, thanks," Mary said.

"You two go on, then," Brother Dennis said. "I'll report to Father Jerome."

I walked Mary across the campus to her room. The bells of the church began ringing as we passed it.

"It's Sunday," Mary said.

"It's always Sunday at this place."

"I meant it's my last day here. My flight back is at two o'clock."

"Oh." I was torn between asking her to stay and begging her to smuggle me onto her plane. I ended up taking a third line. "I'll drive you to Louisville."

"Good. We'll have a chance to talk."

We had a similar chance on the rest of the walk to Guest House, but we didn't use it. Mary kissed me on the forehead when she left me at the front steps. "Come by for me at noon," she said.

A little after twelve, I pulled up at those same steps in Brother Dennis's white Rambler. I'd had three hours sleep, a shower, and a sweet roll, and I felt like I might survive after all. The roll was a present from Brother Dennis, who had used it as an excuse to get into my room to examine the bump on my head. He'd also passed on a summons from Father Jerome. The old priest would talk to me whenever I felt up to it. I hadn't yet.

Mary, when she appeared a few minutes later, looked as fresh and normal as St. Aelred's had on my return. She wore a brown peasant dress over a linen blouse, and her golden brown hair shone in the full sun.

"You clean up well," I said as I took her bag from her.

"Thank you. The secret is getting really messed up first."

When we were in the car, Mary said, "Let's go by St. Meinrad for a minute. I want to say good-bye to Krystal and Brother Dennis."

"They're both gone. The sheriff's people came by for Krystal half an hour ago. Brother Dennis rode along to hold her hand."

"What will happen to her?"

"I don't know. A foster home eventually, I guess."

"At least she'll be able to go back to school."

"That will be the least of her worries," I said, thinking that she'd lost both her family and Michael Crosley.

Mary disagreed. "It's what this business was all about," she said. "You've been chasing around after some sonnet and all the time the key was a little girl who wanted to go back to school."

I didn't like hearing the sonnet dismissed. I still thought it was at the center of everything that had happened. Although I'd lost the goal of finding Crosley through the accident of having accomplished it, I still clung to the poem. It was a way of not admitting to myself that I had failed Crosley and Sarah Morell both.

But I wasn't up to arguing the point. "You talked with Krystal?"

"Last night after you'd left. She told me that she'd given the marijuana to Michael as a way of escaping her father. She was desperate to get away from him."

Mary stopped talking abruptly and stared at the road ahead. I sensed that she wasn't finished. After a mile or so, she said, "She had bruises, Owen. I saw them last night. That bastard beat her."

We drove as far as the state highway without speaking. The car's automatic transmission slipped badly, and it took us forever to match the speed of the Sunday drivers racing past.

When we were safely in the flow of traffic, I asked, "So Crosley never talked with her about the poem?"

"No," Mary said impatiently. "I brought that up last night, but Krystal didn't know what I was talking about. Michael was interested in her, not some family album."

It didn't sound like the Crosley I'd come to know, and that discrepancy suddenly seemed like an important clue. Father Jerome had sent Crosley into the world to expose him to ordinary people. To increase his empathy with the world's victims. The old priest's scheme may have worked. The plights of Sarah and Krystal had certainly gotten through to him. I thought of the prayer on the back of the holy card he'd given Krystal: "Make my heart like unto Thine."

"Krystal couldn't understand why nothing happened after she'd given Michael the pot," Mary said. "I'm not sure I understand myself."

"Crosley didn't know what to do," I said. "He spoke with Karen Koffman and Ronnie about marijuana, trying to decide whether to turn the Morells in."

"Why did he even hesitate?"

We would never know the answer to that for certain, but I thought I might have guessed it. "It was Sarah Morell. She was in bad shape financially. She would have been destitute without the income from that farm. I think Crosley was weighing her situation against the damage the Morells were doing with their pot. That was the decision he told Ronnie he had to make.''

"He got mixed signals from Ronnie and Karen Koffman," Mary said. "It's no wonder he was confused. It's really going to shatter Krystal when she hears that he's dead. I wish I could be there for her.''

"Krystal knows already. She didn't when I first talked with her last Friday. She gave me a message for Crosley that day. But when I saw her on Saturday morning at the courthouse in Randolph, she knew. She was scared to death. I thought at the time that she was frightened of me because of Sarah Morell's murder. Now I think she was frightened for me. And for herself. Somehow she'd found out what had happened to Crosley.''

"She may have heard Curtis and the others talking about it," Mary said.

"Or he might have taunted her with it. That might have been part of the beating he gave her.''

I glanced over at Mary. She looked like she was working herself up to call Curtis a bastard for the third time. I jumped in first. "Krystal transplanted one of her flowers to Crosley's grave in the old family plot. That's how I found the grave. It was rue, an herb that means repentance.''

Mary tied it together. "She was saying she was sorry for involving him.''

I adjusted the Rambler's vent window to direct more air in toward us. "I should have brought you a bouquet of rue," I said. "Sorry I ruined your visit.''

"It was my idea to play detective. I won't make that mistake again. Solving a mystery can leave you pretty empty.''

"This one isn't solved yet. I still don't know who called the Morells to warn them about Crosley. It wasn't Sheriff Yeager. And I don't know where the sonnet is.''

Out of the corner of my eye, I saw Mary turn her head toward me. I knew the look she'd have on her face, a worried, warning, here-we-go-again look. I pretended to study the worn concrete before us.

The Sunday afternoon traffic around Louisville was just heavy enough to keep me occupied until we reached the airport. We parked in a surface lot a quarter of a mile from the terminal and walked to it across new, hot asphalt that gave a little with each step. Inside the terminal, the bright carpeting and the glass and aluminum walls looked unreal to me after months spent in the Gothic stone of St. Aelred's, making the place seem like the set of a space movie.

We traded Mary's bag for a boarding pass and made our way out into a long arm of the terminal to her gate. We'd cut it closer than I'd intended. There were only ten minutes left until her flight's scheduled departure.

It was time for me to speak or forever hold my peace. Time to tell Mary about my troubles at St. Aelred's, about the doubts that wouldn't go away and my obsession with knowing that made living with the doubts impossible.

"Mary," I said. It was as far as I got. Like characters in a farce, we'd spent the weekend carefully not saying what was really on our minds. Now our time was almost gone, and we stepped on each other's lines in our haste.

"Wait, Owen," Mary said. "I have to tell you something before I go. It's what I came out here to say."

We were standing near rows of vinyl seats occupied by sleepy-looking travelers. At a counter in front of the seats, a uniformed young woman was sorting slips of paper. Mary took my hand and drew me closer. She lowered her head slightly and looked up at me through her lashes.

"Harry asked me to marry him. I said yes."

The woman behind the counter announced the first boarding call for the flight. The quiet seating area suddenly came to life around us. We were jostled by the passing crowd as we looked for some sign in each other's eyes.

Tell her, tell her, tell her, I repeated to myself. It wasn't too late even now to make my confession.

"I wish you were still wearing your collar," Mary said, abruptly and disjointedly.

"I could button my shirt up, if that would help," I heard myself reply.

"Harry and I would like you to marry us. It would mean a lot." Mary's eyes were suddenly shining in the dusty sunlight. "If you're able."

That tiny "if" pulled back the curtains for me. Mary knew I was in trouble. She knew without my telling her. Brother Dennis had told her, or Elizabeth Mott, or I had without realizing it. Mary knew, and she was going to marry Harry anyway.

I waited impatiently to hear my clever reply. What finally came out was just "Good-bye."

Mary kissed me quickly and joined what was left of the line at the gate. I selected an empty seat in a row of empty seats and waited until the airliner pulled back from the gate. Then I walked to the window. The runway paralleled the wing of the terminal in which I stood. Mary's plane taxied away to my right, out of sight. I waited patiently until it rushed back into view, lifting off as it came abreast of my window. Then it disappeared into the hazy summer sky.

THIRTY-ONE

I DIDN'T GO BACK to St. Aelred's after leaving the Louisville airport. Father Jerome was at the seminary, waiting to berate me for my fatal curiosity. Waiting to ask me questions about mysteries I might never solve. I outsmarted him by driving instead to the courthouse in Randolph in search of Sheriff Roger Yeager.

I was in luck for once. The sheriff's offices were very busy on that Sunday afternoon. Roger Yeager sat at the center of the activity, watching it approvingly. When he spotted me, he waved me into his office.

"We got them, Mr. Keane," he called out. "The Georgia highway boys picked the Morells up. All three of them are safe as houses."

I couldn't tell whether Yeager had cleaned up and rested since I'd left him at the Morell farm. His uniform was as sweat-stained and rumpled as every uniform I'd seen him in. A pot of coffee on a warming plate sat on one corner of his desk. He poured a cup for me as I sat down.

"Your tentative identification of that body has been seconded by another witness, so there's no need for you to look at it again. Some monk from your school did the honors."

"Brother Dennis," I said.

Yeager consulted a paper on his desk. "That's right. We'll have Crosley's dental records brought down from Indy just to make certain. The early word is he may have died of a blow to the head. One right about there," he said, pointing to my new bandage.

"How long has he been dead?"

Yeager shrugged his round shoulders. "That's guess-work, too, at the moment. It looks like several weeks. My own bet would be he died on the same night the Morells took him away from your school. So if you're blaming yourself for not working it all out faster, you can rest easy. He was most likely past helping before anyone knew he was gone."

"How about family papers? Did you find any?"

"A boatload," Yeager said, indicating a box on the floor next to his desk. "Though I can't see anything among them worth killing anyone over."

He gave me an inventory as I picked through the box. "Mortgage papers for the farm, titles to some equipment, some school papers of Curtis Morell's and the little girl's, receipts for seed and the like. Find what you're looking for?"

"No," I said. I'd stopped on the way to Randolph to buy cigarettes now that I was out from under Mary's watchful eye. I sat back in my chair and pulled out the pack.

"There you go," Yeager said. "That's a good idea." He rummaged in his desk drawer and produced a briar pipe and a leather pouch. "We've got tobacco. We've got coffee. If you want later we can have a bottle of something decent brought in. We can settle back and have us a nice long talk. Start at the beginning and run me through to the end."

It was the reason I'd come to Randolph. I wanted to talk everything out, to list what I knew and what I still had to learn.

"Michael Crosley was in trouble before he ever heard of the Morells," I began. "His father, Martin Crosley, died suddenly last spring. Michael had come to St. Aelred's in the first place to defy his father. Beatrice Crosley, Michael's mother, told me that. Michael thought his father was a loser, a blue-collar worker who had never opened a book. He was wrong. About a month ago, Michael's Uncle John told him the truth about Martin Crosley. Martin had gone into World War II a sensitive kid who wanted to be a teacher. He'd come out a damaged, closed-up man who seemed to despise everything the earlier Martin Crosley had valued. Everything Michael Crosley would come to value."

Yeager had his pipe going. It sat comfortably against his fringe of beard, its wreaths of smoke making him look like an overfed elf.

"That wasn't the biggest bomb John Crosley dropped on his nephew," I continued. "Michael had the idea that it was better to go through life without coming too close to other people. That might have been what attracted him to the priesthood in the first place. He could love everyone in a sterile, safe way without really risking his love on anyone."

I leaned forward to drop some ashes in the tray on Yeager's desk. "He'd gotten his view of human relations from watching his parents' marriage, from observing his father mostly, whom Michael saw as unloving. Uncle John undermined Michael's plans for his life by revealing that Martin Crosley had once had a great love, a woman named Lisa Logan who died while he was in the service."

Yeager shifted his pipe to the other side of his mouth. "So from the get-go this Michael Crosley was wrong about his father and wrong about himself. This uncle really yanked the rug out from under him."

"Yes. That was the state of mind Michael was in when Father Jerome, his spiritual director, sent him out into the world. Father Jerome thought Michael's inability to love would make him a bad priest. He wanted Michael to identify with the people he'd have to serve."

"Sounds like the priest had the right idea," Yeager said. "Sorry I kicked around that spiritual development business yesterday. Guess I could use some myself, at the risk of agreeing with my ex."

"Right out of the box, Michael ran afoul of Sarah Morell and her financial troubles. She told him about some family papers at her farm that contained letters from the English poet John Keats."

"'Ode to a Nightingale' Keats?"

"Yes," I said, taken aback.

Yeager laughed. "You surprise easier than a hound dog with a head cold, Mr. Keane. You're not the only one who's been inside a school. So that's what these mysterious family papers you're looking for are all about. Did Crosley find them?"

"He must have," I said. "Before he disappeared, I heard him recite a sonnet in St. Aelred's pub. I think the poem was part of what he'd found, a lost sonnet of John Keats's."

Yeager whistled. "That's what you were hoping we'd find at the farm?"

"I thought the Morells might have recovered the poem when they kidnapped Crosley."

Yeager waved his pipe at me. "Back up there. You're getting way ahead of yourself. You haven't even gotten Crosley out to the farm yet."

"Sorry. The Morells admitted to me that Crosley approached them about the papers. They told him they didn't have them."

"And of course they couldn't let him search for them for fear he'd discover what they were up to," Yeager said.

"Right. At the farm, Michael met Krystal, Curtis's daughter. She had problems, too, mainly a violent father who wouldn't let her go to school. Michael took an interest in her, coming back to see her at least twice."

"That was your Father Jerome's idea at work, I take it." Yeager then echoed the priest's own words. "Crosley was thawing out."

"Yes. He approached Curtis about letting Krystal go back to school and got a black eye for his troubles. Then

Krystal slipped him a bag of her father's marijuana. She wanted to get free of her father by turning him in.''

"Why didn't Crosley come to us with it?"

I repeated the answer I'd worked out for Mary, that Crosley had been worried about Sarah Morell's desperate finances and confused by the opinions he'd received on the dangers of marijuana.

Yeager nodded. "That's an easy subject to start an argument with," he said.

"In the end, Michael debated too long. The Morells received a phone call telling them that Crosley had ripped them off. Frank and Curtis went after him."

"Hold on a minute now. Who called them?"

"I don't know. The Morells didn't seem to know themselves." I hesitated for a moment. "I thought it might even have been you or one of your deputies."

Yeager didn't seem offended by the idea. "You reasoned it that Crosley could have come to me with the pot?"

"Yes," I admitted. "And you acted awfully friendly toward the Morells the day after Sarah's murder. I thought you might be old friends."

Yeager began to laugh and then to cough until his face was bloodred. He took a long drink of coffee. "Now you're sounding like an Easterner again," he sputtered. "Just when I thought there was hope for you. You probably walk around studying the tops of your shoes for fear someone's going to speak to you. In Indiana we don't expect to be asked for money or mugged by everybody we meet. We actually still say hello and shake hands. The way you saw me handling the Morells was just my standard neighborliness. Doesn't make me their first cousin, thank the Lord."

"Sorry."

"I can vouch for my deputies, too. I'd bet my life none of them made that call. How about the people Crosley quizzed on the subject of marijuana? Could one of them have doubled-crossed him?"

As far as I knew, he'd asked only Ronnie and Karen Koffman. And he hadn't told them he actually had some marijuana. I couldn't see a connection between Green Streets and the Morell farm. "I don't think so," I said.

"Let's get back to your story. The Morells kidnapped Crosley, right? How did they find him?"

"Probably by calling the phone number he'd given them and asking questions. Curtis did the same thing with my number. The old house on campus where Michael lived was usually unlocked. And his room number was listed on a mailbox in the front hallway. They came for him during a storm. The housekeeper told me there were muddy footprints all through the house the next morning."

"Just like in that nursing home," Yeager said.

"Michael left clues to his abductors, but I was a long time figuring them out. One was a book about Keats that he left on the center of his desk. And he dropped the keys to the car where the marijuana was hidden out in the street where they were sure to be found. He deliberately took the wrong raincoat so he could get the keys."

"That was the coat Springer found burned in the old cabin?"

"Yes."

Yeager bent forward to tap the dottle from his pipe into the ashtray on his desk. "Shame all that quick thinking didn't do him any good. That took place weeks back. Then last Friday you showed up at the farm, retracing Crosley's steps. The Morells decided they'd have to stop the tourist trade, so they killed Sarah."

"I'd be willing to bet that Sarah's murder was all Curtis's idea. He was pretty unraveled last time I saw him. Killing Sarah was a low percentage play, likely to direct attention back toward the family and the farm."

"You're forgetting that they had a made-to-order fall guy in Michael Crosley," Yeager said. "They knew he wasn't about to show up to protest his innocence. Of course, they had to have a fatheaded old sheriff to swallow the hook. Lucky thing for them I was reelected."

He tried to pour himself another cup of coffee, but the pot was empty. "Guess I didn't want that after all. So where does all this storytelling leave us? Seems like there are two unanswered questions. What happened to the poem? And who called the Morells?"

"That poem isn't one unanswered question. It's an easy dozen. For starters, how did Crosley get the poem in the first place if the Morells didn't give it to him? Krystal Morell had never even heard of it. If it wasn't for the reading at St. Aelred's, I'd have to believe Michael just lost interest in the Keats papers after he met Krystal. Everything seems to suggest that."

"Why did he recite the poem aloud anyway?" Yeager asked.

"I've come up with too many answers to that. Michael was really worked up the night he read the sonnet. I've thought all along that was because he'd decided to leave St. Aelred's. I started with the idea he'd met a girl and fallen in love. Then I was afraid it was because he'd decided to steal the Keats papers."

"None of which makes sense now," Yeager said, "because, as far as we know, he never intended to leave the school."

He ruffled his beard with the knuckles of one hand. "I don't envy you the job of trying to puzzle that one out. Fortunately for me, I don't need that poem to make a case against the Morells. It's enough that Sarah sent Crosley out to the farm. Doesn't matter whether he found a hundred poems or none.

"That mystery phone call is another matter. That leaves a little hole smack dab in the middle of my case. I surely would like to know who tipped the Morells off."

We sat and thought about it for a while. The moment reminded me of another time when I'd sat in the same chair wondering about another mysterious phone call.

"When I was here yesterday, your deputy told you about a call some Indianapolis banker made to the Good Fellows home. What was that all about?"

"We still don't know. The savings and loan the caller mentioned turned out not to exist."

"Did he give his own name?"

"It wasn't a he, it was a she. And she didn't give her name, or leastways the people at the home couldn't remember it."

"What did she want?"

"The address of the Morell farm. Some made-up story about needing an appraisal. The girl who answered the phone read the information off and that was that."

"Michael Crosley's mother works for a bank in Indianapolis," I said, thinking aloud. "Could Michael have told her about Sarah Morell?"

Yeager shrugged again, grimacing at the same time. "I have to call that poor soul with the bad news. I'll ask her about Sarah if I can work it in. Guess I should do that now."

I recognized the cue and stood up.

"Our steno will be in tomorrow morning," Yeager said. "We'll need a formal statement from you and your lady friend."

"You'll have to get hers long distance," I said. "She's on her way back to New York."

Yeager wasn't pleased, but he took the news philosophically. "Don't expect she'll remember Indiana very fondly."

"No," I said. "I don't expect she will."

The sheriff got up and walked me to his office door. "Thanks for your help, son. And your patience. Guess you priests need plenty of that. I'll give you a call if any iambic pentameter shows up when we search the Morells."

THIRTY-TWO

WHO HAD WARNED the Morells and where was the Keats sonnet? I asked myself those questions over and over again as I walked from the courthouse to my borrowed car, until the pair began to seem like one long, last question. I paused beneath the shade of an old beech tree with my hand on the Rambler's door, wondering if that was just a trick of my weary mind or a genuine possibility. Were those two questions bound so tightly together that they had only one answer, a single name that could explain everything? The tired-looking guy with the bandage on his temple who stared up at me from the car's dusty window nodded yes.

I stood there watching my reflection, hoping it would next tell me where to head. I knew I had to find the missing name before I could face Father Jerome—there would be no time afterward—but I had no idea where to look. The mysterious Good Fellows caller had been a woman. I took that slim lead as my starting point. Would I find her in Indianapolis or New Albany or Shangri-La? Or at sleepy little St. Aelred's?

"St. Aelred's," I said aloud. Mary's arrival had reminded me that there were worlds outside the little school. Now she was gone, and that larger universe seemed to be collapsing inward, leaving only the seminary, a dense, dark core that pulled everything toward it, all the loose ends of my mystery, all my own twists and turnings.

The thought that the person I wanted might be a campus insider reminded me of a detail I'd let slip away in my fascination with sonnets and marijuana. Someone had taken the Keats book from Crosley's room and returned it to the library. I'd never called Mrs. Wilson back to find out if Paula, her overachieving housekeeper, had returned the book. That little omission now seemed like a major misstep.

I left the car and crossed the street to a phone booth that shared one corner of the courthouse square with Krystal's cannon. On my way across the still-hot pavement, I checked my watch. Mary was home by now. Back on the East Coast with the pollution and the muggers and the suicidal drivers, safe forever from crazy Hoosier farmers and amateur detectives. Safe with my old friend Harry. I twisted the knife by rerunning scenes of Mary's visit over and over, getting a head start on a lifetime of missing her.

A few feet from the cannon's black mouth, I slowed to a stop, playing and replaying one scene in my mind. Hidden in the sad retrospective of Mary's visit, I'd found an answer. One I didn't like.

I ran the last few feet to the phone, reaching for my wallet at the same time. In it, I found the scrap of paper on which I'd written the number of the old rectory. The phone there rang nineteen times before Mrs. Wilson picked it up.

"Owen," she said in response to my first hurried words, "have you found Michael?"

St. Aelred's vaunted grapevine had so far missed the biggest story it would ever have. I rudely ignored Mrs. Wilson's question, not wanting to be sidetracked by her grief or curiosity.

"Have you had a chance to talk with Paula?" I asked.

"About the library book, you mean? Yes, I saw her at mass this morning. She said she didn't take any book. She was positive."

"You were entertaining a friend the day Paula was there." I paused for a beat and braced myself against the warm aluminum of the booth. "Was it Elizabeth Mott?"

"Yes, it was. How did you know? She's another campus widow, poor dear. She stops by for tea every now and again."

"Did she go up to Michael's room?"

"Elizabeth? No. She was with me the whole time. Except she did let herself out. We'd talked right up to the start of 'Guiding Light,' and I didn't want to miss any. Why would she go to his room?"

For the second time in that short call, I dodged her question by asking another. "Dr. Mott lives just off the campus, doesn't she?"

"About a mile south," the patient landlady replied. "On Old Sawmill Road. A yellow farmhouse."

I thanked her and hung up.

I drove back to the campus and Old Sawmill Road as fast as Brother Dennis's dying transmission would allow. I had no trouble finding the house. It sat at a turning of the road on a grassy hillock, a yellow, one-story house with white gingerbread trim.

I saw Professor Mott as I pulled into the drive. She was seated in a small garden behind the house. She didn't look up when my tires hit the gravel drive or when I slammed the car door behind me. She was wearing a white dress and a broad-brimmed white hat, and her head was tilted forward slightly. I thought that she was reading the book that sat in her lap, but when I drew closer, I saw that the book was closed.

I stood a few feet away from her chair, waiting for her to look up. When she did, I saw that her eyes were dark and her mouth was set in a tight line. Her round, pink face was drawn down toward the collar of her dress, as though it were softening in the heat.

"Owen," she said. "Father Jerome just called with the terrible news about Michael Crosley. Is it all true?"

"Yes," I said.

"Are you all right?"

"Yes."

"And Mary?"

"She's okay, too. She's gone back East."

The professor's dark eyes looked me over carefully, at the same time taking in the last chapter of the Owen and Mary story. "I'm sorry," she said. "Tell me what happened to Michael."

It didn't take long. I'd already briefed Dr. Mott on Michael's dealings with Sarah Morell and his first trip to the farm. I now added the character of Krystal and the detail of the gift she'd given Michael, the bag of marijuana. I described Crosley's fatal hesitation. Then, without mentioning the warning call the Morells had received, I told the professor how they'd kidnapped Crosley.

She sat with her head down for some time.

"I'll come back on a better day," I said.

"There isn't likely to be one, Owen," she said, looking up at me. "Please stay. Tell me what you want."

The afternoon sun was almost hitting the treetops, but its heat still made me feel lightheaded. "I want the sonnet," I said.

"I see," she replied. "Why did you come to me?"

I understood that she was asking me to describe the evidence that had led me to her door. One mystery buff to another. I looked around me at her garden for a moment in an effort to clear my mind. What I saw were roses predominantly, another variation on the gardening theme that had run through my investigation. Beatrice Crosley's garden had been edible, Krystal Morell's medicinal. Elizabeth Mott's was decorative, a place of carefully ordered beauty. It was just the place to sit and read poetry written by long-dead men and women.

"Someone searched Michael Crosley's room last week," I began. "Someone from St. Aelred's."

"Might it not have been the men who abducted him?" Dr. Mott asked the question with a teacher's objectivity, not disputing my reasoning so much as encouraging me to tighten it up.

"I don't think so. They did their searching the night they came for him. And I don't think they would have bothered returning an overdue library book. I noticed it on my first visit to the room. The book was only important because it might have linked Michael Crosley to the discovery of a lost sonnet. The men who kidnapped him didn't give much thought to poetry."

"Go on."

"Your friend Katrinka Wilson told me you dropped by last Thursday for tea. And that you let yourself out. I think you could just as easily have let yourself up to Michael's room. You could have taken the Keats book—it was returned on Thursday—and found the sonnet."

"What other clues have you?"

"Someone called the Good Fellows Retirement Home a few weeks ago with a phony story, trying to get information about the Morell farm. It was a woman."

"What else?"

"When I first came to see you, you acted as though you barely knew Michael Crosley. Later, in front of Mary, you described him like someone you knew very well. I think you did know him well.

"You were the first person I thought of when I wanted to tell someone about the sonnet. Michael would have thought of you, too, when he needed someone to evaluate his find. You would have been a natural for that job. The one person on campus who would have appreciated a lost sonnet. Or so I thought. But when I came to you with the story about Keats, you discouraged me from following it up."

Dr. Mott removed her hat for a better look at me. She set it on the grass next to her chair and pushed a strand of silver hair backward, away from her face.

"As I recall," she said, "I discouraged you because you hadn't worked out a convincing motive for Michael's actions. This new story seems to have the same weakness. What was my motive?"

"You told me the answer to that yourself," I said. "That first day I came to you. You told me that a young seminarian on the threshold of his life wouldn't be tempted by the poem. It had to be someone disappointed by life who saw the sonnet as a last chance."

"'A last grab at the gold ring,'" Dr. Mott amended. "I'd forgotten I'd said that."

"The day I found Mary in your office, you told me that you'd tried to leave St. Aelred's."

"Tried unsuccessfully," Dr. Mott added. "I've spent too many years in this backwater. My credentials are too dog-eared and mildewed. This was always only a place my husband loved. When he died, there was nothing for me here."

She looked past me at the garden with her hands on the book in her lap. "Now you'll want a statement from me, I suppose. That's how these scenes run, isn't it?"

I found I could only nod.

"Michael Crosley did come to me with news of Sarah Morell's story, as you've guessed. He asked me to undertake the evaluation of anything he might find. I saw the offer as my chance to finally do some substantial work, perhaps even to escape this place.

"That's how it began. But after that first happy meeting, Michael changed. He became moody and preoccupied. He told me it had all been a wild goose chase, that there was no Keats material. After that, he refused to even discuss it.

"I didn't know whether or not to believe him. I'd wanted it to be true so badly that I found I couldn't let the idea go. I called the retirement home. I made up some story to get the address of the farm. I planned to call the Morells to find out if the old woman's story had really been a hoax. But I didn't make the call right away. I was afraid to. I didn't want the dream to end, I suppose.

"Then Jim Carroll came by to drop off his latest manuscript. He told me that Michael had read a sonnet at the Unstable. I thought immediately that it must be from the Keats material Michael had said didn't exist. From the little Carroll remembered of the poem, I knew it was no known work of Keats. I jumped to the same conclusion you later did: that Michael had found a lost sonnet.

"I panicked. All the hasty misjudgments I later reproved you for I made then myself. I decided that Michael had lied to me, that he planned to act as a free agent without regard to me or the Morell family. I'm afraid I started drinking a little in my despair and frustration. I'd certainly had too much to drink the night I called the Morell farm. Without identifying myself, I started to tell them that Michael Crosley was robbing them. That he meant them no good. I was cut off by an outburst of the foulest, most hate-filled invective I've ever heard. It frightened me. I hung up the phone and sat alone in the dark all that night, through a terrible storm."

She looked around the bright garden as though it were filled with lightning-cast shadows. "After Michael disappeared, I should have spoken up. I was afraid something had happened. Too afraid to act. I felt I'd opened a horrible Pandora's box with that call and unleashed some primordial evil."

I thought of Curtis's mad dance around the burning shed. "You had," I said.

Dr. Mott was too deep in her own memories to hear me. "Weeks passed. I talked myself into believing that Michael had only gone away, that nothing really terrible had happened. But I couldn't forget the sonnet. When I thought it was safe, I went to visit Katrinka. I let myself into Michael's room. I took away Bate's book on Keats. I should have burned it, but I've never even been able to write in a book.''

"And you took the sonnet,'' I said.

"The sonnet?'' She stared at me for a moment, wide-eyed. "I'm confessing a murder to you, Owen. I'm telling you that I killed Michael Crosley. I'm not sure how it happened, but I know I'm responsible. How can you still be interested in that sonnet?''

Because I was still curious, God help me. I still needed to know. And I wanted something tangible to show for all my questioning. Something to justify my role in Sarah Morell's death. Like Dr. Mott, I'd been the unwitting catalyst in a murder. I understood her guilt well enough to want to relieve it.

"You didn't kill Michael,'' I said. "A man named Curtis Morell did. When you called that night about the poem, Curtis thought you were talking about some marijuana that had gone missing. He thought you were warning them that Michael planned to turn them in. You had no way of knowing about the pot growing. What happened afterward wasn't your fault.''

"You'll never persuade me that I'm innocent, Owen. I suspect you'll never even be in a position to absolve me of my sin. I regret that, truly. When Father Jerome phoned me yesterday morning to ask me to sit with Mary, he spoke a little of his reasons for sending you after Michael. I'm referring to the odd idea he had that you two were opposites and yet linked somehow, each one half of a complete priest.''

"Celebrant and victim,'' I said.

"Exactly. I was sitting here thinking about that when you drove up. Victimhood is what Michael Crosley lacked, and what he ended up obtaining. If Father Jerome is right, Michael died a priest, albeit an unordained one. You may struggle through to ordination, Owen. You're just stubborn enough to. But I don't think you'll ever achieve the synthesis Michael did.

"It's ironic really. You're a leap-of-faith detective. The evidence that led you to me would have been too flimsy to support any of your paperback heroes. If you could reach out to God with the same intuition that led you to me, you'd be a happy man."

"Where is the sonnet?"

Dr. Mott opened the book in her lap and extracted a folded piece of paper. "Here it is," she said. "Your Holy Grail. Or should I say your Maltese Falcon? Do you remember what the falcon turned out to be made of? Lead, wasn't it? No gold, no precious jewels. No answers. I'm afraid that's the way it's going to be for you and the grails of this life, Owen."

I took the paper from her and unfolded it. It was ordinary lined theme paper, yellowed with age. On it was written the love sonnet, in a large round hand in faded blue ink:

My soul had been too long at youthful ease;
   Slow days had come and passed in languid file;
When I was captured by Eumenides,
   Thy furies sent to torture and beguile;
The voice that has become my sacred muse,
   The orbs that have eclipsed all other light,
The form of perfect grace that has confused
   A lifetime's certainty of wrong and right.
No more will my poor spirit find its rest
   In faery realms of words and games of love;
For now, forsaking artifice and jest,
   Can I but strive to reach the heights above;
While doomed to fall outside that promised land,
With fingers stretching upward for thy hand.

It was signed "Martin Crosley, April 30, 1941." The poem was the work of the sensitive boy who didn't survive the war, written for the girl who died while he was away.

"I found that in an old Latin textbook in Michael's room. It's the poem he recited at the Unstable, isn't it?"

"Yes," I said.

"I should have left it where I'd found it, but I couldn't. I'd wanted it too badly. I'd given too much for it. Almost as much as you have, Owen."

THIRTY-THREE

I LEFT DR. MOTT with her thoughts, taking the sonnet away with me. It was mine by right, as I had been the highest bidder. The professor had certainly put me in my place with that assessment. I'd come to her garden an avenging detective, but I left it a failed priest.

Dr. Mott had been wrong about other things, such as the Maltese Falcon being made of lead. In the movie at least, the bird was made of the stuff of dreams. The wishes, the hopes, the unspoken prayers. That was the good side. The downside of dreams had to be there, too. The doubts, the fears, the dark, unguessed desires. The sonnet was certainly all those things. Martin Crosley had put both sides in it, the vision of happiness and the realization that he would never have it. It might have seemed like a game to that long-ago high school kid, the undercutting of the ideal with the likely. Perhaps he'd just been observing a convention when he'd ended his poem on that sad note, repeating some poetic formula long out of date. Or maybe he'd felt the same cold wind blow through him that hurried me back to the car.

I thought I finally understood Michael Crosley's emotional recitation of the poem at the Unstable. It had been a confession after all, although a very personal one. He'd been admitting that he had sold his father short, that he'd misjudged him harshly. And he'd been mourning Martin Crosley, both Martin Crosleys. The one who had died in the spring and the one who had died in the war.

He had been mourning something else in that performance, the death of a peculiar kind of innocence. Michael had been saying good-bye to the arrogant assumption that he wouldn't fail as his father had failed. For the first time, he'd seen himself as his father's son and recognized his father's unhappy fate as a very real possibility for himself.

Or was I putting my own feelings into Michael Crosley's head? Failure was very much on my mind as I drove back to St. Aelred's. Failure and loss and the idea of living my life without someone I loved. It was enough to make me believe that I might be Martin Crosley's real heir after all, and the sonnet my rightful legacy.

As I parked my borrowed car in its little space behind St. Meinrad Hall, the bells of the church began calling the monks to vespers. I reminded myself that dusk lasts forever in Indiana in the summertime. I could be on my way east before dark.

Trade-Off
Maxine O'Callaghan

First Time In Paperback

A Delilah West Mystery

GIVE HER A SIMPLE MISSING PERSONS CASE ANYTIME

Savvy California P.I. Delilah West hits the horsey set in
Laguna Hills when Benjamin Wylie hires her to find his
missing teenage daughter, Tamra.

Things turn nasty when Delilah discovers the bludgeoned body
of Kate Sannerman, the Wylies' neighbor. Had Tamra witnessed
the murder? Was she another victim? Had she planned to run
off with Kate's husband, now the police's prime suspect?

As the case heats up Delilah's days, a new man puts sizzle into
her nights, and things are getting too hot to handle. But she is
determined to keep her cool, even when trying to thwart a killer
trying to put her on ice—permanently.

"A canny piece of work."   *—The Washington Post*

Available in February at your favorite retail stores.

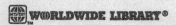

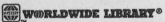

LOVE BYTES
SALLY CHAPMAN

First
Time In
Paperback

A Silicon Valley Mystery

USER UNFRIENDLY

Trading her high-tech, high-stress Silicon Valley career for her own computer fraud investigations agency, Julie Blake embarks on her first case: the disappearance of Arnie Lufkin, a renegade programming genius and suspected embezzler.

Julie and her partner/lover, Vic Paoli, have barely agreed to take the case when her system is broken into and a threatening message left on her screen. Scared, but with creditors snapping at her heels, Julie decides to dig deeper.

A foray into virtual reality proves that the missing Lufkin is not only a brilliant man, but a dangerous, egocentric manipulator. Wherever he is, Lufkin is playing deadly games, making murder a reality.

"[Chapman's] books are not only _diverting,_ they are lucid."
—_Oakland Tribune_

Available in April at your favorite retail stores.

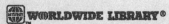 **WORLDWIDE LIBRARY®**

BYTES

KINDNESS CAN KILL

JANIE BOLITHO

First Time in Paperback

An Inspector Ian Roper Mystery

NOT A PRETTY PICTURE

Stunningly beautiful, brazenly sexy, Julia Henderson was every man's fantasy and every wife's nightmare—until her brutal murder rocks the quiet English village of Rickenham Green.

Detective Chief Inspector Ian Roper and his team sort out the clues and conclude this was no illicit one-nighter gone insane. It was deliberate and emotional. Whoever killed Julia knew her well.

So twisted are the sins and secrets of some community members that two will confess to killing Julia. But it's the identity of her true killer that remains as shocking as it is inevitable.

"Taut, psychologically compelling..."   *—Publishers Weekly*

Available in February at your favorite retail stores.

To order your copy, please send your name, address, zip or postal code along with a check or money order (please do not send cash) for $4.99 for each book ordered, plus 75¢ postage and handling, payable to Worldwide Mystery, to:

In the U.S.

Worldwide Mystery
3010 Walden Avenue
P.O. Box 1325
Buffalo, NY 14269-1325

Please specify book title with your order.

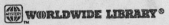

WORLDWIDE LIBRARY®   KINDNESS

A RECONSTRUCTED CORPSE

SIMON BRETT

A Charles Paris Mystery

First Time in Paperback

A STIFF ACT TO FOLLOW...

If playing a dead man could be called a role, Charles Paris has sunk to new lows when he agrees to play missing Martin Earnshaw on the true crime TV series "Public Enemies."

The show has all the hallmarks of a hit: a vulnerable, tearful wife, a sexy female detective and, best of all, dismembered limbs probably belonging to Earnshaw turning up each week just before airtime.

As viewers shudder gleefully and ratings soar, Paris discovers there's more to the whole production than meets the eye...and the climax is a killer.

"A perfect vacation read."   —*People*

Available in March at your favorite retail stores.

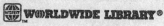 **WORLDWIDE LIBRARY®**

CORPSE

GRIZZLY

First Time in Paperback

CHRISTINE ANDREAE

A Lee Squires Mystery

FAIR GAME

English professor Lee Squires is spending Easter break in Montana as cook for the J-E dude ranch, where friend and owner Dave Fife is hoping that some Japanese investors—plied with home cooking—will pour cash into the struggling J-E.

Lee has come ready to whip up hotcakes, biscuits and chicken fried steak—but not to wrestle her libido over Dave's brother, Mac, a tireless bear activist…or to find a dead body with missing parts.

Another mangled body later, officials are hunting a bear. Lee doesn't buy the theory—but in tracking the truth, she comes face-to-face with a human killer who is nothing short of…grizzly.

"Good character interaction, great sense of place, and steady suspense." —*Library Journal*

Available in May at your favorite retail stores.

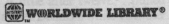 **WORLDWIDE LIBRARY** ®

GRIZZLY